CAIN'S REDEMPTION

BOOK 2 OF THE MASTERS SERIES

A. J. CHAMBERLAIN

British Library Cataloguing in Publication Data

A catalogue record for this book is available from the British Library.

ISBN 978-1-9161758-6-0

Cover Design by Esther Kotecha

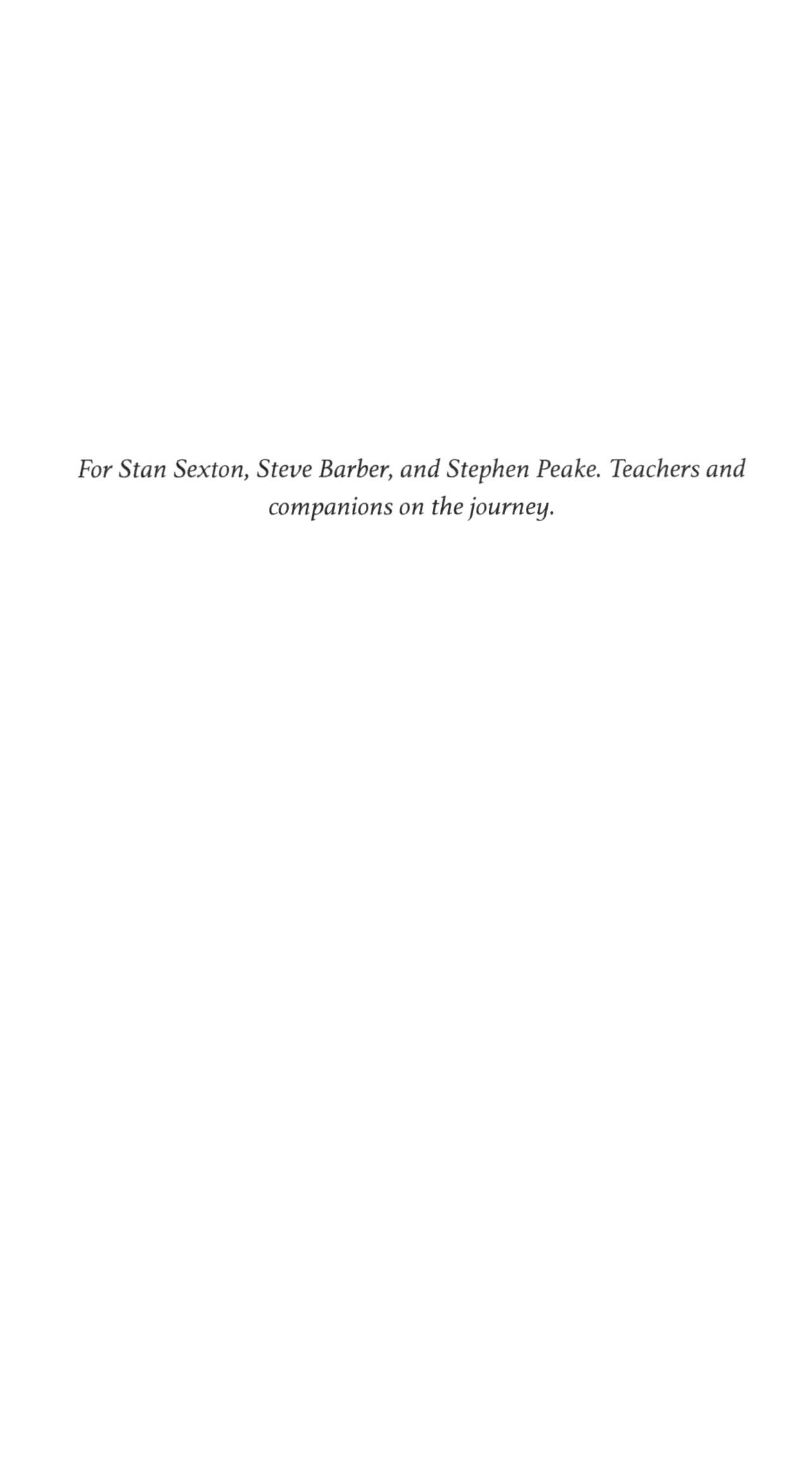

For Stan Sexton, Steve Barber, and Stephen Peake. Teachers and companions on the journey.

Sing to the Lord a new song; sing to the Lord, all the earth.

— Psalm 96 v 1 (NIV)

CAIN'S REDEMPTION

$$1$$

Senate Square, **Helsinki, January**

Darius Lench lost his footing again and cursed the ice. He walked on, crunching across the flagstones and glancing at the ground beneath his feet.

The maintenance crews were sprinkling salt onto the greying slush, and Lench's soft, city shoes slithered over the uneven surface. Before him the floodlit cathedral dominated, the ethereal glow on the masonry hinting at things unseen. Elevated above the square, the building spoke of permanence, the saints stationed at each corner, directing the mortals below to a more righteous calling. In the crisp, cold, air he saw the clean points of the golden crosses, and in his heart he despised it all.

He'd needed to get away from everything so that he could regroup and focus, and an old friend had offered him the space to do that. Here he could clear his mind, listen and submit to the master.

He was looking forward to this moment, despite the promise

of torment. Now, at last, he would find out how to repair the damage, and face the punishment for what had already happened. No amount of success in the other areas of his life would protect him from the reckoning and when it came, and he would offer no excuses.

He looked at the crisscross patterns of stone receding from him in all directions, and felt the freezing water tease its way into his socks.

"I am coming, my Lord," he whispered. "I will submit."

He removed a slim silver case from his pocket, took out a cigarette and lit it. The smoke hung heavy in the frigid air. He rubbed at an ache in his shoulder as he continued to pick his way across the uneven surface, his footsteps rapping out a brisk, uneven tattoo on the stone.

Lench presented himself to the world as a very successful man. He visited the gym regularly and, drawing on sheer strength of will, maintained the brutal regime he had set for himself. He was fitter than he'd been ten years ago, despite his tobacco habit. His body looked good for his age and his mind had lost none of its precision, and his propensity for caustic wit was as strong as ever.

But none of this would be any use to him when he stood before the master to atone for his failings, but like any good leader, he took responsibility when required, and this was just such an occasion.

A year ago he had been humiliated by the SLaM debacle, but since then he had enjoyed professional success and now Darius Lench was a seriously rich man.

His wealth kept him busy; he owned and rented, bought and sold. He had guessed right in the market and made money as others had lost it; and in all this time he had worked and worked on the art of dominance. Darius Lench could be civil when required, but beneath the refinement he cultivated a ruthless edge.

His personal life reflected the same approach. In the last few months he had refined and purged his group. He had driven out the weak people and cast them aside. The process had started, appropriately enough, with Martin Massey.

He had only ever let Martin join the group because of his position in a company called Sound, Light, and Music, or SLaM, as they liked to call themselves. Martin and his colleagues at SLaM had their fingers on the pulse of youth culture, and Lench's Master had determined that these people were a suitable instrument to work his will into that culture. And so, Lench had tolerated Martin Massey's excitable arrogance as the man developed 'SEEKA', a nihilistic, drug-related project that nudged young people towards one of Lench's favorite creeds: do what you will. That was the basis of Lench's life and philosophy.

But Massey had been nervous and stupid, and Lench had always despised him. He had had to endure the sight of Massey's pathetic little ego bobbing up and down with the ebb and flow of the SEEKA project. When that project failed so did Martin's association with the group, and he had been discarded like the trash that he was.

After that, Lench removed some of the others. One by one they had been pruned. Some fell away from the faith; or were tempted by a less demanding regime. There were a couple of New Age "hangers on" who stumbled across his path on their great search, and some who spoke of the master in terms of a vague metaphysics. He had nicknamed them the "lukewarms". These people weren't even sure that their Lord existed; they talked glibly of "forces" and "nature" as if the reality of spiritual conflict would pass them by. He despised them even more than the followers of the enemy. There was no place for such people in his group and he was pleased to see them weeded out, disposed of, forgotten.

The people around him now were of an altogether different order. They had been selected and hardened, and they shared with him a preoccupation for the master's will. These people understood that life was a contest, and winning was everything. There would have been no room for the likes of Massey in the current line-up. Poor Martin would have looked like a little boy, lost in a museum, frightened by the towering exhibits. With these new acolytes, Lench felt more able to fulfil his ambition and to serve his master and exercise power in all its forms.

But even as Lench built up his group, so also SLaM had thrived. Time and again he had felt compelled to track the fate of his enemies; to see whether they had disappeared like a cancer succumbing to therapy.

At first he thought SLaM would wither, as the misfits who took it over struggled to make themselves heard in the cacophony of contemporary culture. He smiled when he discovered they had taken on Lewis Ashbury as some kind of consultant. He jeered as he recognized little Conner Adams and his band achieve some notoriety at the fringes the music scene. He actually laughed out loud when he discovered that the woman, Alex Masters, had taken on her whore of a cousin to dream up bits of merchandise for them. They were a pathetic collection of amateurs and he was confident that their little venture would flounder and die.

But SLaM did not die. Indeed, it flourished and gained something of a reputation for what it did. He watched it all from a distance, and uncertainty stirred in his gut. Perhaps he had underestimated them, this raggedy crowd; perhaps they had more money than he realized; perhaps they would not just disappear into the noise. Over time the derisive laughter stopped, and the smile became a grimace. The success of SLaM was his failure, and so now he felt compelled to present himself to the master, to give an account, receive instruction and endure the appropriate punishment.

He did not immediately notice a man approaching him from the edge of the square, a black outline against the floodlights, coming into his field of vision. When he did see the figure, Lench recognized immediately the bulky silhouette of his old friend Tarmo Ketola. Tarmo lumbered up and Darius Lench took one last resentful suck on his cigarette before dropping it into the slush.

"You are eight minutes late," he said.

In response Tarmo laughed, his mirth turning into a rattling guttural cough. He spat out phlegm before he spoke.

"Darius, my friend, you need two things: decent shoes and a drink."

Lench smiled despite his mood. "Maybe," he said, "but first I have work to do."

The wind blew across the open square and snagged at Lench's thin jacket. He pulled it around himself as they walked together away from the floodlights of the cathedral and into the darkness.

"Tell me," said Lench, "does it ever get warm in this god forsaken land?"

"Not forsaken by the gods though, eh?" Tarmo turned and inspected his friend, like a doctor examining a sick patient. "You most definitely need a drink."

"You do know why I am here, don't you?" said Lench impatiently.

"Ah Darius, you are so clever, but you are also a fool. I will help you to rescue yourself from this mess."

"Don't flatter yourself," said Lench, stamping into slush as the cold seeped into the bones of his feet. "And why are we meeting outside this dung heap of a place? Is this another example of your warped sense of humour?"

Tarmo laughed again. "It's an easy landmark to find. I didn't want to make things any more difficult for a foreigner like you, Darius, now come!" Tarmo picked up the pace and Lench followed on, taking an extra stride to catch up with his friend.

"At least let me get you some proper boots," said Tarmo. "You are not in the City of London now." The big man launched into another coughing fit, and the pair of them trudged on.

"I should tell you," said Lench, "that things have deteriorated again. SLaM is now a running sore. That woman, Masters, has kept the thing afloat somehow."

"Our friend," said Tarmo softly, "is he not able to remove this woman you spoke of?"

"If only it were that simple," said Lench. "She is..." he searched for the right words, "...she is not open to us. We cannot harm her, although we may yet have opportunities to do a great deal of harm to the people she loves. But she is closed to us, and I have spent several hours trying to explain this to Josef."

"Ah, poor Josef," said Tarmo, smiling. "He could never quite grasp the subtleties, eh? I think that's why I am fond of him. He's always ready to slip the blade in first and ask questions afterwards."

"Yes, well that's not always the answer, is it!" snapped Lench. He continued before Tarmo could respond. "Josef has his uses but it doesn't take much to get him into a rage, just someone spelling his name wrong, 'Joseph' instead of 'Josef', is usually enough."

Tarmo nodded and smiled.

"Yes, that's Josef for you," he said, "I know you have to handle him carefully."

"There are other reasons why Josef has become something of a liability," said Lench, "and you know them well enough."

"The scar," said Tarmo, "and the blood."

"Yes," said Lench, "the scar and the blood. The current restrictions are for his own sake as much as any question of strategy."

The hulking figure betrayed no reaction to this; but Lench could sense the disappointment and anger. Josef was one of Tarmo's favourites.

"I am sorry for him," said Tarmo.

"Yes, yes it's a shame," said Lench, "but there it is. Josef's trade carries a certain amount of risk. His contact with the outside world is our point of weakness and it should be minimal. He should move unseen. But that is all rather difficult now that he has been compromised."

"I think you have not told me the half of it, Darius," said Tarmo. "I know he failed with the Bridget Larson job, as did you for sending him there in the first place; but what else is there, what else has he done?"

Lench sighed; he had not intended to spend time going over the Assassin's indiscretions.

"Alex Masters runs a café," said Lench, "and without my permission, Josef visited the place. I understand that he became 'upset' while he was there. He thought I would be asking him to dispatch one or two of them, and so he decided to go on a little reconnaissance mission."

"And?"

"And," said Lench, impatiently, "rather than slip in and out unobserved, an activity in which he is supposed to be an expert, he made a spectacle of himself, frightened the customers, and got himself noticed."

Tarmo sighed. "I did not realize that he had let himself go." He slowly shook his head. "So you have been quite merciful with him really."

"He has been a good servant in the past," said Lench, "and I respect loyalty despite what others might think. But his usefulness is probably coming to an end."

Tarmo grimaced, the pockmarks showing on his face in the floodlight.

"I understand," he said, "but don't discard him just yet."

"Oh, I won't do that," said Lench. "I still have plenty of work for him to do."

There was silence between them as they continued across the square towards a row of parked vehicles.

"Anyway," said Lench, "let's not get too morose, we still have much to do and the service of the master brings both rewards and penalties. Josef has had his share of rewards in the past, and, like me, now has to face the penalties, which I am sure he will take like the man he is."

"He will," said Tarmo.

"But I am not here to talk about Josef, or to decide what is to be done with him. My business with the master is my real concern. I obey his call."

"And the woman is protected?"

"We cannot harm the woman," said Lench, "or that tart of a cousin she hangs around with. They are protected."

"That is a pity," said Tarmo, "but I presume there are others."

"Of course, and any one of them might warrant further attention – that idiot brother of hers perhaps – but I need to identify where the master wants us to direct our attack."

"It will be revealed to you," said Tarmo. "Come, the car is here."

Tarmo's four-wheel drive was warm after the bitter wind of the square, and Lench was soon cocooned in the comfortable, leather interior as they drove away. He was exhausted and he knew it. He had taken an evening flight to come here directly from work, and he feared that Tarmo would find him asleep and snoring when they got up to his villa. It wasn't a prospect that he relished. He needed to remain alert and strong for this encounter.

He thought again about power, his own power, and pride, both of which had been diminished by this *girl*. He used the anger to keep himself awake.

"I take it everything is prepared," he said as the car picked up speed.

"Of course," said Tarmo, "you may spend yourself as extravagantly as you wish." Then with an abrupt movement, the driver's side window glided down and the warmth that had built up in the car fled in a moan of icy air. Tarmo broke into another coughing fit and hawked a gobbet of phlegm out into the racing darkness.

The window purred back in to place again.

"You will have your answers, Darius," said Tarmo, "and no doubt you will pay dearly for them, but maybe you can have some relaxation after that, eh? I have a little wine, and maybe I can arrange for some company for you?"

Lench felt tiredness creeping on him as again the interior of the car warmed up. "Keep your whores to yourself tonight, Tarmo."

The big man grunted and the car lurched across the highway, sloughing through the snow that banked up on the side of the road.

Twenty minutes later, Tarmo's villa loomed before them, a dark grey mass amid the faint glow of the night. A single light shone from the attic room. The car crunched to a halt on an expanse of gravel and Lench noticed the glitter of settled snow on the ground and in the trees.

"Do you wish me to stay with you?" said Tarmo, switching off the ignition.

This was no small offer and Lench did not answer immediately; the world around him was silent except for the occasional tick of the car engine as it cooled. He rubbed his shoulder as pain stabbed down his left arm, adding to the general tiredness he felt.

"No, thank you," he said, "but I appreciate the offer. I have to do this alone."

At the oaken front door of the villa, Tarmo dug into the pocket of an old leather jacket and fished out a formidable collection of keys.

"Again, I welcome you to my house, Darius, I hope you find what you are looking for here."

They walked through to the lounge. The embers of an earlier fire were still glowing in the grate of a soot-caked fireplace and the air was heavy with stale smoke. A large sofa draped with animal pelts sat before the fire, facing the flames.

Lench noted the familiar wood panelling, darkened with the years of smoke, and the trophies of the old gods on ledges and window shelves around the room, memories of the power of deities long since forgotten by the rest of the world. In one corner, he saw a heavy black oak table laden with spirit bottles.

"Lead the way," said Lench. "I want to engage with our master as soon as possible."

He followed his host through the house and up two flights of well-trodden stairs, to the door of the attic room. At the door he stopped and removed his shoes and soaking socks. Tarmo wheezed over and picked them up without a comment, and then he placed his heavy hand on Lench's shoulder. It was an expression of support and Lench accepted it as such.

"I will come and find you when you are finished," said Tarmo.

Lench nodded, then he entered the room alone, shut the door and quickly set about the preparations. He shivered, and stretched his neck left and right against the persistent shoulder ache, and then he sat down on the bare oaken floor, breathed deeply to centre himself, and closed his eyes.

Lench's head lolls to one side, and spittle gathers at the corner of his mouth; he lets slip a low moan as he sinks into the dream.

HE IS LYING on the surgeon's table, and lights surround his body. He is the subject of the procedure that is about to unfold. To his left he sees a green cloth, draped over a stainless-steel trolley. On top of the cloth is a tray and on the tray are an array of instruments of the kind used to part skin from flesh, and bone from muscle.

There is no one else in the room. He is warm and naked except for a thin green sheet, covering his body. There are restraints over his wrists and ankles, holding him to the table on which he is lying. His mouth is dry. The ceiling reflects light from the various instruments lying ready on the tray. Unseen machines are humming monotonously in the sterile environment.

There are double doors at the end of the room and he hears them as they swing open with a light brushing sound. A figure enters the space, gloved, face covered with a green surgical mask. Lench cannot see the figure clearly but he knows who it is.

The adrenaline starts to enter his bloodstream. He suffers an overwhelming desire to grovel as he has done many times before, but he is strapped to the table and cannot move.

Apart from the machines everything is quiet. He knows he must wait and respond only when he is spoken to. The noise of the machines becomes a dull resonance, an insistent whining noise that cuts out as the figure starts to talk to him. He shivers at the sound of the surgeon's voice.

The figure stands at the foot of the table; the features are indistinct, hidden by the surgical mask and the glare of the lights.

"Yes, my Lord." The procedure has not even begun and already Lench's voice is croaking. His desire to bow his head is almost overwhelming. He realizes he has been pressing himself against the restraining straps on the table and he tries to relax. The surgeon continues:

"Yes, my Lord."

Darius shuts his eyes, and nods, he wants to swallow but he just gags on the sharp, clinical air.

"And so it shall be," says the surgeon, spreading his hand in a gentle arc across the array of instruments on the green cloth. He looks across at them, waiting. Every one of those instruments seems to have its own personality; a specialism for each of the tasks at hand – slicing and cutting, parting and stretching and probing. Each may have a part to play in what is about to occur. The surgeon speaks with a quiet voice, but it carries within it the spite of a whip.

"Yes, my Lord."

Darius feels his heart rate quicken again, and moisture forms on his brow. The room is warmer now, and there is another smell that he does not recognize, something sweet, intimate, physical, and devastating.

He hears the sound of an instrument lifted from the soft cloth, the slight disturbance of the material. The blade is balanced in the hand of the surgeon, it rests on his glove.

Lench strains to look down across his body, which is covered except for one square, cut in the material, exposing the flesh. The muscles of his stomach move under the skin as he braces himself. Now he can see the growth, manifesting as a discolouration under the fine hairs on his skin. He sees the shape of a face, her face as he remembers it from those months ago. The face of Alex Masters.

"Look more carefully, Darius," whispers the voice. "I will show you how it is to be done."

Now he can see that the growth is changing, taking on the form of other faces; one of them he recognizes as the whore cousin. Then there's another face that he does not recognize, but it draws and repels him; it's an old man, physically weak but spiritually strong, very strong. Finally, he sees Alex Masters' stepbrother, a young, hopeful and naïve boy, ripe for the taking. There's some weakness in the boy, and Darius realizes this is the first hint of what might be on offer to him.

Just then his neck muscles give out and he smacks the back of his head onto the table. After a couple of breaths, he glances up again.

The blade glints in the surgeon's hand and Lench's fingers creep to the edge of the table. The instrument draws near.

ON THE HARD floor of the attic room, Lench twitches and pumps his left hand, gripping and releasing. He moans, and it is a loud, mournful sound that travels through house so that Tarmo, who is pacing the lounge downstairs, winces when he hears it. In the attic Lench rolls onto his side and then back to face the ceiling.

"DO IT, DARIUS."

The surgeon brushes fingers against the restraints holding Darius' left hand in place, and all of the bonds fall away. Now unencumbered, Lench reaches out and takes the instrument from the surgeon, and passes it to his right hand.

He sucks in the dry air and tastes the disinfectant in his nose and the roof of his mouth; then he releases and sucks in more air. His sinuses register the alien smell again, the sting of the environment, and the roof of his mouth is dry. He gathers his strength of will, and after balancing on the edge of revulsion he slides the blade purposefully into his exposed flesh.

At that moment he feels both the inexorable white heat of the pain and beneath it the sheer sensation of the metal cutting into his body, the blood wells up and seeps into the theatre garment draped over him, dark-stained red spreading into the green. He gathers himself and wills his hand to move, drawing the blade in an arc around the growth in his stomach. The sharp metal passes through his flesh without any resistance and the face that was Alex Masters is now drowned in his own blood.

He is dimly aware of the fact that if this was another man's dream the penetration of the knife would have been enough to explode him back into his waking life; breathless and aching.

But he is not released yet.

The surgeon views the procedure, dispassionately.

"Ye–" He tries to speak the words, but his throat is dry. In his dream he can smell the taint of metal as his blood starts to run down the side of his body. He can feel the moist, sticky warmth of it against his side where it is already starting to congeal. He braces himself as best he can and revolves the blade again, digging further into the wound. He hears the pit-pit-pit of blood dribbling off the table and onto the tiled floor beneath him.

The surgeon steps closer to view Lench's work. The mask covers the face and so Lench cannot guess at the reaction. Lench is aware that the machines have switched off, and there is silence except for the occasional tap of fluid onto the floor. The surgeon continues to inspect the wound and Lench can hear the dull roar of blood loss in his ears. He starts to feel detached from the experience.

Finally, the surgeon holds out a gloved hand. "Give me the blade, Darius."

Lench obeys; passing over the blooded instrument, he braces himself weakly, in expectation of another touch from the blade. The surgeon leans over, inspecting the wound and frowning as if he is unable to discern the result of the procedure. He places the blade on the table and picks up a large object like a saw made out of silver metal. The surgeon leans over the face of the stricken patient.

"Look at me, Darius."

In his mind, Lench speculates on what will come next, and his concentration wavers, his will wavers, and he looks aside from the measureless black eyes staring at him.

But the spiteful voice commands him to return.

Lench concentrates, listening to the will of his master.

"Yes, my Lord," he says, grunting through the agony.

The surgeon nods and gives his instructions.

There will be two separate attacks on the boy. One will be intrusive and personal, an assault on the body; the other will be subtler but no less devastating, an assault on character and integrity, made possible by the boy's own sin and lies. The beauty of the plan is that, just as the boy is attacked at his weakest point, so in the same action, SLaM will be attacked at its weakest point, and come apart.

Lench knows well that the pursuit of one opportunity may give rise to others, and so it is with the instructions he receives. Some of his other enemies may become vulnerable. The surgeon mentions Daisy, the whore cousin whom Lench already knows, and there is another one, a proud man who is full of shame and anger. Even through the pain Lench appreciates the beauty of the attacks, exploiting each victim's vulnerabilities, crippling their effectiveness.

And there is meaning in this casting aside of the blunt

instrument as well. Josef's approach won't do this time, and certainly there is no more room for "freelance activity", no more thoughtless excursions into enemy territory.

"Do you understand all I have said?"

Lench nods; fear and blood loss have finally silenced him. Then the surgeon straightens and turns. Lench is aware of the receding footsteps, and again the quiet brushing of the swinging door. The patter of fluid to the floor has stopped and the warm blood is now drying, fusing him into place on the table.

He waits to see if anything else will be required of him. He is well aware that there will be no premature waking from this dream; he will not be released except by his own hand, and he hears himself whisper in his weakness and despair.

"Let me go, let me go and do this." The pain in his abdomen has blossomed now into a pounding, absorbing ache, drying him, sucking his life, but he finds enough emotional energy to listen for the release.

The silence continues, and he feels himself drying out, dying under these lights.

He summons his will and then reaches out to the table. The already disturbed wound bleeds afresh and he is all but gagging on the pain now. He finds the first instrument he can, an object that looks like a large scalpel with a serrated edge. The end is sharp, and it should achieve his purpose. His breath is in rags and the sweat on his forehead is beginning to trickle into his eyes, making them sting. With an extravagant effort he uses both his arms to raise the saw above himself and holds it above the already gaping wound.

He takes one more breath, and then another, and then aided by the sheer force of gravity he brings the edge of the blade down into his chest and for a moment he knows an altogether different order of pain.

The agony is vast, dimensionless, he is lost in it, stripping thought and identity. It consumes him until he is no more.

LENCH'S EYES SNAPPED OPEN, and in his disorientation he felt the expectation of the agony, but there was nothing beyond the cramp and the ache of his limbs.

By degrees he composed himself, overcoming the breathlessness, and assessing the situation.

He recognized where he was and involuntarily, he cried out, pushing his limbs into a stretch. Then he began the process of relaxing, trying to lower his pulse rate. Within his stomach he felt a dull ache where in his dream he had pushed in the blade and excised the tumour.

He was lying on his back looking up through a small skylight in the ceiling of the room. In contrast to the uncharted void of night he could see two stars twinkling and he was overwhelmed by a sense of the pointlessness of everything he did, as if all his striving, and all his struggles were for nothing. For some inexplicable reason he thought of his mother, and in his mind he saw an image of her, straightening his blazer as he went off to his first day at school. He felt her pride and love again for the first time in many years.

The sensation disturbed him, and he suppressed it. This moping around would do no good. He had to get up and find Tarmo, but the stars drew his attention again. Some people looked to the stars for inspiration, guidance, navigation, but he did not follow these little points of light; he had received all the guidance he needed. He closed his eyes, and recalled the details of his mission. He just needed one more moment to regain his composure, and then he had a battle to prepare for. He relaxed again, aware of the deep sense of exhaustion within himself, and the twinge in his arm and shoulder which surfaced from amongst the numerous aches and pains that was a consequence of lying on a cold, hard floor.

An hour later Tarmo found him, bare footed and shivering in his sleep. The big man regarded Lench with pity and shook his head.

"I trust your anguish has been worth it," he whispered. Then with a grunt he lifted Lench as if he were just a child, and slung him over his shoulder, ready to deposit him onto the pallet bed in his spare room.

2

———

ALEX ARRIVED EARLY, her breath steaming in the crisp dawn air. The sky was shading towards a soft mauve as the winter sun emerged above the skyline of the city.

An empty office always struck Alex as a strange, unnatural place. The whine of the office alarm faltered as she typed in the security code, and the furniture took on a surreal aspect in the silence. Grey, angular shapes stood, waiting for light and sound and the traffic of people to give them function and meaning.

She snapped on the lights, and felt that old sense of reassurance, of being in control by being in early, switching things on, getting everything organized. She might be the Chief Executive now, but some of the habits she developed when she was the PA had never gone away.

In the boardroom, the chairs and the table were already arranged, and she resisted the temptation to adjust the pads of paper she had set out the previous evening. Instead, she turned to prayer, acknowledging that, for all the work she had done, there was so much more that was beyond her control, all of which she would have to commit to Jesus.

Some important decisions would be made today, with consequences for SLaM, and for the people who worked for the company. There was so much to pray about, so many different and conflicting issues and challenges to offer up in prayer, and she wondered if she should get a piece of paper and a pencil so she could write them all down; but when she centred herself, and tried to open herself up to the will of the Spirit, all she could utter was one word:

"Daisy."

And maybe that was right, because whatever else they discussed at the meeting today, the main event was Daisy, her ideas and her future at the company.

Alex continued with her prayers, while outside, the winter sun crept higher above the urban skyline, a golden red glow, silhouetting the office blocks beneath it, defying the bitter wind and frost of a winter morning.

When she was done, she went into the small kitchen just off the main office suite and looked at her watch. She wondered who from her team would be in first, and she didn't have long to speculate before Aiden Kennedy, SLaM's newest recruit appeared at the door.

Aiden was an accountant by training, and he had a sharp methodical mind which had been put to good use as he picked up the pieces of her old company, Sound Light and Music, or SLaM as it had been known, after Alex had bought it from her old boss Lewis Ashbury.

SLaM had almost been ruined by its disastrous involvement in a venture called SEEKA, an attempt to sell merchandise that reflected and glorified the drugs culture. When that venture fell apart Lewis had been glad to sell what was left of the business to his old PA, Alex Masters, and she had drafted Aiden in to stabilise the finances and secure the business.

She had met Aiden through a church contact and although she trusted him, she knew little about him other than the fact that he had trained as an accountant before moving into one of the big City partnerships. SLaM was just one of the companies that he looked after, and she was grateful to have him on the team.

"You're the early bird today, Alex," he said as he dropped his coat and bag onto his chair.

"As always," she replied, "but I bet you had a late night preparing the financial reports for us."

"I might have," he said, and smiled.

Alex always found Aiden's accent comforting and reassuring. He'd been Chief Financial Officer for nearly a year now and his calm, competent approach had been the perfect antidote to SLaM's rehabilitation after the chaos of SEEKA. Aiden was the calming influence that had given the others, especially Daisy, license to dream dreams and think their crazy thoughts.

But even Aiden's reassuring competency couldn't disguise the reality that hung over them all: SLaM was running out of money.

Without saying any more he sat down and took some sheets of paper from his bag. Then he muttered under his breath as his pencil flicked across the columns of figures he would be presenting today.

Alex looked at him and then went back to the kitchen. Where many of her old colleagues needed a cigarette to help them face the day, she preferred caffeine. She brought back two cups.

He was still hunched over the figures when she returned, and when he did look up to take the cup, she looked him in the eye and said:

"Aiden, I want to change the name of the company."

"What? Why?" He put down his pencil.

"I don't like 'SLaM'," she said. "We aren't *Slamming* anything. I want a name that says who we are, what we hope for."

"Well it's your call," he said. "Have you talked to Lewis about this? Branding and image is his thing, and I'll have to work out how much it's going to cost to rebrand, but I think you know that. It's not a small thing, Alex."

Then he turned back to his numbers.

She looked at him for a second longer and frowned as he scanned the document in front of him. What she was saying was important, and all he was doing was adding up the numbers he'd already worked through.

"Aiden!" She almost shouted his name.

He jumped. "What?"

"I need your support, Aiden. I know the figures are important, but I need to have you with me on this."

Aiden leant back in the chair, tossing his pencil onto the table. "Alex, you know you have my support."

She was still staring at him.

"So, what's this really all about?" he said. "Come on, talk to me."

"I want us to stand for something that is full of light and hope," she said, "not aggression and darkness. I see so many young people crushed under the wheels of self-hate and self-harm, lost in all that social media confusion, I hate it. They're in such pain but they have to pretend everything is okay." She paused, trying to think of the words to sum it up. "It's evil masquerading as cool."

"Evil has always masqueraded as cool," said Aiden casually. "It always will."

"Well it makes me angry!" she shouted.

"I know it makes you angry," said Aiden, "and hat's why I work with you, because you get passionate about this stuff and you are trying your best to do something about it." He picked up the sheet of accounts and waved it at her.

"Whatever you might think," he continued, "this is not the

only thing I care about, it's not even the most important thing I care about. None of the numbers mean anything without the vision behind them, and that's you; pulling it together, making it happen. I do understand what you are trying to do here."

"I know you understand," she said, "I know you do, I think that's why I am shouting at you."

"I trust you Alex; that's enough. Really it is."

"Is it though?" she said. "It won't be enough when the money runs out."

He looked at her and smiled.

"That's where you have to trust me." He waved the papers in his hand again.

"Yes, of course," she said.

"So what do you want to call it?" he continued. "What's this new name you want for the company?"

"I want something light. I want a name that speaks hope and joy, and warmth."

"Okay," said Aiden, "we'd better start thinking then."

"We don't need to," said Alex. "I know what I want to call the company: I want to call it Summer Media and Entertainment, or just 'Summer' for short."

Aiden nodded. "If that's what you want to do, you've got my vote."

She noticed he didn't say any more about rebranding costs and she was grateful; that was a conversation for another day.

He finished scribbling some figures on the paper in front of him and handed it to her.

"Here's where we are with the money," he said.

She scanned through the numbers, looking for something that would tell her how quickly they were burning through their reserves.

"So how long have we got?" she said.

"If things stay as they are, we've got about six months, maybe seven or eight at the absolute limit if we ration the marketing spend. Of course, that's worst case. If Conner's album goes platinum, or he picks up a couple of million followers on social media, we could be just fine."

They both smiled, but it was clear where things were.

"If we forget about the hopelessly optimistic scenarios," she said, "how are really doing ?"

"If things stay as they are," said Aiden, "by the summer we'll be finished."

"Okay, thank you."

"But then there's always Daisy's fashion line," he said, smiling, "although that's another case of spending money in the hope that we might make some one day in the future."

He got a copy of the report that Daisy had prepared for them on her ethically sourced fashion line. It was still at the early stages, more a collection of bold colours and lines than actual stock to be sold.

"These are brilliant though," said Alex.

"Indeed, they are," said Aiden, "but like every other part of your business at the moment, Alex, she needs the funds to make it work."

"I know," said Alex. "Let's see what she has to offer us today."

Before either of them said anything else, the door swung open and Caleb Wicks walked in; he was halfway through a conversation with them even as he placed his worn leather briefcase on the table.

"The traffic! Alex my dear, you will have to remind me why we meet here in the middle of town, where there is nowhere to park." He paused and stared at them both. "Oh, excuse me, Aiden. Good morning to both of you, how are you?"

"Very well thank you, Caleb." Alex smiled and moved the seat next to her out from the table.

He sat in the chair, and rubbed at his shoulder muscles, trying to relieve the stress of the journey.

"Maybe you should take the train, or the bus in?" said Alex as Caleb reached into his bag.

"What?" said Caleb. "Oh, perhaps you are right." He paused. "The car is a habit and probably a bad one, especially when there are better, greener ways to travel."

"You said it," said Alex.

"I'll look at the options," said Caleb, and turned to Aiden. "I must say you look a little peaky, my dear fellow; are the company figures keeping you up too late at night?"

"I think you know the answer to that one," said Aiden, with a rueful smile.

"Oh dear, well that is rather unfortunate. You need to get an early night. Mrs Wicks and I always feel the benefit of an early night. Anyway, is the kettle on?"

"We don't do the kettle here, Caleb," said Alex. "We have a hot water dispenser."

Caleb frowned.

"May the good Lord preserve me from hot water," he said gently. "No one can make a proper cup of tea with hot water. Well never mind."

Caleb was just taking his coat off when the door jumped open and Lewis and Daisy burst in, laughing at some private joke. Daisy carried a bundle of papers, and was dressed as ever in her skinny jeans and bright tee shirt. Alex marvelled at how Daisy could be so very thin and yet not seem to feel the cold. Lewis meanwhile looked every inch the civilized gent at leisure, in his corduroys and tweed jacket.

"Hello, you two." Caleb smiled at them. "Are you joining us today, Lewis?"

"The boss wanted me in for this one," said Lewis, nodding at Alex, and then he winked at Daisy who smirked back at him.

"There would be no point in me persuading Lewis to join us," said Alex, "and then not using the benefit of his wisdom."

Lewis laughed. "I don't think anyone has ever called me wise before, but remember, I'm more your music mogul type than a fashion guru."

"I know," said Alex, "but all the same you might say something wise."

He laughed again. "We'll see."

With everyone present, they filed into the boardroom and took their seats. Daisy hooked up her laptop to the projector and stood at the front, fidgeting with a pen.

"Okay," said Alex, "thank you all for coming in, especially to you, Lewis; I suspect we have taken you away from the golf course today."

"For you, Alex, I will miss a few rounds," he said, smiling.

"I'm very grateful," said Alex. "As you all know, Daisy is presenting her fashion range ideas today. She is doing so not only with my permission, but also with my encouragement." She stopped, letting this comment sink in; she wanted them all to know that she, the boss, was behind this one.

"Daisy believes we can tap into the growing market for garments manufactured with fairly traded materials and made by fairly paid workers. That will be part of the appeal and branding for these items. I don't want to preempt what she has to say so without any further delay, Daisy, over to you."

Alex reached over and dimmed the lights, wondering if Daisy felt as nervous as she did.

IN FACT, Daisy did feel as nervous as Alex, and more. This wasn't just one of her good ideas; her work with SLaM was her dream now, and this presentation contained all of her most precious ambitions. After all that had happened, after all the support she had received, Daisy wanted to work with these people, but this was work she wanted to do, this wasn't merely a presentation for her, this was her heart and blood and soul.

The first slide flicked up and she started.

"So this is it. This is how we're going to take the fashion dimension of SLaM to a whole new level."

As she said the word "SLaM" Aiden glanced at Alex, and raised an eyebrow.

Alex shook her head, now was not he moment to talk about a change in the company name.

Images and designs flicked up onto the wall. Collectively they represented a huge step on from the tried and trusted collection of branded merchandise they had been selling. This was a whole wardrobe of styles, designs and colours, and as she progressed with her presentation, Daisy felt the fear inside her turn to excitement.

"I want to bring a diverse, international feel to our collection, both in terms of the materials and style."

"Gracious, I didn't know we were going have a *collection*," said Caleb without any trace of irony. "This is wonderful."

"Why shouldn't we have a collection, Uncle C?" Daisy smiled.

Caleb leant over to Alex.

"Did she just call me, Uncle C?" he whispered.

"I believe so," said Alex, trying to keep a straight face.

Daisy flicked up another image. "This cheongsam is a good example of the kind of thing I want to see us produce."

"Excuse me, what is a 'cheongsam'?" asked Caleb.

"This represents the more formal aspects of what could become our portfolio," said Daisy. "As you can see, a cheongsam is a tight-fitting silk dress, it originated in Shanghai in the 1920s."

"Fascinating," said Caleb, steepling his fingers.

Daisy continued with her presentation, and Alex tasted the

adrenaline in her throat. Was this working? Did they like what they were seeing?

Daisy came to the heart of her presentation with a series of designs that, unlike the previous ones, contained almost no colour at all. Most of them were simple pencil or ink drawings so they gave only the impression of a garment, lacking the substance of firm contours and colour.

"I am also working on some designs for tabards, waistcoats and jerkins. These are at the heart of the whole collection. I know what I want these garments to look like; I just need to find the right material. The right texture and colours." She paused, letting them ponder on her words.

"I have been wondering how to integrate all this with what you want to do here." She glanced briefly at Alex. "And I want to find materials that tell a story, a God story you might call it. So, for example, if I can find a material that in its own environment speaks of God's creation, I could use that. All of these items will have to be integrated with the SLaM branding of course. But that, everyone, is the vision I want to turn into a reality for us."

Daisy finished her presentation and Alex brought up the lights. Lewis and Caleb blinked at each other.

"So, where do we go with this now?" said Alex, picking up the discussion and directing the question at Daisy.

"I need to find some materials, and there is only one place to do it."

"Really, and where is that?" said Caleb.

"Paris," said Daisy firmly. "Première Vision. It's the world's foremost design materials event. The next one will be in a few weeks' time. I need to go there if I am going to pursue this the way I want to."

She took some sheets of paper from her bag.

"Here is a summary of my proposal to the board, in writing."

She handed out the papers and then she smiled at Aiden. "All the likely costs have been stated."

"Thanks, Daisy," said Alex. "Has anyone got any questions?"

No one responded, and Alex wasn't sure if they were amazed, unconvinced, or just bemused by the whole thing.

"Thank you Daisy," said Alex, "that was an inspiration. You had better give us a few minutes talk it through now," she said to Daisy.

"Okay, well I'll be in that café over the road," said Daisy. She got to her feet and hurried out of the door. She felt as if she had just revealed the deepest, most personal part of herself to them; exposing herself to their judgement. She could not have done this two years ago, but still the whole situation made her feel nervous and angry in a way she could not quite explain.

Even as she was walking out, the old nerves and the old condemnation rose in her.

They won't like it, they won't understand it, she thought.

Or they'll like it but there won't be any money. They'll say lovely things about it all and tell me to come back another time, next year, or two years, or never.

By the time she reached the café she was even more convinced that it wasn't going to happen. She wasn't even sure now if she wanted to do this project with them.

"Maybe that's not such a bad thing," she whispered to herself as she hovered outside the door and reached for her cigarettes, "maybe that's not so bad after all."

THE MEETING ROOM door closed and no one said anything; the only sound was the hum of the projector fan.

Finally, Alex broke the silence:

"I want to know what you think, your honest opinion. You all received a copy of Daisy's proposal in your briefing pack. Basically, she is asking for more time within her current role to develop this project together with her existing merchandise responsibilities. Additionally, she is asking for some budget to go to this Première Vision show and buy some fabric samples."

She looked at them, each one in turn, trying to decide which one to ask first.

"What do you think, Caleb?" She hoped her old friend would see how important it was to give Daisy a chance now.

"Oh, it's wonderful, wonderful!" he said, waving a hand in the air. "She is such a talent."

Alex nodded, and smiled.

"But," continued Caleb, "I do wonder if we have the money for it right now. Perhaps it's something for next year? We are rather stretched at the moment financially and I fear that if we said yes it might give Aiden even more sleepless nights. I think what she has here is wonderful, and we must do it, I am just not sure if now is the right time."

Then he added as if as an afterthought:

"The thing is, she will be expecting us to say 'no' so we must say 'not yet, but it will happen'. We cannot let her lose heart."

Alex nodded and turned to Lewis. "What do you think?"

"Well, of course this could be a great idea. It's very exciting, there's lots of energy in this thing. Daisy is brimming with talent but my instinct would be to put the company's money into the music project, and focus her on the standard merchandising for now. Like Caleb said, promise it all to her next year, you know. Now, I know you guys have a different approach to me, not just the profit motive and all that; so you might want to play it differently, but I'm for saying 'no' or 'not yet'."

"Whether we do it now or next year, do you think it would work? Can we make money on this?" said Alex, still facing him.

"Eventually, yes," he said, "a lot of people want their tea and coffee to be fairly traded; maybe enough of them want their clothes fairly traded as well. As for the money, I wouldn't give all this a second thought if my instinct said go for it," he gestured to the figures in front of him, "but you people don't want to fly by the seat of your pants in quite the same way we used to. Bottom line: great idea but you need to be cautious now."

Alex felt the frustration welling up inside her. She had hoped that at least one of the two of them would be supportive of Daisy's plan, and push for them to give her the green light, right now. She'd wanted at least one of them to say as much before she turned to Aiden. During the presentation he'd kept glancing back to the figures, and she wasn't sure how much notice he had taken of what Daisy said.

"Aiden?" Her tone was unnecessarily sharp, as if she were accusing him of something, and she could just see Caleb raise an eyebrow in her direction.

Aiden looked up from the numbers. "Of course we she let her do it. And she must do it now, this year not next year. What were you all thinking, talking about next year? If you tell her that, she'll leave, and it will never get done, and everyone will miss the opportunity."

He said it as if it was the most obvious thing in the world, and they all stared at him.

Aiden looked back to his numbers, and then he glanced up again.

"Anyone disagree?" he said.

Alex burst out laughing, and Lewis shook his head.

"I should have hired you as my accountant five years ago!" said Lewis. "You're as crazy as the rest of us."

"I mean it." Aiden was the only one in the room not smiling. "We need to give her our full support, now. If we wait, that talent will be lost to SLaM forever. And just for the record, I don't think we are going to be calling ourselves SLaM for much longer, are we, Alex?"

Everyone looked at Alex and her eyes widened, she sat forward.

"Right, no we're not," she said, surprised at Aiden's revelation. "We're going to rebrand."

"Are we?" said Lewis.

"Yes," said Alex, "but that's a conversation for another time. Let's focus on Daisy's work. I agree with Aiden, we should approve it now."

"Well maybe this is God's wisdom," said Caleb. "Alex, I wonder if we might pray around this for a couple of minutes. Please do bear with us, Lewis."

"You guys carry on," said Lewis. "I'm going to go outside for a smoke. For what it's worth I think you should go for it, it will be fun to see how this unfolds, but then of course it's not my money."

He got up and looked at them all.

"I confess," he said, "I thought you Christians were a timid bunch, but maybe you've got some drive and passion after all."

"I'll take that as a compliment," said Alex, "thanks."

Lewis chuckled to himself as he left, clutching a packet of cigars and a lighter.

The directors of Summer, as it would come to be known, bowed their heads and prayed.

In the same physical space, angelic beings, the emissaries of the Lord, turned in their own way to prayer. There was one for each person present, and some others, filling the room with unseen light, each of them going about their divine business.

Angel stood in the room listening to it all. The decision to sponsor Daisy now was the correct one; and this moment of prayer would help to ensure that the decision had the necessary spiritual grounding, and was handled in the right way. From

Angel's perspective the humans in the room seemed to look brighter, achieving a kind of dazzling clarity as they prayed, as if Angel had been looking at them all through a dusty window, which had now been flung open.

Angel waited in the silence and the instruction came to him, and to all of them.

Aiden should tell her, and Conner should go with her to Paris.

So that was how it would be. He made no judgement on the merits of the instruction he received; it was the Lord's will. On cue he bent down close to Alex's right ear and whispered something into her mind and heart.

"Well, thank you everyone," said Alex.

"Perhaps," said Caleb thoughtfully, "you might want to tell us what your opinion is, my dear. Everyone else has had their say."

"I think we have made the right decision; I think she should go, I always did. But maybe someone needs to go with her. I want to send Conner along for a couple of days to help her."

"Conner?" said Caleb. "Interesting. Isn't he touring then?"

"Not until after this fashion event," said Alex. "He can take a break from rehearsal and go and see the sights with Daisy."

"Well," said Caleb, "I think that feels like the right decision. We should agree some budget for her, for them, and then someone needs to tell her our decision. Do you have any ideas about who that might be?"

DAISY SAT in the corner of the café, her designs spread out in front of her across the table.

She knew that that they were going to say no, and she was going to sit here until someone came to tell her. She had enough self-awareness to realize she was preparing herself for bad news, defending herself from the shock, but it was still true; she still thought they were going to turn her down.

Looking at it now, all her work seemed flimsy and inadequate. She wished she had added more in terms of colour and detail to some of her drawings; she wished she'd been more assertive in putting forward her case; she wished she hadn't mentioned some of the likely costs.

Actually, she wished she had done a lot of things differently, but it was all too late now.

She didn't see Aiden come in, and wander up to the table where she sat; he had a ten-pound note folded in his hand.

"Do you want another drink, Daisy?"

"No," she said.

"Are you sure?" said Aiden. "We have some things to discuss."

She looked at him for a moment, trying to read his intentions.

"Americano, please," she said.

He returned with two coffees.

"The board have agreed to your proposals," he said, "and that you should get on with the project now, and go to Paris for Première Vision."

"What?" she said.

"Your project is approved," said Aiden, with half a smile. "We need to discuss your travel arrangements and expenses."

She stared at him. "Approved?"

"Yes," said Aiden. "Come on, Daisy, you're up! This project of yours is happening!"

"Oh God, YES!" she said. Customers turned in her direction as she jumped up and flung her arms around Aiden. He blushed and staggered with her weight around his neck, pulling him over the top of the table.

"You're welcome!" said Aiden.

She looked at the drawings on the table in front of her, and she saw them once again as works of genius.

"What did you think they should do?" she said, staring at him.

"I told them your project must be approved, and you should do it this year, now," he said.

She looked back at him, and many things crossed her mind, and she said none of them. She realized as well that she was actually shaking in her excitement and she tried to relax.

This was it. She was going to get a chance to design and make her own clothing. She was going to go to Paris for the greatest fashion material show on earth – Première Vision.

3

___

LENCH'S GROUP GATHERED, as usual, at his country home. They abused themselves and each other in their usual manner, and then disbursed, each of them nursing their own particular form of damage.

They had chatted together immediately after the formal gathering, and the Assassin had been there, standing at the edge of the group while most of the others had their backs to him. He was conscious, once more, of being the outsider, superficially one of the group and yet also the alien amongst them. He increasingly felt this alienation as Lench packed the group with his own types, the rich, the arrogant and the entitled.

From early childhood the Assassin had always been on the outside looking in, kicking hard against the rest of the world. The others in the group sensed this separation, and they both feared and despised the killer amongst them, perpetuating the Assassin's view of life and his place in it. Some of the old members of the group had shown him a pleasing degree of deference, even understanding, but the current lot treated him with snobbish disdain. It was especially true of some of the new women, they were the worst; they really made him angry.

And even in another, darker, plane of existence the Assassin's separation was confirmed. The demon hordes that attended each of Lench's other associates cast their baleful glances at the Assassin and the legion that fed off him; they in turn stared back, bitter, vengeful, held in place by an unspoken and ancient discipline.

Lench had instructed him to be here this evening, to meet with him personally afterwards. If it hadn't been for this summons, he might not even have turned up.

Some of the group grunted a farewell to him as they left, and he nodded to them, distracted from his brooding about the meeting he was due to have with his leader. He knew he would be subjected to the usual indignities that Lench seemed to enjoy provoking him with when they were alone together.

"Not quite the team player, are you, Josef?" he would say, in that arrogant, understated way of his. The Assassin would respond with a look as patient as death, and even Darius Lench could not hold this man's gaze forever.

Josef, or Josef Xavier Durand to give him his full name, considered himself to be a mongrel. He was a racial cocktail of French and German-Austrian blood and for most of his life he had been marginalized because he was not quite enough of any one of these races. When he mixed with the French, they suspected he was German; and when he mixed with Germans, they knew he was French; and in Britain he had simply been treated as *foreign*.

Josef Durand represented at least the third generation of a family schooled in the brutalities of life. He was born and spent his early years in Marseilles. His grandmother arrived there in the winter of 1958. Pregnant and alone, she had been determined to seek some kind of life for herself and the child she carried. She found some accommodation, and the baby was born, a girl who would become his mother. She grew up amidst the sights and smells of the sea and those who lived by it; and the teeming atmosphere of a busy, raw port town was the first and only thing she knew.

Josef's grandmother had died when his mother was fifteen, not quite old enough to protect herself from those who might make use of her pretty smile and slim figure. Dreams of college and a loving husband slipped away before the necessities of survival.

She had become pregnant with Josef during the course of her trade and done what she could to protect him and bring him up, as her mother had done for her. Josef had no idea who his father was; probably one of the lean and restless men who liked to spend a night on shore when their ship docked; his mother had talked about an Austrian sailor who visited her occasionally when he was in port.

As a young boy he quickly learnt the benefits of being useful; running errands for his mother's pimp and finding ways to enter and leave premises unnoticed. He became a proficient thief before he could read or write.

His mother was murdered by one her clients just before his eleventh birthday. He could still remember the overwhelming confusion and anger that came over him when he returned home from an errand and discovered her corpse. It was the most profound feeling, full of loss and rage, a feeling that defined his approach to life from that day onwards. He discovered a new level of motivation, fuelled by anger and the lust for revenge. For the next twenty-four hours he did not sleep; instead he visited all the places where he had contacts and asked questions and kept his eyes open, hoping the murderer had not already gone back to one of the many ships that disappeared out of the harbour each day.

Josef felt a thrill in his gut when, the evening after his mother was murdered; someone whispered to him that the man who had most likely murdered his mother had not yet left port. The vessel he was crewing on was still waiting for cargo and would be leaving in the morning. The police were still in the early stages of a perfunctory investigation when they found themselves with another murder in the city, a body was found on the dockside, a clumsy gunshot from a stolen weapon, and then someone had beaten the corpse, the face and body bruised and swollen. Reflecting on the kill some years later, Josef had disapproved of the clumsiness of it, but had applauded his younger self on his courage and commitment.

The boy Josef found that he had enjoyed the kill. He revelled in it in fact, the justice of it, the fear in the victim's eyes, the finality of the act. That night he became a convert to the idea that it was violence, not talk that achieved results. He continued to look for, and find, injustices meted out against him and his associates, and he used those injustices as a spur to practise his new beliefs in a brutal and uncaring world.

He became an efficient assassin as well as a proficient thief, and although his circumstances changed, the anger that drove him, that made him lethal and ruthless remained constant.

In later years he gradually realized that vengeful anger, like all sinful indulgences, demands a price for the benefits it brings. He had no regrets and paid that price willingly. In his case it was a gradual release of control, and a gradual submission of the will to the other forces within him. Violence and the love of violence had become the taskmasters, driving him with a relentless cruelty and precision towards all forms of destruction, including self-destruction. In the process, his capacity for obedience clashed with his need for violence.

Recently the tension between these opposing forces had tormented him almost to the point of breakdown, and he knew that within the group his reliability was under question; he strived to maintain his usefulness, but the discipline and restraint he need to do his job, to prove himself amongst Lench's friends, was leaking out of him as his character wore away.

It was these doubts about his continued usefulness that plagued him as he waited in the reception hall of Lench's home. He looked around, at the images and the décor. This hall was bigger than his entire flat. In the pictures on the walls, men gazed down with cold, sharp eyes; dressed in the finery of different historical periods. Their lifeless eyes gazed down on him in unforgiving judgement, and some of them seemed familiar to him. There was evidence of Lench's other passion here also, a large glass cabinet holding a collection of very old surgical instruments: blades and saws, needles and hammers. The cabinet was locked and alarmed, and he speculated for a moment on how he would break into it if he had to.

He let out a long sigh and looked around at the trappings of wealth. Just being in this place made him angry in ways he could not define, and still he waited as the minutes passed and the others were long gone. He had learnt to be patient during the course of perfecting his skills, but it wasn't something he was comfortable with. Looking at the paintings again he suddenly realized where he had seen eyes like that before. He remembered again the faces of some of his mother's clients; the clothes were very different, but the eyes had that same hard look about them. He thought about his mother, and to his surprise he found that the memory stirred at the sediment of the love he once felt for her.

The thought of it made him restless and he started to pace around the table at the centre of the hall. On the table was a vase of dried flowers, and he was leaning forward examining the flowers when Lench emerged from his study.

"Fingers off the table, Josef, there's a good chap," said Lench, and the Assassin straightened up and stared at his master.

Lench smiled and walked over to where Josef stood. He indicated the table.

"Do you know what this is?"

The Assassin looked away; here was one of Lench's games, and he wasn't in the mood for any of it tonight.

"It's a Victorian Burr Walnut Sutherland table," continued Lench. "A simple piece in many ways but eminently practical. One might say that it has its place." He paused for a moment. "Come in, Josef, and sit down; we have things to discuss."

The Assassin followed Lench into his study and stood opposite an expansive desk. The leather surface was buried under papers and folders, and there were also a couple of screens tracking markets and prices across the globe. Lench eased into his seat at the other side of the desk and looked at Josef in the way a Headmaster might look at an errant child.

"I'll come to the point," said Lench. "I have discerned the master's will in the matter of crushing our enemies, and now we must act."

The Assassin stayed silent, watching with a steady gaze; maybe the boss *was* about to give him some new assignment. He would welcome that; a little focused activity would be good for him.

"I am ready," he said, "I am ready to get to work."

"Ah, well," Lench smiled with feigned embarrassment, "there's the rub; I'm afraid you are going to have to play second fiddle on this job. You see it's Marie who will take charge of your involvement this time."

Josef stared straight ahead of himself and said nothing.

Marie? He thought. *What could she do?*

Only a slight twitch of his left eye betrayed the confusion swelling within him; he knew of course that protest would be useless. Lench was conveying the master's will, not a point for discussion.

"In fact," continued Lench, "you are going to have to do what you are told, by her."

Still the Assassin was silent.

"Do you understand what I just said, Josef?" Lench leant forward and raised his eyebrows.

"Yes," hissed the Assassin.

"Pardon?" said Lench, who had genuinely not heard the words. At that moment, something broke in the Assassin's mind, some final safety value fractured. Lench stared in shock as Josef's eyes widened considerably and he let out a bellowing scream of a response.

"*I SAID YES!*" As he spoke, the flat of his hand came down, hard, on Lench's desk, making the stacked papers jump and the screen flicker.

Lench was genuinely startled. "Contain yourself, Josef! While you are in this house, you will conduct yourself in a fitting manner. Do you understand?"

The Assassin was silent.

"Do you understand?" said Lench, he stood up and stared straight at the Assassin.

"Yes," said Josef finally, then he took a deep breath and tried to calm his heartbeat.

"Good." Lench took a deep breath too, unnerved by the vehemence of the outburst. "Now, as I said, you are going to have to work with Marie, and do what she tells you. Is that going to be a problem?"

"No." The Assassin clenched his right fist behind his back.

"Do you?" said Lench, coming around his desk to stand next to the Assassin. "I want to be sure that there is no confusion here. No possible misinterpretation of my directions."

"You have made yourself clear," said Josef.

"Good." Lench reached into the top left-hand drawer of the desk and withdrew one of his favourite Don Alejandro Havana cigars. He took his time lighting the cigar, and after three puffs, he called out in a clear, authoritative voice, "Come in now please, Marie."

Josef looked round in surprise as the door adjoining the office opened, and a young woman walked in. She wore a very dark grey executive suit and her brown, slightly wiry hair was tied back, accentuating the sharp features of her face. The suit could not disguise her athletic build, the muscle tone under the clothing. There was determination in her lips, and her dark eyes concealed something of her personality in a way that Josef found strangely beautiful; around her neck on a thin silver chain she wore the symbol of her faith.

"Marie," said Lench casually, "thank you for joining us. I was just explaining the arrangements to our friend Josef here." He turned to the Assassin:

"I want you to understand," he said with mock patience, "we are going to be subtle in our approach this time, and Marie is most suited to the particular requirements of the situation. There might be a role for you, from time to time, if Marie thinks it is appropriate. Is that clear?"

The Assassin could feel the moisture on his brow. The room was warm and the scent of Lench's cigar hung in the air. He didn't want to react to what he knew was a test, an attempt to bait him.

"So, let me be clear as well," he said. "Will she slip in and out of places undetected? Will she dispatch people at your command?"

Lench glanced over to Marie and she gazed at Josef and smiled.

"I will be the judge of who does what," she said, "and you will do what you are told, under my instruction, as you do under Darius." She turned away from him as if the matter was closed.

But the Assassin would not accept this kind of dismissive

treatment from the woman; he took one quick step towards her so that he stood just behind and to the right of her. He was disappointed that she did not flinch or turn to him.

"You will never presume to tell me the master's will, I do not answer to you," he hissed, making flecks of spittle settle on the lobe of her ear.

Still she did not turn. "By submitting to me, you are submitting to the master's will."

Lench observed but did not intervene; this contest had to play itself out, and he was quite confident in the abilities of his new protégé.

A maniac grin cracked the Assassin's face and he moved so she would only be able to see him from the corner of her eye.

"Were it to take my fancy, MAR-EE," he pronounced her name with a deliberate awkwardness, "I could overwhelm you, here and now, on this desk, and take you for myself."

"You would fail in your attempt," said Marie, facing him, "and regret your folly."

Josef looked as if he was about to respond when she whipped her right hand out and caught him across the jaw with her palm. It made a sound like a dry branch snapping. But even as Marie's hand connected with his jaw, he removed a small, thin-bladed knife from somewhere, and sliced first into the blouse of her left arm and then the skin of her forearm, drawing blood.

In the silence each of them stared at the other.

"Very good, very good indeed," whispered Marie. She peeled back the sleeve of her blouse to reveal the wound on her forearm. Blood slid lazily down her arm to her elbow.

She offered the cut to the Assassin who watched impassively as the trickle of blood gathered and formed a hanging drip at her elbow. They both looked at the red drop of blood, but then Josef's gaze went down to Marie's right hand, which hovered an inch from his side and contained a small vial of fluid. A needle from the vial was pressing lightly against the Assassin's shirt.

Josef slowly replaced the knife in his sleeve, and then eased away from her.

"Oh, come now, Josef," she said, moving a step towards him, "don't be shy. You've drawn blood, you know the protocol."

He stared at her.

"This is not the time," he said, his eyes moving between hers and her left elbow still held in front of him.

"Drink," she said.

"But surely..." he stammered.

"DRINK," she commanded, and thrust her arm forward.

With a greedy anticipation, he grabbed her arm, raised it slightly, and ran the tip of his tongue up from the elbow to her wrist, savouring the sticky metal flavour of her blood.

"If we have to have this conversation again," she said as he licked his lips, "you will feel the needle."

Josef stared at her. He laughed and continued to lick his lips.

"Well that was excellent," said Lench, breaking in on them. "Now, if you will excuse us, Josef, Marie and I have things to discuss. You will be told what is required of you in due course."

Josef could still feel some trace of Marie's blood on his chin as he bowed to her, and she returned the compliment. Then he nodded to Lench and turned to leave without waiting for a response. He walked briskly out of the room, out of the front door of the house and into the cold country air.

Outside he looked across at the two remaining vehicles parked in Lench's drive, and the comparison only served to reinforce his place in the world. His car was a scuffed pale blue Fiesta, instantly forgettable, a tool of his trade. Then next to it, gleaming in the dark, he could see the sleek Iridium Silver of Lench's just purchased SLK 350. The boss had boasted about this latest purchase, indulging himself by taking up the offer to fly business class to the manufacturer's premises and picking up the car personally. It was, the Assassin knew, just the kind of ostentatious gesture that Lench would love.

Josef felt a sudden desire to urinate on the bonnet of the Mercedes, but he found the strength to resist that indulgence and got into his own car and drove away.

WATCHING FROM THE WINDOW, Lench drew on his cigar and released the curtains.

Marie placed her hand on Lench's arm; the blood had clotted fully now.

"He *is* spent," she said, simply, looking straight at her leader.

"I will be the judge of that, Marie." Lench smiled and blew more smoke into the air between them, "but you," he said, turning to her, "*you* are most definitely not spent. You are going to get a chance to prove yourself. The master requires your services, and I am relying on you."

"I am ready to do anything that is required of me, anything."

"Good. You understand that we simply can't fail again. We cannot."

Marie remained silent and Lench placed the cigar in a large crystal ashtray.

"What do we need to do?" she said.

"Sit down," he replied, "I have no desire to conduct another stand-up discussion with anyone this evening."

She sat neatly in the armchair opposite his desk, the inverted pentagram swinging slightly before it came to rest against her breast. He could not read her eyes through the dark, almost black irises. Was she impatient or expectant? Indifferent or maybe full of all kinds of hunger, he could only speculate.

Lench was not, as a rule, a man taken with passions of the

flesh, but he did find Marie's intensity, her focus, rather alluring. He considered the wisdom of having her strip naked now right before him, as a kind of test of obedience. The idea lingered in his mind before he dismissed it; she would have done what he asked, of course, and more; but she would know it was a pointless exercise and would not think well of him for it.

He took a photo from his pocket. "This," he said, "is Alex Masters' brother, Conner Adams."

She studied the photo, her face expressionless. "I know of him."

"This is our target, their weakness. If we can destroy him, we will destroy their company. We need to attack both his character and his body, and in the process crush him. The advantage we have is that he is both their weak point and the chief source of income in the next few months. If we can remove the boy, then we remove that income stream, and their whole empire will fall. You and I will each take one aspect of the plan and execute it. I am going to go after his integrity and his calling; but you must go after his body."

"How?" she said.

"You will lure him to the safe house, obtain some pictures of yourself conducting some abuse of him, you will be in disguise of course. Josef can bring him to you, and support you in the process, meanwhile I will do what I need to, to destroy his integrity."

"How much I am allowed to do to the boy?" she said.

"Well, feel free to enjoy yourself," said Lench, waving his arm casually so that the smoke swirled above their heads, "but he must not be damaged too much. Perhaps some light blade work, decorate him, but don't harm him, the devastation has to come from within."

"It will be done," she said.

"Excellent." Lench shifted in his seat. "And now perhaps we could indulge in a little sport I think."

"As you wish," said Marie. "In here?"

"Yes, I think so," said Lench.

It was an indulgence on his part, a rare physical event for him, a diversion, but he saw no harm in it.

"Well, you have come a long way," he said after they had engaged. "The nice Christian girl now serves the master."

"Do not speak of my past, please," she said. "I do not wish to remember."

This was as close as she got to emotion, and Lench thought he could see a flush of anger on her cheeks.

She pulled on her blouse. "They have made their choices," she continued, "and I have made mine." She hung her jacket over her arm, covering the tattered and bloodstained blouse sleeve. The wound had reopened in the midst of their activities, but she had ignored it. He had considered offering to get a bandage for her but had decided she would decline the offer.

"Well, goodnight then," he said.

"Goodnight," she said, and left.

***

CALEB JOLTED out of his dream and stared at the ceiling, the words already on his lips.

He was immediately alert, a state he never normally achieved in the morning until after he'd had a nice cup of tea. He knew he must get up, immediately, but quietly; if his wife woke up and saw him like this she would think he was having some sort of seizure, but the only thing seizing him was an utter conviction that God required his attention, now.

He felt disorientated, and just a little nauseous. It was like this sometimes; when the good Lord completely failed to respect his preferred morning routine. In the past Caleb found himself roused at all sorts of unreasonable hours of the morning often for things that, from his human perspective, might possibly have waited. On such occasions, he reluctantly hauled himself from his warm bed and out of obedience rather than enthusiasm, he wrote it all down, prayed it all through, and then usually, fell asleep again.

Wrapped in dressing gown and scarf, he walked into the study and eased into his most comfortable chair. He reached down and unlocked a desk drawer, removing a thick, dog-eared notebook; the pages interleaved with bookmarks, Post-it notes and thin strips of material.

He laid the book on the leather of his desk and fished for a pencil from one of an array of commemorative mugs before him, and then he started to write.

Thursday 23rd January –
The Lord has stirred me with a portent that
the enemy will strike soon. First, there
was a dream; I saw Alex standing with
her cousin Daisy behind a high and
glittering shield. I am convinced that this
shield was of the Lord's making, a
protection for them both. But on their
faces, I saw horror. Looking further on I
saw a man in the darkness with hot and
vengeful eyes, a scar across his face; but
surprisingly, when I saw him, I did not
feel fear or anger, but rather the Lord's
compassion for a broken soul. I saw him
attached to a set of threads, as if he were a
puppet or mannequin; and the threads
connected to a frame held aloft by another

figure, the puppeteer. As I looked more closely, I saw that some of the threads had become detached from the frame, allowing the man some independent movement. This other figure, the puppeteer, intrigued me, for he is surely the mind behind the enemy's attacks. I should not be surprised that things have come to this. The dark forces are gathering again.

He put down his pencil and looked across the desk to a photo. This was a rare snapshot from a family party, and staring at him intently amongst the crowd of faces were the images of Alex and Daisy. In his vision they were safe behind the shield of the Lord, secure and protected. But what was special about them? And if *they* were protected, who was not?

He leant back and breathed out in a sigh, beginning to wonder what was different about Alex and Daisy. What was it that made them safe?

A thought came to him, like a voice speaking in his mind:

"They have met the enemy and they have overcome."

Of course, they had had their encounter with two of the enemy's people, and they had faced them both down. There was the man who had caused a scene in Alex's café, and the other one who had confronted them by Alex's car.

But these were still dangerous men, and not everyone was safe behind the shield.

Whatever it meant, he knew that after a period of relative calm the battle was, once more, about to begin.

"God have mercy," he said. Then he pulled himself to his feet and headed out to the kitchen.

4

———————

Daisy pushed on through a small group of French speakers clustered around a large stand, jostling them from their discussion.

"Pardon!" she shouted joyfully. "Pardon, monsieur!" Then she took a sharp right, following the edge of one of the exhibition stands round and off again in a direct line towards her destination. Conner trailed behind her, struggling to keep up.

Around her, Parisian couture blended with fabric and design from across the world. Amongst the chatter and the heat, an mélange of ideas and colours met, coming together from different places and cultures, and Daisy's senses buzzed with the sights and sounds of it all.

Conner caught up with her and stared at the splendour around him. Left to himself he would have browsed the stands at his leisure, casually exploring this world of fashion and fabric under one roof, but Daisy was on a mission. She pushed on, clutching a portfolio case and pulling at Conner's shirt as she moved off.

"It's here, here just past these people and..." She ploughed between a pair of smart-suited Italian buyers as if she were determined to interrupt an intimacy between them. They eyed her with a mixture of suspicion and bewilderment. Conner followed behind, trying to convey an apology in his expression.

"Here! Here it is, look," she said, and stopped.

Conner was still trying to give a visual apology to the Italians when he bumped into Daisy, nudging her into a large man who was resplendent in a red and gold waistcoat and green silk cravat.

"Good morning, madam," he said, "admire and enjoy." He moved his right hand in a graceful arc indicating all of the fabrics before them. Conner pulled his gaze away from the dazzle of the waistcoat and ogled at the display before him.

"This is it," said Daisy, "just look at them, aren't they beautiful?"

"Yeah, absolutely, Daisy," he said, and he meant it.

Amidst the bustle and the heat, Daisy stood completely still.

She gazed out at a kaleidoscope of African colour and texture – rolls of material fanning out, the bounty of a continent. She leant forward so that her lips were close to his ear. "I want them all, Conner, all of them. I want to take them home with us."

Conner had a vision of himself staggering back to the hotel, weighed down with bundles of material.

"Is that allowed?" he said. "I mean how much money can you spend here?"

She laughed. "What are you? Aiden's secret assistant?"

"No," he said, "but they did give you some sort of budget, I mean you can't buy it all."

"Calm yourself," she said, "we're just getting some samples."

"Well, you get whatever you want to," he replied defiantly, "but don't expect me to drag it back halfway across Paris."

She looked at him and raised an eyebrow. "Now don't be upset with me, Conner. Just look at this."

She opened the portfolio case and removed a pencil drawing

of a loose-fitting jacket. The vendor peered over her shoulder, nodding slowly at the designs.

"What about that, Conner, what fabric could we use for that?"

Conner blinked a couple of times and peered through the haze at the fabrics in front of him. He was desperate to give her some sort of answer and so he pointed at a crimson material shimmering in the warmth.

"That one's nice, I could see you using that," he said, but he wasn't sure whether she even heard him. Her eyes moved on to some of the other fabrics there.

Daisy could see that Conner flagging, and it wouldn't be long before he was complaining about the heat and his aching feet.

"Come on, Conner," she said, putting her arm around his shoulder, "don't give up now that we are here. Look at this design again and tell me what fabric I should use for it." She pulled another sheaf of paper from her file.

He was about to tell her to work it out for herself, when another voice cut in on them:

"I think you should try using the Kente cloth from Ghana."

In Conner's head, the noise of the exhibition receded, and he heard that single, female voice. He turned to see who had spoken.

She was about Daisy's height, dressed in a cornflower blue blouse and cream cotton slacks, and in the heat of the exhibition she looked as if she was surrounded by her own bubble of coolness and calm. She had clear green eyes, framed by ginger curls, and he looked at her and smiled.

And she didn't notice him, because at that moment Daisy pushed past him and flung her arms around the girl.

"Poppy!" she said. "Oh my God! What are you doing here?"

"Looking at fabric of course," said Poppy. "Rather like you I suspect, although my team are pretty much finished here now. It's wonderful to see you again, what have you been up to?"

"Well," said Daisy, "you'd be so impressed. I'm working as a buyer for a fashion and media start-up in the city, they're going to let me design my own range."

"Wow," said Poppy, "they really must love you, that's so exciting for you, well done!"

"Real clothes!" said Daisy, waving her designs in front of her friend's eyes. "Not just tee shirts and sweats." She paused, feeling the excitement again, and then became aware of Conner fidgeting next to her.

"Oh, and this is my colleague Conner. He works for them too and he's here giving me a bit of a hand. Conner, this is a friend of mine from design college, Poppy Martinez."

"Hi, Conner," said Poppy, "so are you involved in the fashion side of this business too?"

There was a curious movement in Conner's stomach, as if some of his internal organs were fidgeting next to each other.

"Well, no not really," he said, "actually I'm a bit of a musician."

"Really," said Poppy, "what do you play?"

"A bit of acoustic guitar, and I sing as well." They looked at each other for just a moment then Daisy laughed.

"Bit of a musician," Daisy mimicked Conner's voice. "He's very modest," she said. "He's actually the lead singer in a band that the company are sponsoring, they get loads of hits on YouTube and they are going on tour later this year."

"Really," said Poppy, "so what's your band called?"

"We're called Joel's Garden," said Conner. "Pop, rock, a few ballads, that's us."

"Oh, I think I've heard of you guys," said Poppy. "I'll look out for the tour."

Conner blushed and grinned, stupidly.

"Well," said Poppy, "we should all meet before you go, if we can; I want to have a proper catch-up with you."

"Sure, let's do it," said Daisy. "So anyway, what were you saying about some fabric from Ghana?"

"I think you should try using Kente cloth from Ghana," said Poppy. "The material has a deep spiritual significance for those who produce it." She looked at Daisy's sketch once more. "There's a particular fabric from the region, *Nyanknoton*, it means 'God's eyebrow'. It's the name the indigenous people there give to a rainbow; I think it would be an excellent fabric for your design."

The man in the waistcoat eased himself into the conversation.

"We have Kente cloth here, madam," he said. "I can show you the fabric if you would like to see it."

Daisy nodded, and the man bustled around amongst the rolls of material. He returned with something that could only be described as a riot of colour.

"And this is the *Nyanknoton* design. Do you like it?"

"It's beautiful," said Daisy, drinking in the colours.

Daisy stared at the material and tried to picture it within her own design, and then she showed the drawing again to Poppy. They both studied Daisy's sketches and looked at other materials for several more minutes while Conner wandered around glancing at the different stands nearby, and then glancing back at Poppy Martinez.

"Behave yourself, Conner," he whispered under his breath.

Poppy and Daisy finished by fixing a time and place to meet later that afternoon, then Poppy handed them both one of her business cards.

"Now I remember why I always wanted to work with you when we had to pair up," said Daisy, "and work on something together, you always seemed to understand what I was trying to say in my designs."

"And you always designed the best clothes, even if..." Poppy stopped.

"Even if?" said Daisy.

"Even if things weren't always easy for you," said Poppy. "I'm sorry," she added. "I'm so pleased for you, Daisy, these people are lucky to have you, you're going to do great things."

I could do even better if you were working with me thought Daisy but she didn't say anything.

"Anyway, I'd better get back to my colleagues," said Poppy. "I'll see you later, Daisy, maybe you too, Conner, bye."

"See you later," said Daisy and as she went back to the fabrics, she caught a glimpse of Conner's eyes, wide in wonder as he watched Poppy Martinez disappear.

"So, what did you think of my friend Poppy then?" she said.

Conner's brain was just a fraction behind his mouth, always a sign of honesty.

"She was blue and cool. I mean she was dressed in blue and she seemed cool and calm. She's very nice"

"Oh she liked you too," said Daisy, winking.

"Really?" said Conner. "You think so?"

Daisy laughed, clear and loud enough to attract the attention of the Italian buyers they had barged through earlier. The assistant, who had been standing almost next to Daisy, took a small step backwards.

"What's so funny?" said Conner, frowning.

"Oh nothing," said Daisy, "just you." Then she turned to the assistant. "I want to take some samples of this fabric please."

"Certainly madam," he said, producing some scissors.

Conner and Daisy spent another hour browsing the world of materials and fabric before Daisy decided it was time to head back to the hotel. She had a text exchange with Poppy and then they set off.

Meeting Poppy had raised both their spirits, for different reasons, but as they worked their way back along the bustling Parisian streets, Conner began to flag again. He promised himself a hot bath, some alone time, and lunch. He definitely wanted lunch. If he hadn't met Daisy's old college friend he knew would have been feeling a bit sorry for himself by now.

"So who is she again?" he said.

"Who?" said Daisy. "I don't know who you're talking about."

"Stop it," said Conner.

"Her name is Poppy Martinez," said Daisy, "and she was in my year at college. Of all of us she was the gentle soul, not desperate, not striving, and she could just see colours, I don't know how she did it. It's really lucky we met her here, I want to pick her brains about some of my sketches."

Conner was silent as he padded up the busy road, carrying a bundle of fabric samples.

"We have arranged to meet this afternoon for a chat."

"Hmm," said Conner.

"If you want to join us you can but we are going to be talking business, okay?"

"Fine," said Conner.

"Maybe we'll talk business and you can join us for tea, yes?" said Daisy. "So long as you behave yourself."

"I always behave myself," said Conner, and Daisy raised an eyebrow.

"Shut up," he said, laughing.

They walked on perhaps another twenty yards when she stopped and looked at him, he had a grin on his face like a kid with a new balloon.

"Oh for goodness' sake, if you are going to be all goo-eyed over her it might be best if you keep out the way this afternoon. I don't want you playing the love-struck puppy all the way through. Got it?"

Before he could answer, she had turned back from him. He stuck his tongue out at her back, kicked a small stone and watched it skim and bounce across the paving stones and away into the gutter.

"I'm not going to get in the way," he called after her. "I want to see how your designs develop as well. I want to hear what she has to say."

"Sure you do."

"Yes, I do!" he shouted back at her, and the truth was, he did want to see how Daisy's designs would fulfil their potential. "I want to see your vision fulfilled."

"I know you do," she said, "and I want you to be there when I meet up with Poppy later."

They walked a little apart for the rest of the journey; Daisy striding out in front, Conner keeping his thoughts to himself, tagging along behind her.

She stopped at the front of the hotel, the wooden and glass revolving door moved languidly around on its axis. She turned around to see how far Conner was behind her.

"Thank you," she said. "I mean it."

"I know," he said and smiled his cheeky grin at her.

"Are you happy to hold onto this material for now?" said Daisy; nodding at the bag of material he was carrying.

"Sure," he said, "I need to go and freshen up a bit, then we can get something to eat."

"Lunch in half an hour?" she said. "I'll see you down here?"

"Sounds like a plan," said Conner. "Then I'll join you later for tea with your friend."

"Best behaviour this afternoon, okay?" said Daisy.

"Hey, best behaviour is my middle name," said Conner. "I didn't disgrace myself with you, did I?"

"I suppose not," said Daisy, nodding.

"Anyway," he said, "I don't even know this girl, she just seems nice, that's all."

"Oh she is that." Daisy walked over to the lift and Conner followed her. His room was on the ground floor, but Daisy's was on the second. She pressed the call button and the doors opened immediately.

"Poppy's lovely," she added as she got in, "and you do have one thing in common with her." She pushed the button for the third floor.

"What's that then?" said Conner as the lift doors closed.

"She's religious like you, my dear, a Christian. Just like you and Alex and most of the rest of my new friends. See you in half an hour."

And with that the lift doors shut.

Conner walked back to his room, trying to resist the temptation to break into a run in the hotel lobby. Life had just become exciting again.

He was back in the lobby fifteen minutes later. To be five minutes early is to be punctual, to be fifteen minutes early is to show an unreasonable degree of enthusiasm. He sat in one of the hotel's expansive chairs in the centre of the lobby and tried to distract himself by browsing through the magazines and papers collected on a low coffee table. It wasn't a hopeful task, because his grasp of French was, at best, basic.

He flipped through a magazine showing the latest Parisian fashions and then tossed the magazine idly across the low coffee table in front of him. The magazine skated across the glass and landed on the floor.

In front of Poppy.

"Oh you're here!" he said.

"Yes," said Poppy, "Daisy suggested we meet for lunch."

"She did?"

"Yes," said Poppy, "I hope that's okay."

"Of course," said Conner. "I think she's really looking forward to talking to you about her designs."

"So you work for this company, SLaM, is that what it's called?"

"It's called Summer now," said Conner, "we've changed the name. It's a bit of a family thing actually, we are what you might call distant relatives, as well as work colleagues now."

"Well, I'm so pleased to meet her again. I've seen Daisy change over the time I've known her, it's been fascinating to watch it."

"I bet you noticed a change in her during the last year."

"Yes, she changed during her last year at college," said Poppy. "Some kind of weight lifted from her, and her work improved as well. Lots of us noticed it."

There was a pause in the conversation. Conner shifted in his seat and the leather creaked. They both smiled and she lifted the magazine and placed it back on the centre of the table with the others.

"Daisy tells me you are a Christian." He heard himself say the words, and thought, *why did I say that?*

"I am," she said. "I'm from a Quaker family."

"Oh," he said.

"Have you heard of us?"

Conner's mind filled with images of peaceful looking people, dressed in simple clothing gathering in a Friends Meeting House. It wasn't a view he would have immediately associated with Poppy.

"I guess you look a bit colourful for a Quaker," he said, and then inwardly scolded himself again for saying the second dumb thing within a minute.

"Well, it's a common misconception. We are encouraged to live adventurously and to choose a lifestyle that makes the fullest use of the gifts we have. I intend to do that."

"All the same," said Conner, daring to press the point a little further, "there can't be that many fashion designers who are Quakers, do the two really fit together?"

Poppy smiled. "This is what I love to do. I heard someone once say: 'let your life speak'. I want to live that kind of life."

So do I, Conner thought, and then blushed as he heard himself say the words.

"Thank you," she said, and smiled. "So do you enjoy being a musician?"

"That's when I come alive," he said, "when I'm singing and playing music."

"I think we have something in common then," she said.

"I think we do."

"And I have heard of your band," she said. "You know, I'd love to find out more about what Daisy and you are doing, and this organization you work for. My colleagues are going back to the UK this afternoon but I am staying on for another night. Perhaps we could have dinner this evening, the three of us? When are you heading back home?"

"Not till tomorrow. I don't know what plans Daisy has for this evening but dinner sounds great." And it did indeed sound like a wonderful idea to Conner.

"There you are!" said Daisy, choosing this moment to arrive. "Come on, let's get some lunch then you and I, Poppy, can talk business and we'll let Conner have the afternoon off."

They went out into the sunshine and found a local café, and when they'd eaten, Daisy put a large sketchbook down on the table.

"Okay, people, here are the ideas so far, together with some thoughts from what I saw this morning."

She flipped the sketchbook open, and Daisy and Poppy talked about the designs.

Conner tried to keep up with them, but found his interest beginning to wander as the two girls set about examining styles and fabrics, talking in terms that had little or no meaning to him.

Daisy noticed his impatience. "Conner, if you want to do some sightseeing and catch up with us later, that's cool."

"Yeah," he said, hesitating. "Well I think I'll do that." He looked at Poppy. "I might see you later then."

"I hope so," said Poppy, smiling, and then she turned to Daisy. "We were wondering whether the three of us could meet up for dinner tonight."

"It sounds like fun," said Daisy, "but I need to get some more work done on these designs, or this trip is going to look like an all-expenses-paid holiday. Why don't you two go and find somewhere to eat and have a look around, and I'll catch up with you both tomorrow."

"Sounds good to me," said Poppy, and she looked at Conner.

"Let's do it," he said. "What time are you free?"

"Around six thirty."

"Have you ever been to *Les Deux Magots*?" said Conner, with a twinkling smile. He was showing off now, having identified this place as one of *the* cafés in Paris, according to his guidebook. "We can get a drink there and then get some dinner."

"Okay, I know of a little place where we can get something to eat after that," she said lightly.

"See you later then," he said and left them to it.

He went back to the hotel, up to his room and shut the door. Then he lay face up on the bed and images of Poppy filled his brain.

"Oh God, oh God, oh God," he mumbled, staring at the

design on the ceiling. After a moment, he fumbled for his mobile phone, hesitating before he made his next move.

Finally, he sent a quick text message to Daisy:

"Fnd out hs she got a byfrnd!"

Then he tossed the phone onto the bed covers and reached for his guitar, hoping a few notes would distract him. He was playing some lazy chords when his phone buzzed with an incoming message; the noise made him jump.

He grabbed the phone and looked at the screen.

"Don't think so"

He felt his pulse quicken, then another message arrived:

"Best behaviour remember!"

He laughed and fished out the business card Poppy had given him earlier, and then he looked at his watch to see how long he had to wait until six thirty.

He imagined Poppy and Daisy sitting together; maybe they were laughing at him, maybe Daisy had shown Poppy the text he'd sent.

"Oh no, no, no," he said and buried his head in his pillow.

5

———————

WHEN ADAM BRESCO RETIRED, friends and colleagues gathered
to mark the event. There was a party at the House of Commons
Terrace, and the novelty of the venue meant that the event was
well attended.

As well as the revellers from the physical world there was
one other who came. An Uninvited Guest who was able to enter,
unhindered by physical barriers and the security staff at the
Palace of Westminster.

Very much on the guest list was Caleb Wicks. Adam Bresco
had been both his managing partner and confidante during the
last twenty years. Together they had steered a course for the
firm, overseeing its steady growth and expansion in terms of
offices and staff. The reward for all the hard work was a solid
reputation amongst a circle of long-term, trusting clients.

Of all his senior colleagues, Caleb found Adam Bresco the
most challenging and likeable. Bresco was a country Anglican of
the old school, a pillar upon which the church community was
built. He occupied lay positions and was chair of the Parochial
Church Council, the PCC. He liked to think of himself as a
tolerant man who valued liberty and order. His interpretation of

wisdom came through an understanding that for any given issue there were a number of complex and divergent points of view; each of which could equally hold merit. His capacity to identify these points of view, and gauge their relative strengths and weaknesses made him an astute practitioner in law. He was a high church liberal, and he found Caleb's brand of charismatic evangelicalism rather exotic for his own tastes.

Their leisure interests drew them apart: Bresco to his club and the assorted country pursuits that he enjoyed, Caleb to his work with Alex, and to church and family life. But in professional matters they tended to agree, and with different areas of expertise they were able to combine as an effective team and cover a wide sweep of law. It had been a stimulating and successful partnership for both of them.

By securing the House of Commons Terrace for this event, the organizers could be said to be punching "above their weight". It was unusual for such august premises to host the retirement party of a man who was, after all, only a provincial solicitor. But all good solicitors have a network of connections, and Bresco was not just any provincial solicitor; some very important people gave him that most precious commodity – trust.

The evening brought a biting wind off the Thames, forcing the early guests to huddle around copper coloured heaters that did no more than take the edge off the cold. Caleb joined the melee and spent several minutes talking to a couple of the other partners about arrangements for the evening; he was going to make a brief speech and present Adam with a gold pocket watch that they had clubbed together to buy for him.

No one took much notice of the arrival of a small, slight figure who made his way to the hospitality tent without stopping to say hello to any of the other guests. Orlando Shand was a journeyman in civil law, and legal counsel to a number of entertainment people, including the late Bridget Larson. He was also an old acquaintance of Adam Bresco from their university days. Orlando had been an occasional guest at Bresco's London club, but he did not know many of Bresco's colleagues and he felt ill at ease amongst these strangers.

Orlando Shand had felt strangely compelled to come to this event, and so against his solitary instincts he had come along to the party; and now here he was, huddled in a warm corner of the tent, sipping a rather fruity gin and tonic.

More guests arrived and the drink flowed. The general consensus was that the hospitality tent, although rather crowded and oppressive, was the best place to be in the current climate.

The Uninvited Guest moved swiftly and silently as he went about his master's will. He stationed himself on the terrace railing and began to survey the group. He was looking for one man in particular. The fact that most of the guests were huddled in a tent did not deter him; he could see through the thick PVC material to identify them all. He scanned each of them, registering the conversations, and neither the icy wind nor the winter darkness impacted on him as he listened and concentrated; his head held at a slight angle. He moved his attention from the tent to the few people who were braving the cold. His eyes alighted on an old, slightly overweight man with a greying moustache. This person was standing not far away to his left and peering down into the river.

The Guest stared at this man and the voice of the Spirit came to him:

"This is the one."

CALEB STOOD close by one of the heaters, and looked across the river to the lights of St Thomas' Hospital. He was questioning the wisdom of standing outside, and thought about making a retreat to the bar when he felt a compulsion instead, to move to the edge of the terrace, to the railing that overlooked the river. Slightly puzzled by this desire to be even colder than he already was, he nevertheless shuffled over and gazed down into the dark and murmuring Thames. The bitter wind made his eyes water.

At once the angel moved with athletic speed along the railing to where Caleb was lost in thought and in one graceful movement he bent slowly so that his lips were a few inches from Caleb's left ear:

"You will meet a man here called Orlando Shand. You must speak with him."

Caleb started from his reflections as the sound floated through his mind. He looked around to see whether anyone had walked up to him unnoticed, but there was nobody.

He had never heard of anyone called Orlando Shand, and he did what he always did in situations like this by keeping the name in mind and then going about his business. On this occasion his business was getting back into the warmth, and he was pleased to see someone waving to him from the entrance to the marquee.

It was David Maples, another of Caleb's colleagues and the main instigator of this event.

If the firm had a social secretary, David was it. He'd suggested the House of Commons Terrace as it was, in his words: "a fitting tribute to Adam Bresco's manifold and diverse contributions to the firm." David, who was even better connected than Adam Bresco, always spoke like this. Caleb had never been able to work out how his colleagues managed to cultivate so many friendships in so many areas of society; but then they were the ones who went to clubs and played golf.

David Maples bounded up to him, full of his usual loud familiarity.

"Ready to deliver a fitting panegyric then, Caleb?"

"A what?" said Caleb.

"A few complimentary words about the old man." David waved his glass in the air. "Something fitting to express our affections."

Caleb smiled. "I have prepared a little speech, yes." He patted his top pocket.

"That's excellent," replied David, then he leant in towards Caleb. "Don't make it too long, old chap, or our guests will start to get restless." He followed this remark with a conspiratorial wink.

"Anyway," he continued, "how are you getting on with your pop stars and media celebrities? SLaM, is that their name? Adam tells me you are an indispensable part of the business now. Quite the adventure for you I would have thought."

"Well, yes it is," said Caleb, "hobnobbing with the stars, I feel quite giddy sometimes. It's now called Summer Media and Entertainment, and we are all doing fine at the moment."

"Very exciting I am sure, so how's the remuneration?" said David.

"Well it's a bit of a labour of love at the moment," said Caleb, "but when some of our young talent goes viral, we'll all do very well; and honestly, I do find it quite invigorating being around these young people. We have retained the old CEO, but we did need to change the company name."

"I should think you did after all the nonsense with that drugs raid. I remember the news stories at the time, weren't their ecstasy tablets all over the place when the police raided their offices?"

"I think the tabloids might have embellished that part of story to give it a bit of edge," said Caleb with a pained smile.

"Well I dare say," said David, "but still, it's a good job they have you there to keep things on an even keel."

"Of course," said Caleb, mildly surprised that his colleague remembered the story from so long ago. "Water under the bridge now though; I think most people have forgotten about it."

"Oh I am sure they have, Caleb, and I expect you make sure these youngsters are behaving themselves, not too much alcohol and early nights all round. Speaking of booze, do you want to come in for a drink? I'm fairly near frozen here."

David Maples turned on his heels and headed towards the scrum at the bar, with Caleb following on. At his shoulder the Uninvited Guest pierced his mind again:

"Orlando Shand, ask about Orlando, now." The voice was urgent, insistent on compliance, now.

"I say, David!" said Caleb, almost shouting above the noise of the crowd. "I don't suppose you know a chap called Shand, do you? Orlando Shand?"

David stopped and looked back at his friend.

"Oh yes, dear old Orlando, one of Adam's chums from way back. He's here this evening actually. A friend of yours?"

"No, I just want to make his acquaintance."

David thought for a moment. "Do you know what," he said, "I think you two might get on well together. He looks after one or two of the *beautiful people* himself; it's certainly his line of trade. Let's get a drink and then I'll introduce you."

David refreshed his own drink and furnished Caleb with his requested lime and soda, and then led the way to a corner of the marquee where a small insignificant looking man was tapping at his phone.

Orlando Shand was slightly startled as David burst in on him:

"Orlando! Glad you could make it! There's someone I want you to meet; let me introduce my friend Caleb Wicks. Caleb is currently legal adviser to some entertainment company, *sex and drugs and rock and roll*, all that sort of thing, but without the drugs and possibly without the sex." He chuckled. "Anyway, it should give you two something to talk about, shouldn't it? See you later. Remember, old boy," he nodded at Caleb, "brief is beautiful." He winked at both of them and bowled away towards another little knot of guests.

Orlando Shand stared at Caleb, as if trying to work out if they had met before.

"Well it's a pleasure to meet you." Orlando extended a small, smooth, hand.

"A pleasure to meet you too, Mr Shand," said Caleb.

"Please, call me Orlando. So you are legal counsel to an entertainment company?" said Shand.

"Yes, the board has appointed me as Company Secretary," said Caleb. "A bit outside my area really, I focus on commercial property normally, still one does what one can for a favoured client."

"Indeed one does, Caleb." Shand nodded vigorously, as if the comment contained some hidden meaning for him.

"Quite an infamous outfit in its day," continued Caleb, remembering the divine nudge he'd received just a few minutes before. "They're called 'Summer' now but their previous name was SLaM."

Orlando stared at him for a long moment.

"Your client now owns what is left of SLaM?" he said.

"Yes," said Caleb, "have you heard of it?"

Orlando Shand stared at him again for so long that Caleb said, "Are you feeling okay, you look rather distracted."

"I wonder," said Orlando, "did David tell you that I once advised the late Bridget Larson, a former director at SLaM."

"He did mention that you had some connection with SLaM," said Caleb, "but he did not tell me the nature of it."

"Bridget was a personal client; I never represented the company itself. I assume you are advising the business rather than any of its officers."

"I act for the business and I advise one of its directors on an informal basis."

"Really," said Shand, again he was lost in thought.

"What a coincidence," said Caleb, certain that this was the kind of conversation he was here to have. "I am sure my client has mentioned Bridget, I expect she worked with her. I understand the police never traced her killer. It was an outrageous act."

Shand's thin eyebrows converged and he gazed out into space; clearly some strong emotion churned within him. He stuffed the phone into his pocket and looked straight at Caleb.

"Absolutely outrageous, a despicable act." He was whispering but Caleb heard every single word. "A heinous crime perpetrated against my client. The police have released photo-fit pictures of a man they wish to question, a window cleaner apparently, seen near the building at the time of her death, but I do not believe that they will ever catch him."

"Why do you say that?" said Caleb. There was something here, he felt this man needed to tell him something, and he did not know what it was.

"There has been no progress with the enquiry in the last year, they have nothing further to work with."

"And do you have any ideas? Not that I wish to pry or encroach on confidential matters, you understand."

"I have precious little in the way of ideas," said Orlando, placing a hand on Caleb's arm, "but I do have a warning. Perhaps we could step out onto the terrace for a moment."

"A warning?" said Caleb, frowning.

"Could we speak outside?" Orlando walked towards the fluttering canvas of the marquee entrance.

Caleb followed him, and they left the warm moist atmosphere of PVC plastic and alcohol and stepped out into the cold river breeze. Following Shand's lead, Caleb moved across the terrace to the railing and looked out over the dark waters.

Orlando Shand stood next to him and they were both silent for a few moments before he spoke. His voice wavered, he seemed to be engaged in a struggle to contain himself.

"I should tell you now that my client left explicit instructions with me in the event of her death, and I am resolved to follow them to the best of my ability."

"Of course," said Caleb.

"She left a will and appointed me executor. It was a modest estate; you see, she was not a woman of permanent possessions."

Caleb nodded and shivered involuntarily.

"Now I have carried out her wishes as best I can, as many of them as I have been able to," he hesitated, "but not long before she was murdered she sent me some additional documentation with a covering note, detailing some action I should take in the event of her demise."

Caleb frowned.

"Can you tell me about this documentation?" he said.

"Oh, it wasn't the documentation that was so damning," said Orlando, "I shared that with the police. It was just some reports written by a previous director of SLaM, implying that the company should cash in on the drug scene, take advantage of the misery being caused by these drugs to young people. The reports were embarrassing for the company, damning even, but it didn't cast much light on her subsequent murder, and the police didn't pursue it to prosecution."

"But these reports contained something that you wanted to warn me about?" said Caleb.

"She sent a note with the reports," said Orlando, "and at her specific request I didn't share it with the police, but I think it is right that I share its contents with you. In fact, I think I am bound to, for your sake and the sake of those remaining at SLaM."

"What did it say?" said Caleb, frowning.

Orlando leant in towards him and spoke, quite quietly, above the murmur of the river.

"Two things, Caleb," he said, "but first a little context. My client had been conducting an affair with a member of staff at SLaM; his name was Martin Massey. She told me she thought Mr Massey's character had changed, for the worse, and that the relationship was now finished. It had not ended well."

Caleb nodded. From within the tent the sounds of happy chatter died down, and a single human voice could be heard. The speeches would be starting soon, and he didn't have much time left.

"The two things I want to say to you now are these," said Shand. "First, my client told me she thought she was in some danger, she drew my attention to an incident that occurred some weeks before. She happened to be passing Martin Massey's office and he was on the phone. Evidently, whoever he had been speaking to was angry, possibly with him. She heard the voice of the man Massey spoke to; he must have been shouting down the phone. Apparently, he told Massey only to call in future well after ten thirty in the morning. My client recalls looking up at the clock; it was ten minutes past ten in the morning."

Orlando knitted his brow into a frown, unsure whether it would be wise to say any more.

"And the second thing?" said Caleb.

"Oh yes," said Orlando, "well you can read it for yourself, but I'll tell you now, my client thought that Martin Massey had got mixed up with some cult, some violent group whose existence was a threat to anyone connected to SLaM, including herself. I believe that the existence of this group is connected to her murder, and that they might represent a threat to your client still."

"Did she say any more about this cult?" said Caleb.

"Not really." Orlando rummaged in his pocket. "Look, here's my card, email me and I'll send you a copy of the note, there's also a photo-fit picture of the murderer."

"I think the police showed me that at the time," said Caleb.

"I expect they did," said Orlando, "but what they won't have shown you are the CCTV images I obtained some months after my client's murder."

"I contacted the owners of every building within half a kilometre of Bridget's apartment block," said Orlando. "I pestered every security company, every property management company, every residents committee, and finally after three months I received a few images that I am convinced show Bridget's murderer."

"Did you take these to the police?" said Caleb.

"Of course!" said Orlando. "To their credit they were most grateful, but this extra evidence did not help them to identify any suspects."

"I am not sure what I can do with these images, but I'd be grateful to see them," said Caleb.

"What you can do," said Orlando, leaning forward, "is look at them, study them. I believe that they show the murderer before and after he committed the act. I have studied them carefully, and in the images from after the murder I think there is just a trace of a scar on the man's right cheek."

Orlando pressed some well-thumbed photos into Caleb's hand.

"Look at these," he said, "these are CCTV images from the cameras in the building opposite the block where my client lived. I obtained these through my own enquiries and shared them with the police. Admittedly they are not very clear at all, you couldn't identify someone from them, and the police didn't feel it was much more to go on, but I'll share them with you."

"The scarred man," said Caleb suddenly.

"Yes," said Orlando. "The scarred man. Look at these images when I send them to you, use them, find him."

"Thank you," said Caleb, "please send me anything you can."

"In truth, I wish I could be more helpful." Shand sighed. "Nothing can bring my client back, and maybe she won't get the justice she deserves, but if I can stop others getting hurt." He stopped and stared out at the river. "Write to me, Caleb."

"I will," said Caleb. "This week, I'll send you an email and…" His sentence was curtailed as the hulking figure of David Maples loomed towards them from the marquee. He was sweating slightly and clutching a drink.

"Gentlemen, the speeches have started, do come and join us! Come along, Caleb, somebody's got to give the old man that watch."

David Maples led them back to the tent at a brisk pace. They found a place towards the back and Caleb listened to the banter and anecdotes of his colleagues. He was glad that he would not have to say much at the end of it all.

He dug around in his pocket for the package containing the rather elegant gold pocket watch that the partners had bought for Adam. On the back, engraved in delicate lettering, were the significant dates in Bresco's career; his arrival at the firm, then his appointment as partner, and managing partner, and finally today, his retirement.

Caleb wanted to rehearse his speech in his mind, but instead his thoughts were on the information Orlando Shand had given him. Who was the man who shouted at Massey, and why would he only want to receive calls after ten thirty? He sensed not just a threat, but something spiritually poisonous in this information.

He turned to Orlando who had walked into the tent behind

him, wanting to ask one more question, but the man had quietly slipped out of the marquee and was now gone.

Caleb sighed, and forced his mind to think about the speech he was about to make. He heard David Maples' voice call out his name:

"...and finally, ladies and gentlemen, I want to ask the other grand old man of Fenton and Fenton, to say a few words; Caleb, come up and join us."

There was a ripple of laughter and applause as Caleb stepped up onto the raised platform.

"Ladies and gentlemen," said Caleb, nodding to David Maples, "please excuse this 'grand old man' whilst he finds his glasses and his notes."

More laughter rippled through the crowd, and with exaggerated care Caleb put on his glasses, rustled a small piece of paper with a few scribbled lines on it, and began.

6
____

Conner tucked himself into a corner of *Les Deux Magots* and watched the crowds outside as they passed the café windows. His eyes flicked to the door and away again, and he tried not to show his impatience. He took it all in, fascinated by this enticing tableaux of another country and another life. Here was Paris on a plate with all of the delightful sights and aromas that the city offered. He felt the prickling of shame as he found himself trying to listen in on conversations that he could not understand.

Poppy Martinez was three minutes late.

He decided that this was, after all, an appropriate place to meet a lady, and this was the table to sit at with her in the privacy of a corner, and positioned next to a stand of graceful white lilies. He glanced up at one of the *Magots*, the Chinese dignitaries who had given the café its name, the little figure brooding over his box of money. Overhead, he could see the details of the petals and exotic birds carved into antique stone tiles.

In the midst of all this metropolitan energy, he was still able to discern a kind of sadness, an undefined sense of regret. Great writers and artists from the past had been here. He could imagine Hemmingway and Picasso sipping their coffee, and he fancied he sensed some of their intensity, some of the urgency that drove them as they sought to express themselves in their art, hunting the elusive quarry: purpose, joy and peace.

Not that he possessed these things himself in any great quantity at the moment. He reflected on all of the innocent sounding self-justifications he had for getting to know her, all the reasons except the true one.

I would like to get to know her, he thought, *maybe we could be friends. It's good to meet new people especially from different parts of the church.*

He didn't know more than two or three things about Quakers, and she had already demonstrated that some of what he thought was knowledge was only prejudice. And yes, she was a nice girl, and indeed it was fun to meet new people but in the end he could not really deceive himself about his motives. There was more to this than finding out about the wider church, and he knew it.

He wanted to be alone with this girl for a while because she was lovely and she made his heart skip from the moment he saw her – the way she dressed, the way she spoke, the words she said. If he wasn't careful he was going to find himself captured by his own thoughts about her.

He sipped the now lukewarm *café au lait* and resisted the temptation to look at his watch, and then he wandered downstairs to the bathroom again. The concierge recognized him as a recent visitor and smiled.

"She will be here soon, I am sure."

"Yes she will," he answered without thinking. *Was it that obvious?* He grinned like an idiot and dropped a coin into her collection.

"You like her, yes?"

"Yes I do." *I love her, no I don't; I like her. I could love her, one day.*

He retreated into the bathroom; shocked that his mind should stray so far from the defences he used to keep himself safe.

Standing there he could taste his own breathlessness, and he knew his body was telling him something when he found that it took several seconds for him to start to pee.

What is the matter with you, Conner? Get a grip!

He returned to the warm leather couches and polished brass of the café, and tried to say a useful prayer, to steady his nerves. But he did not gain that familiar sense of perspective that usually came with prayers. All he got was the spiritual equivalent of static; he was too close to it, too emotional, not centred enough in the will of God to gain anything further than a vague notion that this was okay, but good behaviour was required – as if it wasn't always! One of the bow-tied waiters had taken his cup, but he could not bring himself to order another; he would wait.

Poppy Martinez was eight minutes late.

Outside the rain fell. Little drops of water weaved their way down the glass frontage of the café. The sight of it made him feel safe and warm as he watched people outside leaning into the wind of the city, huddled. He felt detached from all of them.

He began counting the small tiles that combined into a mosaic on the floor, and then he tried to regulate his heartbeat by breathing deeply while keeping his eyes off the revolving door where each movement held the potential of her arrival. For the first time he noticed the scent of the white lilies.

Poppy Martinez was ten minutes late.

Had he given her the right directions? Was she delayed? Had she called him and he had not heard the ringtone? He dug out his mobile. There were no messages. Then he remembered that he hadn't even given her directions because she said knew this place already.

The entrance door continued to spin, and Conner continued to look away determined not to jump at every new arrival. The waiter asked him if he would like to order anything else.

"I'm waiting for a lady," he said.

The waiter gave a conspiratorial nod, and disappeared. The café was filling up, bustling with customers and noise and the aroma of the lilies and espresso. He looked out on to the shiny wet of the cobbled road and the indistinct, bulking silhouette of Saint-Germain-des-Prés across the road.

Poppy Martinez was eleven minutes late. He would have to order something else soon, either that or leave.

The door spun again and Conner looked up, expecting to see a stranger.

But it was her; he recognized her and he waved. She spotted him and hurried over to the table.

"Hi! I'm so sorry I am late," she said, slightly breathless.

"Don't worry, I have only just got here myself." It sounded like the pathetic lie that it was. He scolded himself and promised to himself that he would tell her the truth from now on.

And immediately he forgot about the brass and the leather and the tiles, and the *Magots* and his money, and he focused in on her. She took off her coat, and he could see that the rain had made her hair damp so it shone under the café lighting, and she smiled at him.

He stood, and she leant forward towards him, and as she kissed his cheek he felt the warmth of her and the press of her hair damp against his ear. He drew in the scent, which might have been perfume but could also have been just her, and something in him, deeply embedded, came to the surface and embraced everything. He closed his eyes and drew breath and then, fortunately, opened them again in time to see the bow-tied waiter approaching.

They shared coffee and warm milk and Poppy talked about her own work, and Première Vision, and the delights and disappointments of the fabrics they had seen.

She talked about her work, and Conner told her more about his band and their forthcoming tour. He could hear himself chatting, laughing, engaging in his familiar banter. He was here but he was also somehow disconnected, running on automatic, cruise control, but also intensely present. He tried to tell himself to calm down, but that was only a partial success.

He studied her movements in the most particular detail: the corners of her eyes and the movement of her hands, artist's hands, the play of her hair just above her eyebrows. It was an enticing and dangerous pursuit. Each time she sipped the coffee a faint trace of moisture rested on her upper lip.

The café was warm and humid and she took off her sweater, and he looked aside as she did so. She wore a different blouse, but the style looked similar to the one she had been wearing earlier.

"Do you like it?" she said, waiting for his answer.

He looked at her, and he said, "Yes, it's lovely..." ...*on you,* he added in his mind.

"I made it myself over Christmas last year. Something to do after eating all that turkey."

He laughed with her and noted the reference to turkey; he had assumed she was vegetarian.

The lilac blouse was embroidered with tiny autumn oak leaves. He stared at the variegated colour of the leaves, and was just starting to stare again at the rest of her when some sense of self-preservation called him back. They had been talking about simplicity and beauty and she leant forward slightly.

"Do you think," she said with a reflective tone, "that a simple design can reflect beauty in the same way that a gifted composer might reflect beauty in a simple piece of music?"

"Absolutely," he said, as if this were one of his fundamental beliefs, "if the designer is skilled enough, or the composer is talented enough, the right simplicity can say much more than complexity."

You are lovely, Poppy, he thought.

"That is what I want to do, more than anything else in my work," she said, leaning forward. "Find the genius in simplicity. Simplicity can bring beauty to any art form. It could apply to music, literature, dance, or design. The challenge is to find the beauty within."

"You have to have a gift for it," he said. "The best artists in any discipline make their art seem simple, even if it isn't, perhaps especially when it isn't."

You really are lovely, Poppy.

The words came into his mind, unbidden.

She smiled at him. "Some of what you said about the Friends is right," she said. "When I was a child I wore good clothes, but they had no colour, no life to them. They performed a function, but they celebrated nothing, spoke of nothing. When I compared what I wore then to the variety and beauty of nature I see now, especially in the autumn, there's no comparison."

"Beauty is elusive," he said, "and I don't think everything in the natural world is beautiful though, some of life's colours are dark." He turned and looked around him seeking to lighten the tone of the conversation. "There is beauty all around, though, if you look for it."

"So what do you see that is beautiful here?" she asked.

He looked around and saw the white lilies, and was grateful for choosing this spot in the café. Her eyes followed his and alighted on them too.

"Surely," he said with a half-smile, "not even Solomon in all his splendour was dressed like one of these."

They both laughed.

"They are beautiful, yes," she said, "and they prove my point: simplicity can be beautiful."

"I suppose," he said, "if we were to look around Paris we might see other things that were beautiful in their simplicity."

"Well, let's see if that's true, shall we?"

"Yes, let's do that," he said, and drank the last of his coffee.

Poppy insisted on settling the bill and they ventured out into the cold, bracing themselves against the urban chill of Paris in February. The rain was easing off and she took his arm with an easy informality, and they crossed the cobbles outside the café, making their way through the side streets and on to the pavement markets of the Left Bank. They passed another café frequented by real Parisians – office workers and local residents – and amongst them there was none of the leisurely confusion that marks out the tourists. The frontage of the café was tiled with the image of a clown bearing a tray of glasses, standing within a spiraling peel of orange. The rain was easing but the clouds were still heavy and ominous above them.

"Now look at this." She laid her hand on his arm and he saw her, peering into a shop window at some Indian materials and jewellery.

"Come on." She pulled him into the shop, and he was immediately confronted by the interplay of smells – incense and wood – mingling in the warmth. Around him, stacked on trays at regular intervals, were trinkets and fabrics, necklaces and earrings; all crafted with a kind of bold beauty, as if each stitch in the fabric and every hammer blow on the metal carried with it the confidence and talent of its creator.

He watched Poppy as she moved between the different artifacts, studying them in detail, and the aroma of the place brought up memories for him; reminding him of times past when he believed in a false Nirvana that had betrayed him. He stepped outside and took a couple of cold breaths to recover himself.

She tapped on the shop window to attract his attention, and pointed to a tray of earrings she had been studying. Poppy beckoned him in to look at them. He took one final breath and went back in to the shop. The tray contained pairs of small earrings carved into the images of different animals, all made from a dark grainy wood.

"Do you wear earrings, Poppy?" As he said this, he looked up and tried to get a glimpse of her ear lobes beneath the light ginger hair.

"Sometimes," she said, "and these would be good because I could also wear them to the meeting."

"Meeting?" he said. "Do you mean church?"

"Yes," she said.

"So do you have earrings you wouldn't wear to church?" said Conner.

"A few pairs, yes," she said.

"Why wouldn't you wear them?" said Conner.

"Because they might be a distraction for some, and I don't want to be responsible for that."

"Really? Isn't that hypocrisy?" he said, rather shortly.

"Why should it be?"

"Well if you are going to wear something outside church shouldn't you wear it in church as well?"

"Not necessarily. I choose not to give offence."

"Isn't that hypocrisy?" he repeated.

"No, that's consideration, there's a difference."

He looked at her and realized that she was completely right.

"Of course, it is," he said. "You're right. I'm sorry."

She smiled at him and took a pair from the tray. Holding them up she studied each one intently, and then she placed them on the palms of her hands and showed them to him. He found himself looking past the jewellery, at the little creases that traced across her palms, and the texture of her skin. Those criss-cross patterns that were part of her history and that would have started to develop even while she was being formed in her mother's womb.

"What do you think of these, Conner?" She was holding two little Indian elephants carved with a detail that gave each figure its own personality. Now that he looked at the earrings, he could see how much beauty there was within them.

"I think they are the best ones on the whole tray," he said, and it was true.

How had she picked these out? In a few seconds she had spotted them amongst all of the others. Maybe, he thought, the act of her choosing them had made them special in his eyes, or maybe she had simply seen the good taste and simplicity innate within them, and she had seen it immediately because that was her gift.

The sky seemed very dark now, against the luminous warmth of the shop, and far away the wind blew a spatter of drops from an awning against the window. He watched Poppy as she studied the little elephants, and he suddenly remembered Alex's carved elephants, sitting on her mantelpiece, once owned by her parents. His eyes smarted with sudden moisture.

"They're lovely," he said, and he found that he had to clear his throat. "Are you going to get them?"

He smiled and then blinked and rubbed his eyes.

"I think I will," she said, and then she looked at him. "Are you okay?"

"Yes, I'm fine, and I think these are wonderful." He nodded at the earrings.

She took them to the shop counter and paid for them.

Dusk yielded to darkness, and as they made their way down to the Îsle de la Cité, the rain gave way to an icy wind. An old man with a bush of beard scuttled past them, clutching a brace of plastic bags. Poppy took Conner's arm again and they walked together, and she pointed out over the shimmering darkness of the Seine, washing past the Pont Neuf. The eastern face of Notre Dame flooded with a pale light and they went down into the Metro.

"I know where we can get some dinner," she said, and he nodded.

Poppy knew exactly where she was going, and Conner was happy to follow. The train arrived and they boarded, the carriage was crowded and as it rattled and swung, she held him to steady herself.

They ended up at *Le Troyon*; she had seen a positive review of the place in a British national newspaper a couple of weeks before.

When they arrived there was a table available for them, and they were not disappointed as they enjoyed the mood of the place with its subtle sights and sounds: soft light, smooth jazz, a New Orleans backdrop to French cuisine.

They ordered from a chalkboard, choosing the special, and Poppy talked some more about her passion for design and colour, clothing and the complex simplicity of the natural world.

If Conner was nervous, then this was a sweet fear; and the excitement of being with this girl was all the more pleasurable because he didn't know what was happening, or where this would go. He realized in the half-light of the restaurant that what he faced now wasn't a temptation to lust but an invitation to take a risk, to expose his character and history, to re-examine old wounds. Occasionally, he would find himself in the mood to be honest, to say what he really felt. What scared him was the fact that this normally happened with people he had befriended over time, with people he could trust. Now he found himself slipping into the mindset with Poppy, a girl he had only just met. What would he tell her tonight?

"You remind me of my stepsister," he said.

"Really?" she said. "That's Alex, isn't it?"

"Yes, that's Alex, she has a bit of a vision as well; her dream is to bring God in to the arts; into music and drama and writing and painting, and fashion I suppose through her work with Daisy."

"We should all dream if we can," said Poppy, "Daisy dares to dream about her work; that's why it's so good she was able to come here this week. To fulfil something that is deep within her."

"Tell me about Daisy, if you can," she continued.

Conner smiled, and shook his head in feigned exasperation.

"What can I say about Daisy? She's on a journey. You know, she used to be really hard, I mean emotionally hard. I remember seeing her at a big family party a few years ago, and she seemed thin and hard and angry, like she hated everyone and everything but she couldn't have told you why."

"But she has changed recently," said Poppy. "You can see it in her. She used to behave like someone driven by some internal bitterness, now she is different, happier, more relaxed. It's difficult to describe. She isn't burdened anymore. What happened to her?"

"Something did happen to her," said Conner.

"Can you tell me about it?" said Poppy.

"It's a bit weird," said Conner. "Just tell me about it," she said.

"Do you believe in demons, Poppy? I mean real personalities not figurative ones?"

"You're not suggesting that Daisy was possessed are you?"

"Not possessed, I tend to think of it more as, well, harassed."

Poppy looked at him unsure of what he meant and, actually, unsure of her own thoughts on the subject. She had never experienced anything that she would call demonic.

"So you think she was *harassed* by demons?"

"Yes I do, but they've gone now."

"Gone? Like they've been cast out of her?"

"Something like that."

There was silence between them for a moment. Demonic possession was not a subject either of them had been expecting to come up in their discussions.

"What does Daisy think happened to her?" said Poppy.

"I don't think knows for sure," said Conner, "and perhaps it's better for her to answer that question. But I think she would say she's happier now, a lot happier."

"Yes I think she is," said Poppy. "So tell me about Alex."

"Well, she is passionate, and determined, and kind of fragile, as well. She loves young people. She wants to bring something to them. She has a hunger to bring Christ into popular culture."

"Is she married, or does she have a partner?"

"No. She keeps busy with the firm of course, but she's on her own."

The food arrived and they both discovered they were hungry. They ate for a few minutes before continuing their conversation.

"How did Alex end up living with your family?" said Poppy.

"She lost her parents in a car crash when she was just ten, so I kind of gained a big sister."

"You seem to be surrounded by adopted sisters, Conner."

"I wouldn't want it any other way!" he said. "I love them all." And it was true now that he came to think about it. First Alex, and then Daisy; they were both precious to him. He found he could love Daisy even more once he had worked out that his true feelings were for her as a brother not a lover. And as for Alex, she had always been special to him.

"Alex is very precious to me." He felt tears forming at the corners of his eyes again as he spoke about her and he clamped down on them, he didn't want to get too emotional this evening

Poppy watched him closely.

"It's good that you care so much for her," she said, and smiled.

And as she spoke, Conner experienced a sensation, like falling over the rim of a great waterfall; and now he wanted to tell Poppy everything, all the secrets, all the desires, all the hopes and fears.

"I have always cared about Alex," he said, "I even went through a phase when I didn't know what I thought about her. For a while I forgot that she was my sister."

Poppy looked at him, waiting for him to say something more.

"I don't know why I'm telling you this," he said and laughed, "but there it is. I remember that she had just bought her flat. She had a little money from her parents' estate and she had a job. It was enough for a deposit and she moved out of our home."

He was whispering now, beneath the level of the softly flowing jazz. She almost had to lip read to make out what he was saying. He never usually talked about these things, and he didn't know why he was doing so now.

"When she moved away I missed her so much, and I didn't really know why; it was just the way I loved her, I had to work it through. I'm okay about it now."

He couldn't believe he'd shared this deepest and most intimate thing with a stranger, but he had done.

"Relationships are so complicated," she said. "On the television, characters are thrown together like little play bricks, stick them together and then pull them apart, as if it was that simple. But people can't live like that. People can't just be ripped apart and stuck together."

"Does anyone really believe it is that simple though?"

"Yes, I knew some people at college," she replied, looking sadly at her plate. "They carried on thinking we were all just pieces of biology, able to fit together and pull apart. They ignored the pain in themselves, and others."

"Sometimes people ruin what would have been a good friendship," he said, "spoiling it with lust and regret

"Is that why you and Daisy never really got together?"

He was surprised by her question, and he looked at her.

"She's told me a lot about you, Conner," said Poppy.

"Yes," he said, "I suppose so, I mean my faith stops me from going too far with someone, even if I do like them, and I did think I liked her like that, for a while. I mean, I wanted to sleep with her, at one stage, I always knew it would be wrong, but the thought was sweet." He ate a mouthful of food to stop himself saying any more.

"What about you?" he said after a moment. "Since we are being honest here; you must have had some relationships, or at least the potential for them."

Poppy smiled and said nothing.

"I'm sorry," said Conner quietly, sensing this really was a sensitive subject. "I mean it's okay if you don't want to talk about it. Let's not turn being honest into a kind of macho game." He placed his hands on his heart.

"I'm gonna reveal more about myself than you are!"

"No *I'm* going to be more honest about myself than *you'll* ever be!"

"What are you doing?" she laughed.

"Oh no you won't. You don't know how honest I'm going to be."

Some of the other diners glanced at him.

She laughed. "Daisy said you were like this sometimes, a bit of a clown. But I don't mind telling you about my relationships, not that there is much to tell; the conversation would be finished well before dessert. I have only had one boyfriend."

"Well, no I tell a lie, I have had two boyfriends, but the first one was at primary school and I was six at the time," she said. "I remember playing with him in his garden once and we cuddled each other for ages. We were sitting under a tree and we just hugged each other. To us the whole thing was a huge secret and I never told anyone. His mother had seen us from the house and thought it was quite endearing."

"Wow, young love!"

"Yes, but that one didn't hurt."

"Oh," said Conner, "so maybe the other one did?"

"In my last year at sixth form college, and my first two years at St Martins I was with a guy, another Quaker. His name was Marcus, and we had grown up together and one day we were friends and the next we were more than that."

Conner remained silent and raised his eyebrows.

"We're not together now," she said.

"I'm sorry," he said. "Let's talk about something else."

"No," she said, "it's okay. The summary of it is that we just grew apart, it was a bit sad but we both got over it."

He nodded.

"I don't think I have experienced life like Daisy and you have," she said. "When I was at college I was aware that there was this great circus going on with boyfriends and girlfriends, all that sex and intensity. But I spent my time watching it rather than getting involved, and by the time I got to my third year at St Martins I'd missed my chance in some ways; and then there was the fact that I was a Christian, and I only wanted a relationship with another Christian. It rather narrowed the field in terms of partners."

"I can imagine," he said.

"That's it really, so like I said, I certainly haven't lived life like Daisy has," she said.

"Well, the sin and the sorrow it causes isn't anything to be pound of," he said. "If you've got this far without being damaged too much, that's a good thing."

"So what about you then, Conner," she said. "What happened to you?"

He fiddled with his cutlery as he spoke:

"I left school at eighteen, and over the summer after my exams I was in a band. We played in some pubs and it was fun. One time we went on a tour. We just had a week away, but we called it a tour. It was a laugh. I started doing the things the others did. I mean drugs; we did grass, and E and to be honest with you we were just messing around, certainly I didn't care."

He stopped and forked up the food in front of him.

"Then I found out a couple of them stole things from shops. It was really stupid, and I told them as much, stealing is such a cowardly, selfish thing to do. I never did it, and it was one of the reasons I moved on from that group, that lifestyle."

He looked at her, trying to pick up any hint of disapproval, but as far as he could see there was none.

"Let's settle the bill and then we can walk down to the *Arc de Triomphe*," she said. "You can tell me some more as we go."

"I'm not sure there is much more I can tell you, is there?"

"I don't know, is there?"

"Maybe there's more we can say to each other," he said and smiled.

They came out onto the street. The traffic created its own breeze as the bitter cold of the night set in. In the distance they could see the floodlights shimmering around the *Arc de Triomphe*.

"So tell me about the band you are in now," she said.

"Well, it's different from the crowd I was with after school.

We have released two albums, put some of our music onto the internet, on iTunes, and now we are about to go on tour, a proper tour this time. And then if that's a success we'll stay together and put out a third album, we have most of the material for it."

"So are you going to be a famous rock star?"

He laughed. "There are no really famous rock stars these days," he said. "Most successful musicians get famous in their own niche and that's where they stay. That's what I want to do. Life is fun at the moment, but I don't know things are going to work out, it could all fall apart, if Alex's business doesn't survive."

"I think you'll be okay," she said, and somehow he simply believed her.

They walked on and the *Arc* loomed ahead of them, an island in a sea of traffic. Conner and Poppy took the pedestrian subway to reach it, passing through an underground bubble of trapped warmth beneath the road.

When they climbed the steps, Conner stood beneath the vast stone pillars and looked up at the bulk of stone arching overhead. Carved into the walls, like shadows in the floodlight were the names of the places where French blood had been spilt and French lives lost. He found it helpful to look at it, to bring his own problems into perspective, and to remind himself that at the most basic level he was still alive, and there were still opportunities out there. His courage returned and he found himself smiling against the wind and roar of the circling traffic.

Poppy stood at the foot of the grave of the Unknown Soldier, and Conner stood next to her. His eyes were drawn down the *Champs Élysées* where the white headlights moved towards them and red lights moved away. He was about to make a comment when he saw the light reflected on Poppy's face, the glow reflected in the tears on her skin.

Her eyes were fixed on the flickering flame that bobbed and fluttered at the centre of the tombstone. He wondered whether as a Quaker she was also a pacifist, and this thought threw the impact of the *Arc* into perspective. She would mourn the soldiers and consider their sacrifice and the sacrifice of their enemies as such a vast pointless waste. Conner could see in her face a reflection of all the loss, all the young men, smashed and wasted.

Just above the roar of the circus of traffic he whispered in her ear, "I know. I'm sorry. This futility."

She turned to him, tears still reflecting on her cheek. "Futility?"

"I'm guessing you are a pacifist."

"I hope to God it's not just the pacifists that are moved by this."

"So do I," said Conner. "If this doesn't make us think, then we've lost something precious that makes us human."

She nodded and then reached out and took his arm in hers; comforted by the evidence of their understanding.

The wind pulled at them, whistling across the stone. Holding on to him, she leant in against his shoulder, and they stood still together.

"This is beautiful as well," she said at last, gazing at the flame. "It's a sad beauty, but some of life's colours are dark."

Conner stared at the flame and felt tears coming to his own eyes as he was transformed by the poignancy of the moment. The elements conspired to create beauty out of the sorrow. The race of the wind against the stone, the fire flickering unquenched before her. Poppy's presence made him pay attention to the colours around him, the navy ink darkness of the night, the yellow folds of the flame, and the white and red of vehicle lights sailing back and forth before them.

"We have enough darkness in the world, Poppy, so you do what you can to add to the beauty for us, that is your gift."

She waited a moment and then she leaned in close to his ear and whispered.

"In his third year Marcus had to choose between a Commission in the Royal Air Force and me. The man I loved went off to war, just like these young men did. I understand he has done very well for himself. I am pleased for him."

Conner closed his eyes and a shapeless jealousy appeared in his heart, but he refused to entertain it, and it passed.

"In the restaurant," said Poppy, "I think I said something like 'it was a bit sad' when we parted. That wasn't true, it was actually devastating, it hurt me so much. It wasn't just that I lost him, it was like I never had him at all."

She held on tightly to his arm.

"For a while I didn't know what to do, what to think," she continued. "I was surprised at how much it hurt me, it made me wonder who I was, what my identity was. But I found a way through it."

"Maybe one day," he said, "if you'll come with me, I will take you to the place where I go when I need to remember who I am. It's not the most awesome spectacle in the world, but it's where I find myself again."

She looked up at him and he could see the question in her eyes.

Where? Where is this place?

He leant forward and whispered to her over the traffic:

"Harrison Stickle."

"What?" She stepped back and frowned in puzzlement. "Harrison who?"

"Harrison Stickle; it's a mountain in the Langdale Pikes, in the Lake District. Although strictly speaking," he continued, "it's a fell, not a mountain, but we won't worry about the technicalities."

"No let's not," she said, smiling.

"From the top," said Conner, "you can see Scafell Pike, Crinkle Crags, Bowfell; and on a clear day if you look to the northwest you can see Scotland, Dumfriesshire. I love that place. Like I said, it's not the most spectacular view in the world but like all of the Lakes the Pikes have their own kind of intimacy."

"Can a mountain be intimate?" she asked.

"Have you been to the Lakes?" he asked.

"No," she answered.

He smiled.

"I'll take you there one day," he said, "and then you'll see what I mean. You'll be designing things the colours of grasses and heather, mosses and slate for weeks afterwards!"

He stepped back from her and put his hand on his heart

"I promise," he said, "that one day we will be at the top of Harrison Stickle, standing on the little grass ledge that faces out to the northeast, behind the rocks of the main summit. I'll take you there and show you."

"I'd like that," she said. "I'd like to see the colours there."

"I haven't told this to anyone before," he said. "Alex knows I love going to the Lakes, I mean we all did as a family, but that specific place; I've never told anyone just how much it means to me."

He turned away, staring again at the whirl and roar of the traffic.

POPPY LOOKED at him and wondered at the intimacy between them. They had each given something of themselves, risked a bit of their private lives with each other, and it had worked, they had each accepted what the other had to offer. She tried to evaluate the consequences of it but found that she couldn't, not right here and at this moment. So instead she gave herself one more thing to reflect on when she thought it all through later, and she kissed him on the cheek, and when she did so her lips lingered on his skin for a just a fraction of a second longer than when she had kissed him earlier that evening.

"I think it's time for us to head back now," she said, and she took his arm again and they went back down to the subway.

7

WHILE CONNER WENT to the Lake District to find his place of peace, Poppy found it by gathering with her people. She found peace when she needed it at the Friends Meeting House where she had grown up, amongst familiar faces and a gentle style of worship and reflection. There was no embarrassment for her to be here with her family, no sense of regression to something of childhood. She had been to college, she had flown the nest and seen all that the city had to offer, and now she was an independent person. And it was still a pleasure for her to sit with her parents and her sisters, and the wider company of Friends.

In the silence she nurtured her ideas about beauty and simplicity. She could see these values in the symmetry of the plain wooden panels that made up the walls of the meeting room; and the four groups of chairs, each facing in towards a central point where the Bible stood open on a square table. For Poppy, God filled this place, His presence was manifest in the quiet peace that makes everything perfect, balanced, whole.

But on the Sunday after Première Vision, Poppy's mind was not peaceful. She was plagued, again, by the old restlessness and fear that incubated inside her, and manifested itself when she felt doubt, or even sometimes, as now, when she dared to hope.

In her imagination the designs for all kinds of garments came to her, another, and then another, abstract in form. The colours were clear and bright and obvious, and as she imagined each item, she could see those colours, bold and sure in the light; but up close each garment was elusive, as they always were when she conceived them like this. Poppy knew colours, they were her companions, she lived with, slept with them, ate with them; but the simplicity she craved in design was only something she could recognize, and never fully emulate.

Of course, Poppy could design clothing, she could create anything, but she never seemed to be able to capture the essence of that beauty, and order and symmetry that was the quest of her heart.

She closed her eyes and tried to centre herself in the reflective calm of the Meeting House.

"Come, my Lord," she whispered, under her breath, expecting to sense that familiar peaceful presence.

But not this time.

Wholly unbidden by the conscious thoughts, she saw not the symmetry and order that she craved but Conner Adams! The disorderly boy, whose voice she enjoyed listening to; the boy who looked as if he couldn't be neat and orderly if his life depended on it.

She tried to focus back onto the designs she had been working on, but her thoughts were interrupted by the colours of Parisian traffic, red and white lights sailing back and forth, and the flickering yellow of a flame and the blue shadows of the *Arc*. She remembered the coffee table in the hotel, and Daisy's designs, some finished and some still little more than ideas. She remembered how some of Daisy's sketches were not much more than lines on a white page, and yet somehow they captured it, the spirit of that simplicity, the style Poppy knew when she saw it.

One of Daisy's designs achieved clarity in her mind; she recognized it as the tabard Daisy had just started to work on, and Poppy's mind coloured it with rich turquoise. It rotated smoothly like a 3D image in space, and Poppy was guided to different parts of it so that she could identify the seams, the lining, the style and cut, even the design of the buttons. She could see it all.

The tabard vanished, to be replaced by one of Daisy's tunic designs. Again this image adjusted and filled with colour. Not a single colour this time but a riot of hues in orange and purple, with a thread of gold; she recognized it as some of the Kente cloth that Daisy had found. She could see it all, how the component parts of the garment would come together, and how it would look when it was finished.

Poppy let out a deep physical sigh that carried across the heads of the congregation. She opened her eyes and felt the colour come to her cheeks. A few of the people around her were glancing in her direction; some clearly wondering if she was in pain, or some kind of discomfort.

Her sister, Louisa, who was sitting next to her leant and whispered, "You okay?"

She nodded, and then said, "I think I could do with some fresh air."

"Shall I come with you?"

"No, I'll be fine."

And with that she stood, grateful to be at the end of one of the rows of chairs, and left.

Outside, she breathed in the early spring air. Daisy's designs hovered in the back of her mind, like ghosts, like water building behind a dam. She coloured them all, and it came to her then that she could only do this because there was, in fact, so little colour in Daisy's work. It was just like the days at Central St Martins when they complemented each other in their work.

She walked home, brisk, distracted, and she didn't even take her jacket off as she took two steps at a time, up to her room.

When she arrived she found tears running down her cheeks, so she reached for a tissue with one hand while with the other she swept everything off her desk so she had a space to work in. She picked up her sketchpad and flipped over the used pages so she had a blank sheet in front of her. To her right on the desk was a large coffee tin, brimming with pencils, charcoals and pastels.

She shut her eyes and prepared to let Daisy's designs come to her again.

"Okay," she said, and the floodgates opened and in a moment she was lost in a furious industry of design and colour. Some of it came upon her so quickly that she only had time to sketch an outline. She annotated the designs with a manic, rushing script, hoping she would be able to decipher it all later; she sketched briefly and with impatience, resisting the dam-burst of colour long enough to capture something of the form before the shades and hues gave it life. When it was finished, she tossed the sheet onto the floor and stared at the next blank page.

This was the cheongsam. She knew it was an adventurous piece of work. The image of it filled with pinks and cream, a scattering of cherry red, and then it was discarded and next came the jacket, and then the culottes, to which Daisy had added a chequered design that shocked Poppy, but she did not dare pass judgement on any of it. And then, improbably, there was a scarf, and it spoke of the ocean, of greens and blues in the sunlight, and a fabric that would be soft to touch, and so it went on, one after the other, as she took the raw material of Daisy's designs and gave them the colour they were always meant to have.

Eventually she stopped because her wrist hurt so much that she could not hold a pencil properly. She leant back in her chair, and cradled her arm like a baby at the breast, and she cried and looked down at the furious scattering of paper on the floor and she flexed the fingers of her aching hand and the tears fell until, eventually, she regained herself and she stood up, walked over to her bed and collapsed into sleep.

She woke about thirty minutes later and the house was still quiet. She stood and stretched and gathered the papers up from the floor and laid them neatly on the desk. Then she took one more sheet of paper and wrote on it:

> *"Dear Daisy,*
> *Your beautiful designs came to me in these*
>   *colours, and I had to draw them, and send*
>   *them to you. I am full of the memories of*
>   *when we worked together, and I can't help*
>   *but put colour between the lines you draw.*
>   *Forgive me.*
> *With love,*
> *Poppy"*

Then she took the whole lot, pushed them in an envelope and sealed the flap.

The post office, she knew, would be open at nine o'clock in the morning.

Daisy is asleep, and dreaming.

In her dream she sees moments from her life appearing on a screen in front of her. As she witnesses these moments she senses some of the emotions that went with them, she's watching the screen but she is also the principal actor.

There is an image of herself as a small child; she has fallen down the stairs at her parents' home. Daisy sees the little girl, in a state of bewilderment, as her orderly world turns over and over, full of shock and pain as she falls. She is looking up at the steep steps, like staring at a mountain.

The expectation of sympathy and attention is instinctive. She is waiting for the mother and the father to arrive. The little girl has generated noise by the lung full, a penetrating, piercing scream. The scream is flooding a house where the adults are already at their wits' end. It passes through walls, doors, humming through the rafters of the roof; it is irresistible.

The father emerges from behind a door. She focuses on him as a source of compassion; but there is something in his manner that seems disconnected from her, he stands near to her but does not touch her, comfort her. She cannot understand why he is not coming to her, giving her the attention that she craves right now.

Now the mother appears, and the girl switches her attention from the father to the mother, awaiting attention. Her body is still in shock, there is pain all over her, and she is frightened. The mother is coming, but somehow she is deflected; the father figure has drawn her away and now they are making their own noise. Daisy feels the pure frustration of her physical limits. She cannot go to the mother, she cannot go and reclaim the attention and so she pours all of her will and anger and despair into her voice, the limit of her human reaction in the world. The noise is pure urgent energy, transcending everything else.

Success! She has reclaimed the attention of both the mother and the father; they are both turning to her now; this is a rich vein, both parents are looking at her and the father is moving to her. She feels the exhilaration of focus again; he is coming to her quickly.

There is an eruption of feeling in her head which she does not immediately associate with the father, even though he is there standing over her. And then some things happen and she cannot identify what they are. The noise at her command is blended with the father's noise and it scares her The mother's noise joins them, and at the same time, with the father next to her, the feeling in her head, which started as sensation, mutates into pain, and the noise which was the mother rises and rises with the pain in her ears and her head, and the father moves away quickly. She sees him in a blur of tears, and she is confused, and above all else, she is alone, cast adrift from the people who, even at this age, she knows should be there for her, but are not.

The scene changes and she is in her bedroom, the door is shut. She is fifteen. In the dream she is completely naked and she is standing in the half-light, with the curtains drawn. She has placed a small rubber wedge under her door so nobody can get in and disturb her. She is looking at herself, using a small hand mirror. She is moving the mirror around so she can see different parts of her body. Some parts she is examining closely, and for other areas she moves the mirror away so she can encompass more of herself. The act of examining herself, piece-meal like this, dislocates her from her own body, allowing her to examine it in a way that she thinks is dispassionate, objective, but is in fact full of judgement and condemnation.

She has weighed her own body on the scales, and found it lacking, guilty. She feels the familiar sense of solitude wash over her. She is alone with a solitude that was initially forced upon her, but is now also hers by choice.

Watching this on the screen of her dreams, Daisy feels a prickling of compassion for the girl that she was: the girl with the dull eyes, and the thin body; the girl who thinks she lacks so much but in fact lacks only one thing really, the love and compassion that has been missing from her life.

The image moves on and now she is in a small study bedroom. There are posters on the wall, and there is music; it is urgent and loud, and it crowds out the thoughts in her head. This is not her room but she recognizes it immediately. This scene has more clarity and precision than the previous two because she has a much clearer memory of what happened here. This comes as something of a surprise to her because she knows that at that moment she was quite drunk. Not helplessly, but enough to make her feel a little detached, as if the words she says are spoken by someone else. She is sitting, slumped, on a bed. The music is loud and she cannot make out any words or tune. There is someone else in the room and she knows who he is. He moves around the room and then he lies down next to her, and his hand moves over her stomach, her shoulder. Somewhere within her mind she is trying to decide whether she wants this physical contact now, whether she is enjoying the sensations she is feeling, whether she would choose to let this happen.

The process of assimilating the experience is slow. His hand feels strong and urgent. His touch is full of hunger, and it takes rather than gives as his fingers press on the fabric of her shirt.

There is so much sensory information pouring into her mind, the smell of his clothing, the noise of the music, the cascade of pressure on her body, all of these senses compelling her, commanding her to comply, to submit.

The pressure applied by the hand increases, and it provokes her into some kind of response. She might not always be averse to this experience, but at the moment she feels threatened, forced. She does not want this to happen now.

She can hear herself saying no.

No.

Now she feels other parts of her body being touched, manipulated. She is becoming more sober. Perhaps the adrenaline is working, kicking her body into action. She articulates her reaction more strongly, pushing the hand away. She is now clear that this is not what she wants.

Daisy is right handed, and for a fleeting moment she feels strong. His hand digs under her shirt, ferreting away, and as it does so she swings her right hand round, trying to swing her body at the same time. It's a lucky shot, and she slaps hard into the cheek and mouth of the boy. She hears a sound like a gunshot, even above the crashing chords of the noise around them, and his head flicks away from her; the hand that was under her tee shirt pulls free. With her other hand she pushes him completely away.

NO

She repeats the word.

NO

Somehow the room manages to become silent, the sound continues but everything is still. The boy stands motionless, staring at her, caught between anger at her slap and shock at what has happened.

The shock has given her the energy to get up and make her way to the door; she thanks a suddenly manifested God that she doesn't have to walk past him to get to the exit. The boy does not move. She opens the door, exits and starts to walk, and then to run down the corridor. Her tee shirt is untucked, it feels uncomfortable, but she will not deal with the discomfort until she reaches her room.

The scene changes.

She is in her room, just a few minutes after the incident. She is shivering. The door is locked. Her right hand is still stinging from the impact on the boy's cheek. He is probably feeling more pain than she is now.

Good.

The shock of the incident has been replaced by a sense of indignation. She is sitting on her bed, headphones on, playing her favourite CD, with her dressing gown wrapped around her. There is a conflict within her; she feels anger at what has happened, but also a sense of worthlessness, that even if she had allowed him to do whatever he wanted, it would only have been what she deserved. Even knows this is a lie, even if it is one she's tempted to believe.

What she does think is true is that she is alone, but in this belief she is wrong. Even now, as she looks on in her dream Daisy knows it's a lie, and for the very worst of reasons.

In her sleep Daisy twitches and shifts in her bed. Still looking in on the same scene she sees something that, until recently, she has never seen before. She isn't alone as she huddles into her gown and loses herself in her music. The dark companions are in there with her, under the dressing gown; right in there, under her skin, in the blood and the bones, fingering her, more invasive than the unwanted hand of a drunken boy.

The scene changes again.

Daisy is looking at a row of cubicles in a public lavatory. The wall tiles reflect the dull luminous strips on the ceiling and she can hear the remote gurgle of a cistern. There is a strange peacefulness about the place.

Suddenly a door flies open and there she is, clutching a little bag and running into the nearest cubicle; crashing into the door which swings violently, hitting a rubber stopper and ricocheting back to hit her shoulder. Watching in her dream Daisy feels that pain in her shoulder now. She has never dreamed this moment before, and she is intrigued and terrified by the thought of how it might play out in her mind now.

She sees herself push round the door, slam it shut, and force the lock across. Then her knees seem to buckle and she collapses onto the cubicle floor, weeping and weeping so that the tears fall noiselessly onto the floor tiles. Her body is shaking with the discharge of emotion.

In her dream she can see herself hunched over in silence, jerking with every sob. As she watches herself she sees three forms materialize in a triangle around her. They pause for a moment, these three figures that she has never seen before, human forms in grey hovering over her, touching her, stroking her back and her arms. Daisy watches in fascination and horror, feeling the revulsion well up inside her.

But she knows that something else is about to happen; if the dream plays out as a copy of reality then she might be about to see the impact of Caleb's prayers for her.

One of the three forms leans in closer and seems to pick with a thin finger at her forehead. The finger has worked itself into her head, just a couple of centimetres, but then the scene is transformed by a deluge of liquid light, pouring like clear water down onto her and over her. The light drowns out the artificial glow of the fluorescent tubes, and it is clean and urgent and alive.

At its touch the three figures recoil as if stung, and flatten themselves against the walls of the cubicle. The edges of each figure seem to bubble and dissolve becoming insubstantial, fraying under the proximity of this new presence.

Daisy remembers this moment, she remembers seeing a vision of Caleb Wicks; and he is there in the dream again, as in the vision, except she sees him more clearly this time. He is kneeling rather painfully on the floor and is wearing a rather faded chequered dressing gown. He is leaning on a desk with his fingers intertwined and clenched. Although he is perfectly still, he gives the impression of being engaged in combat. In her dream she can hear his prayers as inaudible whispers; they are prayers for her and she is embarrassed and thrilled to hear them.

She stares at the praying figure for a moment longer, and only now she sees there is someone else, a man, standing beside him. The man is short, and with a kind but plain face. He is no more than five and a half feet tall, and with wavy dark hair and olive coloured skin. He stands next to Caleb, and has his hand on Caleb's shoulder. Daisy looks at the hand and sees a ragged hole through the base of the palm; it looks like someone has dug a hole through his flesh with a potato peeler. The hole is large enough that the material of Caleb dressing gown is just visible through the wound.

The presence of this squat looking man in her dream seems to banish, for a moment, Daisy's sense of loneliness. She feels his presence as if it were the presence of not one but many people, a great and joyful company, countless millions beside her, laughing, delighted by the truth of their being, who they are, and where they are going. They carry Daisy along with them, pleased to accept her into their company, and she is not alone, and will never be alone again.

***

DAISY KNEW that something had woken her up, a familiar noise. She guessed it was the post dropping onto the mat in the entry hall downstairs. She wanted to go and see if it was for her, but the bed was warm and her body wanted to stay there, and so she lay for a couple of minutes more before she began to fidget and her curiosity got the better of her.

She eased out of bed, and picked up the same old dressing

gown she had wrapped protectively around herself five years ago after the attack. Hugging the gown to herself, she padded down the stairs to look at the scatter of envelopes sitting on their door-mat. There, amongst the detritus of junk mail and pizza menus, she found a large handwritten envelope, generously covered in stamps, and marked "1st Class – please do not bend." It was addressed to her. She recognized the writing as Poppy's and she felt an echo of that sense of company, of companionship that she'd experienced in her dream.

Still standing in the hallway she opened the envelope and found within it a treasure of coloured drawings together with a little note from Poppy. She clutched them to herself and leapt up the stairs back to her room.

She emptied the envelope and spread the drawings out across the table, and her eyes began to water. Here were her drawings, her concepts, now given breath by a kaleidoscope of colours. There was the tabard sketched and coloured with the Kente designs, as she had wanted it. Daisy stared at it all in wonder.

"Like a coat of many colours," she whispered to herself, and laughed at her own embarrassment.

Here were the answers to questions she had been asking herself. She'd seen the colours, known their potential, but there had been something missing, they had been like bodies, perfectly made, but Poppy had brought them to life.

It was just like their time at college, the way they comple-mented each other, and created between them something greater and truer than they might have done on their own, and she knew immediately that it was absolutely essential that Poppy join her in her work.

8

As WINTER GAVE way to the light and life of spring, SLaM joined in the change of seasons by transforming itself into a new company and a new brand: SUMMER. The legal transformation was relatively easy but the brand shift would require a lot more work.

These were the challenges occupying Alex's mind as she arrived for work one morning in early March. As usual, she was the first one in, and as she settled at her desk the morning post arrived, dropping into the postbox outside the office door.

Alex still loved getting post, and so she went to see what had arrived. When she opened the postbox she saw, amongst the other letters, a pastel blue envelope with a handwritten address. Its warm colour contrasted sharply with the brown anonymity of the other items around it.

The envelope was marked for Conner's attention, the address written in rounded, precise, characters, Alex judged by a woman's hand.

She brought the letters in and turned her attention back to the business of the day. Daisy was going to report back on the Paris trip, and had promised "an adventure in colour, a new vision for SUMMER". It had, Alex knew, inspired Conner to buy Daisy a pencil with a multi-coloured lead centre and an orange tassel at the end; she had responded by teasing him with loaded comments about Paris being the *city of love*. Alex had picked up that Conner might have made himself a new friend while he was away, and she made a mental note to stay alert for any more information about the girl in question. Intriguingly, it seemed to be one of Daisy's old college friends, but she knew no more than that.

Alex had called them all in today for Daisy's presentation, including Conner and Lewis. Conner had been in the office for a few minutes when she handed him the blue letter, and he grunted some acknowledgement. He was hunched on the corner of Daisy's desk, picking over some receipts from the trip, wondering what he could claim as legitimate expenses. He took the envelope from Alex, sniffed it, and then ripped it open. Inside, he found a handwritten request from one of his fans, apparently she wanted him to do a solo gig at her birthday party, and she was going to pay him a very decent fee for it.

"Daisy, look at this." He passed her the letter and she scanned through it.

"What do you think?" he said.

"Have you seen the fee they're offering you?" she replied and passed the note back to him.

"Yes," he said, "do you think I should do it?"

Daisy looked at him as if the answer was obvious. Conner was feeling fairly poor at the moment and as he considered it, the prospect of a solo gig, with him taking the fee, was very enticing.

"I'll do it," he said.

"Of course you should do it," said Daisy airily. "Unless it's a con of some kind, and all they give you is a beer and a slice of birthday cake."

"Cynic!" he replied, and nudged his receipts towards her. "So how many of these can we claim for do you think?"

"Well," said Daisy, "I don't think you can claim every penny when you spent half of your time entertaining ladies." She winked at him.

"I had to eat something while I was there," said Conner, "and I think she enjoyed my company."

"Of course she did," said Daisy. "A man of your sophistication and wit, what lady wouldn't?"

"Shut up!" he said, laughing. "So what about these receipts?"

"Later, Conner," she said, "I'm up for my presentation in a few minutes," she waved a hand full of design drawings at him, "so stop being so loved up, and give me a hand to get set up."

She collected her papers and laptop and juggled the whole lot into the boardroom.

"I'm coming." He picked up the letter and read it again, but it was only the fee they were offering him that really had his attention. He lingered over the figure, and then looked at the rest of the invitation, there was only an email address to respond to.

"Conner," Daisy's shout grabbed his attention, "get in here and help me with this projector, will you?"

"Yes, sure." He started humming to himself as he trotted into the boardroom.

He switched on the projector and connected Daisy's laptop. A giant image of Paris appeared on the screen.

"Perfect," said Daisy, opening her presentation. "So how much are they offering you for this gig?"

"Five hundred," said Conner.

"Five hundred pounds?" said Daisy. "For a day's work?"

"That's what they say," said Conner.

"Well," said Daisy, "you've got every reason to be cheerful, you might need that to finance your social life."

"Just when I need some cash, eh?" he said, winking at her,

but she didn't hear him, instead she was frowning at the computer screen.

"You okay?" he said.

"Yes, of course," she said.

"I was just saying," said Conner, "it will be handy to get some cash just at the moment."

"What?" said Daisy. "Oh yes, it will be."

"You sure you're okay?" said Conner. "Is it this presentation?"

She looked up, her face betraying a lack of sleep. She moved past him and pushed the door closed so that they were alone.

"I'm sorry," she said, fishing a packet of cigarettes from her pocket, "it's not even just this presentation; it's all of you. I mean, I love you guys, but you're all so *Christian*, and I feel different, separate."

Conner opened his mouth to speak but she continued:

"I really do appreciate you guys, but this is so intense." She pulled a cigarette out of the packet. "I mean, do you think they even have a smoker's room in heaven?" she said, taking a lighter from her other pocket.

"Daisy," said Conner, staring at the cigarette, now between her lips.

"Don't worry," she said, "I'm not going to light it in here."

"I don't know if there's a smoker's room in heaven," said Conner, "but if they don't take sinners, we'll all be camped outside with you."

"I'm going to ask them to take on Poppy for a while," said Daisy. "I need her, as a consultant."

"The company hasn't got any money," said Conner. "You know that, don't you?"

"Yes," she said.

He looked at her. "Whatever!" he said, and laughed. "Ask for it, they can only say no."

She smiled and shook her head slightly. "I'll be outside." She waved her cigarette.

THE LIGHTS WENT DOWN and Daisy stepped forward. She looked at the faces in front of her: Alex, Caleb, Aiden, Conner and Lewis, and then cleared her throat.

"So," she said, "first I want to thank you for letting me go to Paris, and letting me take my assistant with me." She nodded at Conner who waved back at her.

"So," she continued, "here's what I discovered at Première Vision, and what we made of those discoveries."

They all stared as the colours appeared before their eyes. Designs poured out onto the screen, image after image, presented in detail, ready for mockup and production. Jackets and shirts, tunics and culottes, all individual, but all sharing a theme, a mood that spoke of the light and warmth of Summer.

"These designs are the basic ideas," said Daisy, "and I have material samples for some of them, they just need a bit more work to be ready for prototypes and then production."

She carried on through the presentation, encouraged by the attention she got from them all, and the grunts of wonder and approval from Caleb.

"And that's it," said Daisy at the end. "But you need to know that these drawings are the work of two people." She paused and looked at them all. "One already works for SUMMER, that's me, and the other we should employ as soon as possible."

She watched Aiden to see if he would frown, or even twitch, but he kept perfectly still.

"I've prepared these designs," continued Daisy, "in collaboration with an old student friend of mine, Poppy Martinez, and I want to show you why I think it is so important that she join us. Look at this design."

On the screen they could see a simple sketch of a jacket, something they hadn't seen yet. There was no colour in the image, and only a hint of detail at the collar and sleeves. One or two notes had been added to the design, but these were illegible.

"This is what I started with, and it's what I showed Poppy when we were at Première Vision. A few days later she sent me this."

Another design appeared on the screen. Here was the same garment, but now turned into a tabard, sleeveless, daring in bright yellow with flashes of emerald green at the hem, and notes about the particular materials used as well as suggestions for slightly different hues of colour, all written in a neat hand around the edge of the design.

"This is all I need to mock up the design and create something for us," said Daisy.

ALEX FELT a tremendous sense of excitement as soon as she saw some of the designs, something she judged to be beyond her own human reaction. She decided then that Daisy and Poppy must work together, but she said nothing.

It would cost money, and that was what they didn't have much of right now. It was so reckless to think of taking on someone else, so naïve, and yet it seemed so *right*. She wondered what Aiden would make of this, and she hoped Caleb would sense the rightness of it too.

"These are wonderful," she said. "Tell us more about your friend Poppy."

"She is a really talented designer," burst out Conner, and the assembled heads turned back to him. "She is wonderful, she really is!"

"You're familiar with her work?" asked Caleb.

"Well," said Conner,, "I mean, based on what I've seen I

think Daisy and Poppy can work together are a great team. They were at college together."

"The flower girls." Caleb chuckled. "It's lovely; and if Daisy and Lewis will bear with me, I would dare to say that what we are seeing here is divine inspiration. I admit I don't know much about fashion, but aren't these lovely? This is God at work unless I am much mistaken."

"Sure is," said Daisy before she could think about what she was saying.

"We need to talk to Poppy and see if we can come to an arrangement," said Alex. "What's she doing at the moment?"

"She has a contract with a Fair-Trade clothing business, but that's only three days a week."

"Might I say something at this point?"

All eyes in the room turned to Aiden, who had been quiet so far.

"When we first saw Daisy's designs," he said, "and she shared her ideas with us, I thought we should encourage her, indeed I pushed for us to let her go to Première Vision, as you all know. It may be that she is still with SUMMER because I pushed for her to be allowed to go to Première Vision this year."

The room was silent.

"However," he continued, "what I didn't expect was that, as a result of it all, we would consider hiring *another* employee, and spending more money to do so. You are all talking about this without giving it any serious thought."

Everyone was silent. The projector fan hummed, intrusive and breathy, churning the air.

"It worries me," continued Aiden, "that some of you, even you, Caleb, would pronounce on whether this is God's will or not, without giving any thought to the financial implications."

"My dear fellow," said Caleb gently, "I believe that God is in this. Even if our accounts were in a poorer state than they are now, I would still believe that God was in this. But that does not mean we should rush into this blindly; we need to be wise as well."

"Well I am glad to hear you say that," said Aiden. "I want you all to be aware of the facts. Until we get some proper income from Conner's forthcoming tour, the cupboard is pretty bare. We have enough money to keep us going for about four maybe five months at the moment. Like you, I think these designs are delightful, but if we take on Daisy's friend, that four or five months just shortens again."

Daisy stared at him and kept her mouth shut.

"These are wonderful designs, Daisy," said Aiden, "and it's a wonderful idea, but it's my job to remind people of where we are as a business with our money. I don't think we can take anyone else on right now."

Alex watched them all talking, and their voices seemed to drift away from her. Inside her chest there was a heat building, her breathing was faster but she didn't feel scared or jittery or nervous. She knew what this was.

"We must do this," she said suddenly. "I know what you are saying, Aiden, and it is your job to say it, and you are right to say it, but we must do it. Don't worry," she added, "I have a feeling Conner will come good for us."

They all stared at each other, and Daisy from her vantage point at the front could look at them all, seeing them weighing their faith in God against the risk.

"And we need to offer Poppy a contract," said Alex quietly, "but we need to be honest with her about the state of the business. We can offer her three months work, two days a week, under Daisy's direction."

She looked at Aiden. "I will cover the costs myself," she said.

"Okay," said Aiden, raising his hands, "you're the boss."

The room was silent again.

"Well," said Caleb, rather loudly, "I think that went very well. Thank you, Daisy, for your work on this, a great job. But I fear I have to go now, my other employment beckons. I will see you all soon."

He got up, picked up his bag and coat, and, humming a totally unidentifiable tune, he left the room.

Lewis got up and followed him out. "I'll be back later," he said, glancing at Alex.

Daisy left next, followed by Aiden. Alex wanted to speak with him, but the boardroom wasn't the place to do it. She sighed and headed back to her desk.

Alex was just sitting down again when the phone rang, she picked up and heard a voice that was vaguely familiar, but she couldn't place where she'd heard it before.

"Can I speak to Alex, please?"

"Speaking," said Alex.

"Alex! This is Bernice Templeton, we were at school together. Do you remember me? Bats Templeton, that's what everyone called me then."

Alex stared out into space as her brain sifted through all the old memories of school, the light that came through the tall windows in the assembly hall, the smell of books in the library, the tang of the chemicals from the science lab, and the people she'd known, the other girls who'd been there; and she remembered Bernice, larger than life, Bernice, a bit reckless, very sporty, always up for an adventure.

"Bernice! Wow, I haven't talked to you since, well I don't know. It's great to hear from you! So, how are you?"

"Busy, as ever, you'll not be surprised to hear. Still alive though, and that might be more of a surprise to you."

Images came into Alex's mind – Bernice, the missionary's daughter, fearless as anything, always game for a laugh.

"So," said Alex, "what are you up to these days? Still doing the fencing? What was it, foil? And do people still call you Bats?"

Bernice's initials, B A T, had led to her picking up the affectionate nickname "Bats" at school.

"Oh God, no," said Bernice, "I haven't been called 'Bats' in ages, shame really. I'm a bit more sensible these days, and I'm not fencing anymore, I'm sorry to say."

Bernice had been British Youth Champion and had carried on with the sport even when an accident had nearly blinded her; Alex could still remember the scar, like a teardrop beneath her left eye.

"I've settled down a bit these days," continued Bernice, "just a bit of free climbing and amateur kick boxing, that sort of thing."

"Well thank goodness some things don't change. So how are your parents doing?"

"Oh, still out in the middle of nowhere, I haven't spoken to them recently; I think they are okay."

Alex remembered that Bernice didn't see too much of her parents, away in the mission field as they were. With their absence, and Alex's situation as an orphan, the two girls had occasionally found themselves together for weekends at the boarding school where Alex spent her sixth form years. Their friendship had grown over that time as they had spent time together talking about anything from boys to God to music.

Alex was distracted from the conversation as she looked out of the office window and saw Aiden sitting in his car. He did not seem to be getting ready to leave. She wanted to go and talk to him, but Bernice had her attention for now.

"Anyway," continued Bernice, "I've tracked you down for a reason. Your social life is about to move up a gear."

"Really?" said Alex, suppressing a smile.

"Oh yes; I am planning a do. A big do." Alex remembered

Bernice's excitement at the prospect of any social event, especially parties, and especially parties with boys. "You remember Harriet?"

Alex wrinkled her brow trying to remember the name.

"Vaguely," said Alex, "I think."

"Well anyway," continued Bernice now in full flow, "I've stayed in touch with her, and a couple of the other girls; you remember Samantha, don't you, anyway, Samantha has a brother called Tim; and well you can guess the rest."

"Can I?" said Alex after a moment.

"Of course." Bernice seemed to be working herself up into a fever pitch of excitement now. "Tim and Harriet! They're an item! Can you believe it? I couldn't at first, I thought Sam was pulling my leg when she told me."

Alex could now almost remember who Sam was, but as she kept listening, her attention was diverted again to Aiden's car. Daisy was now standing next to the driver's side door, waving her arms, evidently involved in some kind of conversation with him.

"So anyway," continued Bernice, "the reason I'm phoning, is first of all to say 'Hi!' of course, but also to ask if you want to come to this party."

"Party?" said Alex.

"Yes," said Bernice, now very animated, "try and keep up, Alex! I'm having a party, which is wonderful in itself, obviously, but Tim wants to propose to Harriet, right there, at this party, and thank God I know she's going to say yes, so there won't be any embarrassment, oh it's going to be so romantic, but don't tell anyone because this proposal thing is a huge secret!"

"If I can come I will be there," said Alex. "I'm sure it will be a massive blast!"

"Of course you'll be there," said Bernice. "Oh, and while I

remember, isn't your brother some kind of singer now? Isn't he in a band?"

"Well yes," said Alex, "he is, they're called Joel's Garden, have you heard of them?"

Conner, who was sitting at one of the other desks, still poring over his receipts, sat up when he realized Alex was talking about him.

"Who is that?" he whispered to Alex.

"Yes, we'll both come to the party," said Alex into the phone.

"Wonderful," said Bernice, "and maybe we could get your brother and his band to play?"

"I'm sure they'd love to play at this event," said Alex.

"Who is that on the phone?" hissed Conner, a bit louder this time.

"Hang on a moment Bernice," said Alex, and turned to her brother. "Conner, I am on the phone talking to one of my friends about a very important social engagement, and she might want you and the boys to play at an event."

She brought the phone back up to her ear, and as she did so she glanced outside and saw that Daisy and Aiden were still talking to each other.

"Wow," said Conner, "tell her yes we'll play at it!"

"Was that Conner you just spoke to?" said Bernice. "Is he interested in playing at our event? Can I have a quick chat with him?"

"Please do," said Alex. She glanced out of the window again, just as Daisy was turning away from Aiden's car; he looked as if he was about to leave.

She passed the phone to Conner and headed towards the door. When she got down to the car park she could only watch as Aiden's Saab pulled away, and Daisy had gone. She walked back to the office, frustrated at the opportunity missed.

Back in the office, Conner and Bernice were exchanging

numbers, and then Alex took the phone back from him. She promised to stay in touch with Bernice, said her goodbyes, and then put the phone down. Alex was pleased that she'd been able to reconnect with her friend, but she was really thinking about what Aiden and Daisy might have said to each other.

"Hey, Alex, I've got two gigs today," said Conner with undiminished enthusiasm, "and this one is going to be five hundred!" He waved a piece of paper in front of her.

"Good for you," she said impatiently. "Now I need to get on with some work so go off and do whatever it is that you do."

"Sure, I'll see you later." He was surprised by her abrupt manner. "You know you are my favourite sister, don't you?" he said, coming over and putting an arm around her shoulder.

"Not now please, I'm not in the mood, okay?"

"Okay sure." He was confused but he decided to back off. "Well, I'm off to practice with the guys, I'll see you later."

When the door shut, Alex let out a long, heavy sigh. Now both Conner and Aiden were upset with her.

The office door opened and she turned, not wanting to see either of them, or Daisy right now.

But it was Lewis, and she found herself relieved to see him.

"You okay?" he asked as he slumped into a chair next to her.

"Yes, it's just that...well you would know, it's not easy running a business, is it?"

He laughed. "Heavy lies the head that wears the crown, Alex. That's how it is. If you want to achieve something it nearly always costs. Part of your problem is that you've got some of your family and friends working for you. Mixing business with pleasure or family is always trouble. I found that out."

"Have I done the right thing?" she asked him, surprising herself with the question.

"Well, I'm not connected to the divine network like you lot." He smiled. "I can only offer my opinion."

"I want your opinion," she said. "I value what you think, since you've been in the chair."

"Okay," he said, "if you mean the whole business, then of course you've done the right thing. You've got your dreams and you need to pursue them, what else are you going to do? But if you mean about taking on this girl Poppy, well I don't know. I think maybe you have done the right thing, if Daisy and her can get these designs sorted, prototypes done, and a manufacturing deal delivered in the next three months, then maybe you've done the right thing, but it's a big ask."

"Thank you," said Alex.

"It could all go wrong," said Lewis, "but, hey, go for it!"

She nodded.

"Of course," he continued, "I can afford to say that, it isn't my money, it's yours."

She stared at her desk and tapped a pencil onto the wood. Her diary was open at the date where she had written in details of the party Bernice was organizing.

"Do you want to get a coffee somewhere?" she said eventually, "I still want to talk to you about the marketing for Conner's band."

"Sure," he said, "I'll get the coffees, you can bring the spreadsheets."

CONNER ADAMS CURLED into a corner seat in the back row of the night bus heading home. The vibration of the engine beneath his feet had a soporific effect; floating his mind from the comfortable maleness of the boys in the band and out into the intriguing, unknown territory of Poppy Martinez. Whatever else was on his mind, whatever else he was doing, his thoughts always came back to her, the colour of her eyes, the scent of her, the feel of her against him when she hugged him at the café. He leant back his head and let out a heavy sigh.

This girl had severely messed with his head, and at the moment he was not at all sorry that she had done so. All that time and effort he had put in to building some emotional defences, knowing he needed to be a bit careful with girls, patrolling his boundaries, priding himself on how good he was at this sort of thing, and along came Poppy Martinez, a girl who seemed to be able to find her way under his radar with unnerving ease. He'd resisted the temptation to make a fool of himself with Daisy and in the process they'd developed a wonderful sibling relationship. He'd been especially proud of how resisting some initial stirrings had helped them find the right way to relate to each other, even if it did mean she teased him mercilessly. But with Poppy things were different. It amused him to think that he had resisted one flower, only to fall for another.

His thoughts were interrupted by a vibration from his phone. He tried to pull the mobile out of his pocket and in the end he had to stand up to do so, and by then the ringing had stopped. He put the phone back in his pocket and the rumble of the wheels lulled him into sleep.

When a jolt over a pothole woke him, he found he'd missed his stop. He pressed the bell and when the bus again pulled up he stumbled off, pulling up the collar of his jacket against the cold.

He remembered the call he had received and dug out his mobile. There was a voice message, just three seconds. He watched his breath steam out into the night as he raised the phone to his ear and listened:

"You are Cain."

He looked at his phone as if he expected it to explain itself.

As he stared, it buzzed again into life and he almost dropped it. He answered the call.

"Hello?"

There was no answer.

"Hello?"

Again, silence

"Who is this?"

He fancied he could hear breathing at the end of the line. It was probably one of the guys from the band, Mark or Baz, having a laugh.

"Okay, sunshine," he said loudly, "you've had your fun, goodnight."

He was about to switch off the phone when a voice, clear and precise, spoke into his ear: "You are Cain, and your offering is unacceptable."

Then the line went dead.

He frowned at the phone, expecting it to do something else, but there was only a passive silence; whoever had called him had withheld their number, so he couldn't call back.

He walked on for a couple of minutes and then he listened to the voice message again.

"You are Cain."

It didn't sound like anyone from the band; it wasn't even a voice he knew. If it had been one of his mates they would have done something stupid like phone him and pretend to be Poppy, pledging him undying love.

But this wasn't a joke; this unnerved him, it felt more like an attack. This was from someone who sounded serious, and intent on harming him in some way.

As he put the phone in his pocket it hummed the arrival of a text message:

"You are Cain, and your offering is unacceptable."

He thought back to Sunday school classes he'd gone to, to

Cain and Abel, and the first recorded murder. But which one was Cain? Was he the one who murdered his brother? He would never murder anyone; that didn't feel right, that idea had no power over him, so that wasn't the sting in this attack, so what was it?

"You are Cain, and your offering is unacceptable."

Wasn't Cain the one whose sacrifice had been rejected by God?

Conner stopped and looked at the stars. Was that it? But that didn't make any sense. How could his offering not be acceptable to God? He tried to make himself walk on, continue home but the stars above him drew his attention. Was there something wrong in what he was doing? Was it this thing with Poppy?

He continued to search the skies for an answer, for some reassurance. His offering was his music, was that what this was about? Was there something wrong with his music? Surely that made no sense, did it?

And yet there was something in that, and he knew it; there was something wrong with his music, or his performances of his music.

Conner felt a sickening feeling growing in his stomach as he thought about the songs he had written and played over the years.

Above him through the crisp clear air he saw the white pinpoints of the stars, some randomly scattered, others appearing in patterns or lines, their precision seemed to judge him, and he called out to the one who had put them there.

"Isn't my offer acceptable to you?" he whispered. He continued to look up and listen, but then the stars began to blur and swim around in the inky blackness, and he found there were tears in his eyes.

9

LEWIS ASHBURY SAT at his desk and sucked on a cigar. When he had been a young man, and thought he knew everything, this activity would give him a superficial sense of calm, and confirm him in the illusion that he was in control of his life.

But now that he was older and perhaps a bit wiser, he knew enough to be aware of his ignorance. He knew enough to know that he was not in control. Gradually, everything in life and love and business had slipped from his grasp, so that now, helping out this misfit set of Holy Joes led by his former Personal Assistant had become the defining purpose in the life. And even that could not disguise the creep of fathomless grief that still came upon him more frequently these days.

He looked down at the desk, at the two photos of the only woman he was sure he'd ever loved.

There were two images of Bridget, each displaying different facets of her character: on the one hand there was Bridget his business partner, with all of the courage, intelligence and determination she brought to the company, and on the other there was Bridget the lover, full of charisma and passion.

He didn't have to be a master of self-awareness to know what was gnawing at his gut. He'd buried the truth quite thoroughly and it had stayed buried for months, but now it was rising to the surface, digging itself out of the grave he'd put it in, coming back to him to collect its due.

That truth was as simple as it was devastating. He'd loved Bridget. He'd always loved her, when they were lovers he loved her, when they were just business partners he'd still loved her, even when he'd pretended he hated her, he loved her.

But now Bridget was gone, and her death had affected him more profoundly than he expected, and he could not rationalize or deny this fact any longer.

She'd been murdered, possibly by the shadowy forces that his colleague Martin had got himself mixed up with, possibly even by the maniac who had caused a scene in the café Alex owned.

Whoever it was, he could feel the grief rising in him, mixed with a hunger for vengeance. He didn't want to admit his feelings because he hated the idea of having the weight of the past hanging around his neck, dragging him down. All his working life had been spent looking forward, pointing forward, away from the mistakes and consequences of the past, and on towards new beginnings, fresh opportunities. His desire to stay ahead of the past had always driven him on to find the next new thing. He believed in re-launching his life on a regular basis, like a new marketing campaign for a well-established brand; reinventing and redefining himself, and pushing on so that he didn't so much solve the problems in his life as simply leave them behind. That was why, after Bridget's death he was happy to pass what was left of SLaM over to Alex, another woman he loved, albeit in a completely different way.

But now, for the first time in his life it wasn't working. He couldn't rebrand himself and move on from his feelings for Bridget. She was dead and he had loved her and he still loved her, and he had not grieved her loss because he had not dared to. He had not wanted to admit to himself how he felt, and so he suppressed his emotions, held them down, believing that in time, they would simply go away.

But they had not gone away.

Instead they'd come back to haunt him, and not just a sorrow at her passing, he was also taken with a fierce desire for revenge, a desire with much more potency and hunger than anything he'd felt at the time of her death.

He sucked hard on the cigar and looked at the pictures, and felt nausea churn inside him, and at last he confessed to himself all the feelings: anger, sadness, remorse, love, revenge. He indulged himself in the free flow of memory. He recalled the times they had been together, the challenges they had faced together. The smoke made his eyes sting, as it curled up towards the anglepoise lamp, and he bowed his head. He wanted to pray, but there was nothing there to pray to.

All of the feelings were still there, boiling and curdling inside him, especially the anger. Anger because someone had crushed the life out of her with a spray of bullets, anger at the nagging suspicion that this hadn't just been a burglary gone wrong, that she had been targeted, or worst still, killed by accident.

As he thought about these things, a new resolve bubbled to the surface within him. He stubbed out the cigar and reached for his address book. He would visit a former employee, and return something he had been looking after since the fall of SLaM. That, of course, would be the pretext for the start of a journey towards something else: the truth, justice, and maybe the vengeance he thought he wanted.

Grabbing his car keys he walked briskly out of his apartment and into the cold evening. In his left hand he carried a briefcase, locked and unopened since the day he received it.

Martin Massey, former head of music at SLaM, had done rather well for himself in the last twelve months.

After the SLaM debacle he'd left the country with some haste, and at short notice, he accepted an invitation from his brother to go out to Greece to work on an olive farm. His brother's track record in business had convinced him that the whole scheme would end in failure, and would inevitably cost him money at some point, but he had to leave quickly and he didn't have a lot of other offers, and so he had scurried to the airport, and flown out to Athens.

When he arrived at the farm, he was amazed to discover that the work was light, the investment was sound, and his brother was not the impractical dreamer he'd once been. Martin provided the capital for his brother to buy land from a neighbour to expand the business, and he returned months later with a suntan and a quarter share in a busy and productive olive farm. These had been happy times, a golden period after the chaos of working at SLaM and associating with Lench and his cronies. He'd secured some consultancy work via a media contact, and paid off most of the mortgage on his apartment, and, quite unexpectedly, life was good.

Like his old boss Lewis Ashbury, Martin was well versed in the art of only looking forward, and the SEEKA project, with all the mess it created, was now a distant memory.

Life in the sun had helped Martin to regain some of his old confidence. He had lost his fear of evening callers, and registered only mild curiosity when the intercom system buzzed at around nine thirty one cold evening at the end of February. He'd been casually watching a programme on true crimes, but now he flicked the TV off, walked into the hallway and stabbed at the intercom.

"Who is it?" he mumbled.

"Martin, it's Lewis. Lewis Ashbury, I've got something of yours."

Martin frowned at the sound of the voice.

He wondered whether he could simply ignore this ghost from his past, cower by the intercom and wait for him to leave. But Lewis did have something of his, something he had forgotten about, and knew he wanted to get back, and these days cowering was not his style.

The intercom buzzed again.

"Do you want this brief case or not?" said Lewis.

Martin took a deep breath, and reminded himself that he was not now the man who was scared of people like Lewis Ashbury or Darius Lench. He released the lock and moved over to his front door, resolving to take back his case without asking Lewis to come in.

He heard his old boss, striding up the stairs, and then there he was, a little older, a little greyer but still unmistakably Lewis.

"Hello, Martin," said Lewis, "you're looking very tanned."

"Hello, Lewis," said Martin, "I wish I could say the same of you."

"And I'm very pleased to see you too," said Lewis, making no attempt to hand over the case.

"I see you've brought my briefcase back," said Martin. "Thanks for that."

He stepped forward and reached out his hand.

Lewis moved back slightly, still clutching the briefcase.

"Aren't you going to invite me in?" he said.

"No, I don't think so," said Martin.

"We do need to have a chat, you know," said Lewis.

"Do we?"

"I think so, just for old time's sake," replied Lewis, still holding the case.

They stood at the top of the stairs like a pair of lovers having rather public tiff.

Martin began to feel embarrassed, eventually he mumbled, "Just give me the briefcase and then come in."

Lewis paused before handing it over, waiting a second before releasing his grip.

They walked into a spacious lounge; the furniture, all oak and leather, had the clean, confident look that comes with recent purchases on a generous budget.

"Looks like you've done alright for yourself," said Lewis, looking around.

"I've been abroad making money," said Martin, "quite a lot of money actually." They both smiled. Everyone at SLaM had always been able to agree on the importance of making money. Martin poured them both a generous slug of whisky.

"Not too much for me, I'm driving." Lewis took the glass and sat down. "So are you working in the media again?"

"Just a bit of freelancing," said Martin. "Jingles for social media videos, it sounds niche but there's a lot of money in it right now."

Lewis eased himself onto Martin's smart new sofa; the cushions were broad and firm and they made his coat look scruffy and out of place. He didn't care, he wasn't going anywhere for a while yet. Martin sat in the armchair opposite him.

"So, what are you up to now?" asked Martin.

"Oh I'm working with Alex Masters again. You remember Alex, my PA? She's got her own little company going and she asked me to help out."

"Of course," said Martin, "you always did have a soft spot for her, didn't you." He had a sly smile on his face, and he couldn't resist teasing his old boss.

"So are you sleeping with her?"

Lewis was surprised at his own sense of indignation.

"No I am not," he said, trying not to sound too offended, knowing it would just play into Martin's hands. "You always were a cynic, Martin."

"Oh come on, Lewis," said Martin, "don't play the offended innocent with me, you would have her if you could, and you know it."

"It's just professional," said Lewis impatiently. "I'm doing some work for her company, that's all." He wasn't going to mention that that company was the remnants of SLaM.

Martin swallowed his whisky. "So what is she doing that requires your help?"

"She's setting up her own media business – music, fashion, cafés – she has all kinds of ideas. It's small at the moment but it will grow. I'm helping her with the marketing."

"Wasn't she religious?" said Martin, frowning. "Is this some kind of Christian media outfit?"

"Yes, that's right," said Lewis daring Martin to make another snide comment, which, of course, he did.

"I bet you stick out like a sore thumb amongst the righteous, don't you?" said Martin beginning to enjoy himself. He had been right all along, there really was no reason for him to be afraid of Lewis Ashbury at all.

"I'm not the only heathen they've employed," said Lewis, "and Alex knows what I'm like."

"I bet she does," said Martin, sipping his whisky. "So, what did you want to talk about, apart from your latest career move?"

"Do you keep in touch with any of the old crew from SLaM?" said Lewis softly.

"No." Martin shook his head. "Why should I? I mean, there really was only you, me, that idiot Somerville..."

"And Bridget," said Lewis.

"Yes, well Bridget's dead, isn't she." Martin took another gulp of whisky, and then he realized that he shouldn't drink too much while Lewis was still here.

"Yes, Bridget is dead," said Lewis.

"So is this what you really came round for," said Martin, "to talk about Bridget?"

"I came to return your briefcase," said Lewis, "and talk about old times."

"You," said Martin, "you want to talk about the past? That's not you at all. So what about Bridget though, are you missing her?"

He was speaking quietly now, in a tone that sounded almost like sympathy.

"Yes, as a matter of fact, I am," said Lewis. "And I mean to catch whoever killed her, and I want you to help me."

Martin sniggered and then shook his head.

"I can't help you there," he said, "I don't know anything about it, and I don't know why you would think that I do."

"Really?" Lewis leant forward. "Is that really true? Do you really have no idea who might have killed her?"

"Lewis," said Martin, fidgeting, "look, I am grateful to you for bringing my case back, but maybe now you need to go before you say something really stupid."

"I thought you might know who killed her," said Lewis, still seated and staring up from the sofa; there was silence between them.

"Well, you thought wrong then, didn't you," said Martin.

"I think you do know, Martin. And you are going to tell me." Lewis' eyes were glazing over, as if some great emotion were passing through him.

"And I think you had better leave." Martin stood up. "If *you* know something about Bridget's death I suggest you go and tell the police about it."

Lewis stood up and took a step towards Martin, who

appeared to be swaying slightly. They faced each other, just a few inches apart.

"I wanted to tell you about it first," said Lewis.

"Tell me about it?" said Martin, frowning. "What more is there to tell?"

"I think there is plenty more to say," said Lewis.

"She's dead, Lewis," said Martin softly. "Some burglar broke into her flat, and she surprised them, and they shot her; and now she is dead. She's been dead for over a year, and you're carrying her memory around like a ball and chain. You need to let her go."

"No." Lewis shook his head slowly. "I will not let it go."

The two of them were eye to eye now; the only noise their breathing in the silence.

"I can't let her go, Martin," said Lewis. "I still love her, and I won't let this go."

"Then grieve for her," said Martin. "Grieve for her and allow yourself to be upset, but face the truth that she is not going to come back, and nothing is going to bring her back. I'm sorry, I really am, but that's it."

"You're sorry, are you?" asked Lewis, acid creeping into his voice.

"I've got nothing more to say to you, Lewis. You had better go."

Martin moved towards the front door; it was time to see this guest off the premises. He attempted to move past Lewis, who at that moment reached out both arms and pushed him, hard. Taken by surprise, Martin toppled over onto the couch, the remains of the whisky splashing over the sofa cushions.

"What the hell is the matter with you?" shouted Martin.

"I want to talk to you, Martin, so don't be an ungracious host. I want you to tell me who killed Bridget."

Martin scrambled back to his feet, his anger sobering him.

"You had better get out, before I throw you out."

Lewis stared at him.

"Okay, Martin," he said, "okay, I'm going. But while I am gone, I want you to have a long hard think about Bridget, and who might have wanted to kill her."

He placed his own glass in Martin's other hand, turned and headed to the door, letting himself out. Martin followed him to the door.

"I don't need to do anything for you," said Martin to Lewis' back, "but let me give you something to think about; if you pursue this thing, it's not me you'll need to deal with. Who knows who did it, but if they had a gun they won't be afraid to shoot you either."

Lewis looked back at him. Martin's face was red, his breathing laboured. He looked angry and scared.

"Goodbye, Martin. I'm glad we've had this chat, perhaps we'll do it again some time."

Martin listened for the faint boom of the main reception door to the apartment block closing behind Lewis Ashbury. He drew great comfort from that sound and began to count, *one, two*...God but Ashbury had a nerve coming here tonight... *four, five, six*...he looked over at the sofa, now standing at an odd angle. He looked at the dark stain of the alcohol, the smell filling the room...*eight, nine.*

He moved to the curtain; and watched his visitor walking away down the road, and then he heaved the sofa back into position.

After that he took a long deep breath and picked up the case.

"Well at least I've got you back," he said, smiling at the case. The irony was that in bringing this back, Lewis was helping Martin to distance himself still further from Bridget, and her death, and the group he used to belong to.

He topped up his whisky, and took the case into his study. He remembered the combination immediately, it was her birthday, and even though he'd cast her off in the end, there were some things he did not forget.

He spun the numbers and slid the catches across. The flaps at the front of the case popped open with a small "click", and he lifted the lid and stared at the contents.

It all still seemed to be there, the papers and folders, and the data tag. He picked up the tag, plugged it into his laptop, and switched the machine on.

The machine ticked and hummed as it roused itself.

"Come on, come on!" He slapped the keyboard, which continued to whine, ignoring his petulance. His mobile rang, and he ignored it. It stopped ringing as the machine recognized the tag and opened the file directory.

There was just one file on the disk. Martin clicked on it and some text appeared before him.

Bridget,

I am not sure I will even give you this note, but if you do get it, treat it seriously, and then destroy it, properly. If knowledge of its existence is discovered then I will be dead. So I ask you first of all to get rid of this, the only copy that will ever be made, for your sake and mine.

This is not about our relationship, this is about your life. You must understand that some people are not motivated by money or status. I belong to a group who have an interest in seeing the SEEKA project succeed as I do. They will let no one stand in the way of the success of SEEKA but they have decided that someone within SLaM poses a threat to the project. That someone is you. Because of this they...

Rereading it now, he remembered how glad he was that he had not finished this note. This tag held the only copy of the message, he'd deleted it on his PC long before the police took any interest in SLaM. He didn't know why he had still kept this copy, it had been a stupid idea to do so, but he would not be keeping it for much longer. He was formatting the tag, wiping it clean when his mobile rang again. On instinct he picked it up and answered it.

"Yeah?"

"Don't run out on me, Martin." It was Lewis' voice. "I'll be back soon."

Martin just laughed, and the phone went dead. He tossed it over his desk, and it skittered over the edge and on to the floor; and then his computer told him that the data tag was clear. Another little piece of the past had gone, and the papers he'd kept from his previous life would be soon to follow. He now felt confident that he, and his former associates, were free of any connection with Bridget's murder.

SEVERAL MILES TO THE NORTH, on the other side of the city, Orlando Shand sat at his desk and scanned the short email he'd received from his new acquaintance, Caleb Wicks. He hadn't answered it straight away, and was still struggling with his decision to share his findings.

He had taken digital copies of all of the files, and all of the images, although it was probably only the CCTV footage that his new acquaintance would not have seen before. His finger hovered over the send button, and he tapped it gently.

Then he thought of Bridget, his client, murdered in her own flat and the familiar indignation shook him. He hit the send button with some purpose and muttered to himself.

"There," he said, "it's done, it's done."

10

———

Conner stepped down from the train and stared at the little pot plants neatly placed along the back of the station platform. Alex had told him to be careful and for once he hadn't laughed at her; the recent prank calls and text messages had spooked him, and for the first time in his life, he was feeling vulnerable.

But he was not going to submit to fear, and he'd told the others he was fine to do this, and now that he'd arrived he was looking forward to it.

"Just enjoy it," he told himself, "and think about the money."

The weather was mild for late March, heralding the coming spring, and Conner took a moment to look around.

"Quaint," he murmured, under his breath. This was the kind of place that might still have its very own Station Master, equipped with a bright red flag, a peaked cap and a very loud whistle.

He tried to relax, and thought about the set he'd be playing for this gig. This girl, Jessica Smith, his adoring, fee-paying fan, had sent him a deposit, which meant they were serious, and now he felt very good about how this was going to go.

As he walked out of the station he sent Alex a quick text to reassure her that he'd arrived.

"Mr Adams?"

A voice called to him as he emerged onto the station forecourt. He looked up to see a bearded man with a khaki jacket and a flat cap, driving gloves, and sunglasses. The guy was waving at him from beside a black Volvo estate.

"Mr Adams?" the man repeated; there was something about him that confused Conner, as if looking at the guy for too long would give him a headache.

"Yes, that's right," said Conner, smiling and lifting his guitar slightly.

"Jessica has sent me to collect you."

The driver opened the rear passenger side door, and Conner slid his guitar in and then sat down, buckling the seat belt across himself.

"We'll be there in a few minutes," said the driver as they pulled out of the station car park.

Conner frowned as he tried to place the man's accent, he was about to ask where the guy was from but decided that this might be rude, and so he kept quiet.

They were soon out of the village and heading west into the countryside. Conner tried to keep his bearings, but he wasn't brilliant with directions and after about fifteen minutes he was hopelessly lost.

They drove on and a few village names slipped into and out of Conner's mind. The driver had the radio on quite loud, so conversation with him was impossible.

Eventually there weren't even any village names, just meandering country lanes, one after another. Hedgerows streamed past him, fields like great patchwork quilt squares. Conner's eyelids began to droop and he felt himself drifting away.

He woke with a jolt as the car swung into a small driveway

that led to a cottage, where a couple of balloons hung limply from the front gate, suggesting that some kind of event was due here.

The driver opened the car door for him without comment and led him to the front of the cottage; somewhere inside there was music playing.

The front door was open, and Conner walked into a narrow hallway. The place looked empty, and smelt clean, even sterile. The music was louder now but Conner could not recognize it. The sound was atonal and brutal, and it made him nervous.

"This way," said Josef, and led him down a bare hallway and into a room at the back of the cottage. Somewhere outside, a dog barked. The windows of the room looked out onto a garden, where Conner could see the grass had recently been cut, but the surrounding beds were given over to a competing environment of weeds. Josef's voice caught him again.

"The guests will be here soon," he said. "We have somewhere for you to get changed and freshen up a bit."

Conner tried and failed, again, to place the accent.

"The birthday girl may want to come in and see you for a few moments," said Josef. "Humour her if you would, please." He smiled crookedly and Conner smiled back.

"Sure," he said.

Josef nodded and left the room, closing the door behind him. The music that had resonated around the cottage stopped playing, and Conner found the silence more unnerving than the noise. He suppressed the urge to pick up his guitar and just leave.

Conner looked around the room he'd been left in. It looked like it should be a living room of some kind, but there wasn't much furniture; just a rather incongruous chaise longue standing against one bare wall, its surface covered with blankets and drapes. The floor was boarded and not even covered by a rug. On a laminated table in one corner he could see a large bottle of mineral water that looked as if it had just been taken from the fridge, and some glasses. The air had a faint odour; it reminded him of the incense sticks that Daisy sometimes used. He frowned as he looked around the room; something about this place made him feel uncomfortable, and he couldn't work out why.

"Oh come on, Conner, get a grip," he said and busied himself with getting his guitar out and reviewing his set in his mind. The girl had specifically asked for a couple of his songs, and he was confident he could give a good rendition of them, but one more practice would not go amiss. He didn't touch the water.

As he was tuning his guitar the door opened, and a young woman who must have been Jessica came in. She was wearing a lacey turquoise dress and her blonde hair was tied back away from her face. She looked physically strong, well built but not heavy. She looked older than he had expected her to be, and he was also struck by the idea that there was some vast sadness hanging over her. She smiled, but it seemed to Conner that her eyes did not smile with her.

"Conner Adams, I'm so excited to meet you." She held out a cool hand and he shook it. Something in her accent suggested she was well educated.

"You must be Jessica," he said.

She smiled again and moved towards him. "That's right, I'm the birthday girl." Her dress made a little rustling noise as she came closer, and when she leant her cheek towards him he instinctively kissed her. Her skin felt warm and faintly moist against his lips, it was not an unpleasant sensation.

She went over to the table and he watched her pour out a glass of the mineral water.

"You want one? I can get you something a little stronger if you want."

"How old are you today, Jessica?" he asked.

For just a moment she looked at him, as if he had asked a question that made no sense, then she spoke.

"Twenty-one; do you want some?" She gestured to him with the bottle of water and he watched her sip some.

"Please." He was actually quite thirsty after the journey. "So when are your guests arriving?" He drank deeply from the glass she handed to him.

"Guests should be arriving in about half an hour," she said.

He asked if he could use the bathroom and she indicated a door opposite the lounge.

He went to the bathroom, and when he returned she was gone. He drank some more of the water, but he felt a little dizzy and suddenly panicked, he didn't want to get ill just before a gig. He stood up with some effort and went over to the window, opened it and breathed in the cool spring air.

Why did she call me Conner Adams, he thought, *that is odd, why not just Conner? What fan of Elvis ever met him and said, "Elvis Presley, I am so pleased to meet you."?*

His head was definitely spinning now, and he flopped onto the chaise longue. He stared at his guitar floating around in his field of vision, as if it had a life of its own.

"What the hell is the matter with me?" he whispered, shutting his eyes.

He heard a voice, it was Jessica's voice, and another voice, which sounded like the man who had driven him here.

And as his senses began to shut down, Conner realized that something was indeed wrong. He thought about calling Alex, and then he whispered a slurred prayer:

"Lord, have mercy, on me..."

And then he was gone.

Marie stared at Conner's inert form for a few moments, looking for signs of movement. Finally she was satisfied.

"Thank God he went to the bathroom before the drug kicked in," she said as she moved towards him. "Come on, let's get him stripped and set up."

With deliberate care, Marie closed the guitar case and moved it to the side of the room. Neither she nor Josef spoke as they pulled at Conner's inert form, stripping the clothing from him. Then Josef arranged Conner's limp body over to the chaise longue, left arm over the back of the chaise, right leg hanging over the front, with Conner's foot brushing the floor. Then he left the room, and came back a moment later with a camera and tripod.

"Help me get out of this dress," said Marie when he had returned.

Josef grunted and fumbled with the little plastic hooks that held the garment to her. He struggled with the final hook, ripping the dress as he pulled it undone.

"What the hell are you doing there?" she hissed.

"Keep still," he said.

"You are such a *grunt*," hissed Marie, "it's a wonder Lench finds use for you. Have you got the camera?"

"Of course I have the camera," he snapped. "I know my job, you make sure you know yours."

She looked back at him, naked now, pitch-black eyes staring at him. Her nakedness reminded him for a moment of Bridget in the moment before she slashed him.

"I'll get everything set up," he said. A stirring of lust made him pause but he pushed it away.

IN THE SPIRITUAL world the angels of God see all too clearly how things are, and Conner's angel watched, full of fascination and horror as her precious charge was prepared for the abuse. It was all noted, all recorded, including the details of Conner's drug-spoilt, incoherent prayer, which even now filtered up into the heavenly places.

Conner's spiritual guardian was prostrate, and doing the one thing she did best – worshipping her God, anxious to submit herself yet again to the Lord. From the start she had known this situation was deeply wrong, but she had not guessed how this would play out. She was horrified by the seething legion attending the driver of the car, barely keeping their victim on the leash. She sensed the spiritual stench of this place they were in, where desperate and destructive acts had given license to the enemy to establish himself here. Then of course there was this girl. When she saw at first hand the Spirit that infested her, she had simply closed her eyes and turned away.

The demon sat just above Marie, presenting itself as a little girl of maybe nine or ten years old. Its top half, above the torso, was a replica of Marie as she might have been when she was that age. The same sad dark eyes, set in a younger face, hair tied back in a ponytail, wearing a floral summer dress. The angel noticed that the likeness was uncanny, and unusually detailed, with one supplementary effect. Across the girl's forehead, above the sad and lonely eyes cut into the skin of the forehead was the word: "ABANDONED". The cuts were deep and seemed to go all the way through to the bone of her skull, and a dark liquid oozed from the wounds.

Below the torso, the demon made no attempt to present itself as human; rather where there might have been legs, it seemed to have something like roots that reached down into its host, digging into her brain and heart.

The demon viewed the angel dispassionately, seemingly

unconcerned by her cries to God, then it looked down at its host, and at Conner's inert body spread out before them, and grinned.

In the physical world, Marie placed a mask over her face and donned a pair of surgical gloves. She straddled the inert form of Conner's body and mimicked a number of sexual acts in a systematic and preplanned choreography. Josef worked the camera, moving it occasionally to get a different view. Outside, the dog barked again, and the sound of birdsong drifted in through the open window, a counterpoint to the sound of Marie moving over her victim's skin, and the occasional squeak of the chaise longue as it took their weight.

Marie was comprehensive and methodical; she took her time and Josef filmed it all with the professional patience he'd developed over a lifetime.

Conner's guardian continued to pray, averting her eyes from the site of the abuse; but even as she did so the Spirit that infested Marie leant forward, almost casually and spoke to the angel. There was no bravado, none of the bluster and arrogance that Josef's horde might have exhibited.

"I am alone," it said quietly.

The angel looked at the demon, knowing that she had no power to banish it, or stop the actions of its host.

"And I am not," said the angel quietly, *"and neither is he."* She pointed at Conner's naked form.

The demon stared at the angel as if she'd just said something embarassing at a dinner party. Then it twitched and rearranged its roots, before composing itself again.

"Look at my host," it said, and spread a child's hand out as if introducing Marie to Conner's guardian angel.

"See how disappointed she is," it continued. *"A constant well of frustration and anger; disappointed to be left alone; disappointed to be abandoned by them."*

The angel considered for a moment: *"Them?" Who were the "them" it referred to?* Although she already had her suspicions.

"They were always there for the others," the demon continued. *"Where were they when she needed them?"* It closed its eyes and seemed to suck at the host, feeding again on the vast reservoir of brokenness within.

In the physical world, Marie looked up from her work and sighed. With all the activity, Conner's drugged form had slumped down further and further, the fingers of his right hand touched the wooden floor.

"Let's get on with the next phase," said Josef.

"Patience," said Marie, "pass the equipment." She pointed down to his left.

Without comment, Josef passed her a small translucent plastic box.

The angel turned her attention from the demon and prayed again:

"Lord, hear Conner's prayer."

The demon sniffed and wrinkled its little girl nose.

Across the void, Conner's single, disjointed prayer had indeed been heard; and at around that time, Alex Masters saw the text message from her brother and sent a quick reply.

"HOPE ALL GOES WELL. IF THEY GIVE YOU CASH PAY IT INTO YOUR ACCOUNT!"

She sent the message and switched off her phone.

Sitting over Conner's body, Marie removed the lid to the box. Inside were a selection of small scalpels and a syringe. She decided to start with the cutting.

Removing one of the smaller instruments from the box she held it in her hand and watched the light play on the edge, then carefully she brought the blade down to Conner's chest and drew a line across his skin. She massaged the cut, and blood beaded up at the wound. The camera rolled. Then she lifted her right hand and touched the blade to her palm, watching as a single red bead appeared in her hand. The camera stopped, and the birdsong faded for a moment, and then the oppressive silence was shattered by the sound of a high brash voice, speaking with the cowboy accent of the American West:

"This town ain't big enough for the both of us!"

"What the ...?" said Josef, instinctively slipping one of his own blades from its holder.

"Ignore it, it'll be his mobile," said Marie, still holding the razor, the blood welling on her palm. She looked down at the red line of Conner's own blood.

She was about to bring her hand down on his chest when the voice cut in on them again.

"Reach for the sky!"

Beneath her, Marie felt Conner stir.

"Josef, quick," she said, "we need to put him under again."

"No," hissed Josef, "another dose is dangerous, we stick to the plan; we agreed one attempt at this, and another dose only for the journey back." His voice went quieter still. "And no names, remember?"

They stared at each other, and were only interrupted when Conner twitched slightly. Marie turned her attention back to the blade, drawing it across his chest again, making another bloody track next to the first one. Again Conner shifted slightly, and his right leg began to slide off the edge of the chaise longue so that his foot hit the floor with a dull thud. The ragged line of blood on his chest began to congeal. She leant forward examining his face through the mask.

"It will have to do," she said, and then and then in an act of dominance, rather than affection, she kissed his cheek and his eyelids flickered as she moved away from him.

"Let's see if we can turn the phone off," she said calmly, standing up from him.

Josef reached down to Conner's jacket with a gloved hand, and took out the phone. He pressed the off button and slid it back into Conner's jacket.

"Let's get him dressed," she said, standing up. "Then we can give him another dose for the journey."

They pulled the clothing back on him, his tee shirt smearing the blood from the cut on his chest. Marie picked up the dress and then looked back at her victim. He was lying perfectly still now, mouth open, a couple of red patches showing against his shirt. Marie took the syringe and administered another dose into his arm. She held his wrist as she did so and looked at the little band hanging there: purple letters on a light green background.

"WWJD," she said.

"What?" Josef stared at her.

"Never mind," said Marie, "you can take the short route to the station."

He said nothing as he unscrewed the camera from the tripod. He'd had enough of people telling him how to do his job, especially this woman.

"Okay, a copy for him, a copy for us." She indicated the camera.

Josef ignored her, and walked into the kitchen. The surface of a small breakfast bar was covered in computer and camera equipment. The blinds across the window were heavy and drawn.

He eased the chip out of the camera and slid it into a waiting laptop. File names appeared on the screen and Josef clicked on an icon, whispering under his breath. He copied the files to a waiting data tag.

"Come on, come on," he whispered to himself.

A series of images flicked up on the screen, and he couldn't help grinning at some of them.

The door opened behind him, and she entered.

"He seems to have quietened down now," she said.

"You should stay with him," replied Josef without turning round. "If he revives now I will probably have to kill him."

She was looking at him, and he could feel her contempt, boring into him. He turned to face her, looking into the black soulless eyes.

"He will be fine, and you," she actually pointed at him as she spoke, "need to do your job."

He looked back to the screen and released a long, slow breath. The tag indicated that the file transfer was complete. He pulled it out of the computer port and handed it to her. She turned and left, and the little dress, now ripped at the collar, brushed against the floor.

"Oh yes," he grinned, "I'll do my job, Marie." He switched off the laptop and packed the camera away.

Marie was waiting for him when he returned. She'd managed to prop Conner up against the chaise longue; his head flopped onto his chest. Josef picked him up like a rag doll and carried him out to the car; the body was satisfyingly limp as he strapped it into the front passenger seat. She followed on behind with the guitar, and put that on the back seat.

"How are you going to dump him without arousing suspicion?" she asked.

He just smiled at her as he started the car.

"As you requested," he said, "I will do my job." Then he floored the accelerator and the car lurched across the gravel drive, spitting tiny stones in an arc as he drove away.

Conner woke with a dry mouth, and aching head.

Immediately, he knew something was wrong. He tried to remember where he was. There had been a girl, and a cottage, but now he was outside. He could remember the girl, and drinking some water, and going to the bathroom, but nothing else, no party, no guests, no music set. He reached out to his guitar case, which was lying beside him, and his ribs ached. His clothes felt odd, like they they'd been pulled around, and in some undefined way he felt dirty, violated.

He opened his eyes and tried to take a deep breath.

It was late afternoon, the light was fading and he was sitting on a bench, opposite a station, the station where the bearded guy had picked him up earlier.

He looked at his watch, but he could not focus on it in the half-light, maybe it said five thirty. His head was hurting and he needed to go for a pee, badly. Feeling confused and scared, he wanted to get away from this place, now.

He reached for the phone and scrolled through the messages and missed calls. The first text message was from Alex.

"HOPE ALL GOES WELL. IF THEY GIVE YOU CASH PAY IT INTO YOUR ACCOUNT!"

"God, what happened to me?" He tried to speak the words but his voice sounded rusty and alien.

And his chest hurt. It definitely hurt, and it wasn't just the fact that he ached; there was a sharp stinging pain there. He looked down at his tee shirt, and thought he could see a string of dark patches dots, bloodstains spaced like a constellation across the material.

"What the...?" he croaked.

What had happened to him?

My God, he thought, *what did they do to me?*

He lifted his shirt, and the wounds stung where the blood had stuck the material to his chest. There were angry looking red tracks across his chest. He stared at them and repeated the thought.

What did they do to me?

He remembered a man's voice, and the woman; they'd spoken to each other at one point.

I need to go home.

He summoned his strength, stood up and stumbled across to the station. He still had his wallet and he eased himself delicately onto a seat on the platform. He was lucky; there was a train back to London due in about fifteen minutes.

It was only when he got back to his apartment and was unpacking his bag that he saw the data tag.

Someone had stuck a caption across the label side:

"Conner Adams, porn king. More on the web"

They hadn't even spelt his name right.

He slid the tag into his computer.

The images were very clear, and well lit. He stared, fascinated and horrified, at his naked form. Above his body, a female figure in a devil's mask straddled him, seemingly engaged in a sexual act with him. It looked like it was the girl who had called herself Jessica, but the mask did a pretty good job of obscuring her face.

What had she done? What had she done to him?

He went into the shower and ran hot water over himself; the wound on his chest stung, and began to bleed again as he tried to clean himself off.

What had they done to him?

The question kept coming to him, and then more questions; what if he was infected? What if they had done other things to him? What if she'd given him some kind of *disease*?

My God, he thought. *My God.*

What would it all mean for Poppy and him?

And at that point, under the cover of the noise of the shower he screamed out in anger and despair.

The tears mixed with the jetting water around him, and amongst it all he did not hear his mobile phone go off again, showing off his new ringtones.

"Meet you at the watering hole!"

It was another message, something familiar to greet him when he emerged from the shower.

"You are Cain."

11

CONNER SAT on the edge of the plastic chair, hands clasped around a polystyrene cup, pushing it out of shape. Caleb sat on one side of him, Alex on the other. Caleb was scribbling a note in the margin of a typed sheet. Across the table from them, two policemen sat forward in their own seats frowning. A tape whirred languidly in the machine placed between them, and Conner was silent,

"Can you remember anything about the journey in the car?" said the Sergeant, a shiny man with small pale blue eyes and cropped grey hair. He had the look of someone who had spent too much time listening to people who he knew were lying.

"We were in the car for about half an hour, maybe an hour – a black Volvo estate, I think. I didn't look at the number plates. We drove around in the country; I'm afraid my sense of direction is bad, I'm sorry."

Conner adjusted his gaze away from the walls of the interview room and faced his questioners. Then he looked over at Caleb.

Still he said nothing.

"Okay," said the Sergeant, "tell us about the guy who took you to the house."

Caleb leaned in towards Conner.

"The way out of this is to go through it," he whispered, "you can be the brave man that I know you are. The people who did this to you have taken nothing that is really important from you, nothing."

"What?" said Conner, "but they…"

"You," interrupted Caleb, "are made in the image of God, everything you do and everything you say should be inspired by that fact."

Conner looked at Caleb, and then at the police officers, who were now staring at him.

"I think he was wearing brown corduroy trousers," said Conner, "the driver, I remember that, and a jacket, it was kind of green, like a military jacket, and he wore a flat cap, pulled down over his eyes." I

"What about his features?"

"I'd say he was in his fifties. Beard, sandy coloured hair, rough skin, and maybe a scar on his cheek, I didn't really get a good look at him."

"Did he speak with any kind of accent?"

"Yes, actually he did, like he was German maybe. I think the girl called out his name at some point: Jeff or Joseph, Joseph I think."

"Okay," said the Sergeant, "let's talk about this girl."

Conner nodded and sipped the black coffee they'd given him.

"Can you describe her for us?"

"She looked strong, athletic, I'm guessing she was early twenties, she said it was her twenty-first birthday. And she had blonde hair, tied back, and dark eyes very dark eyes; I'm assuming the girl I saw first is the same one who, well…"

"...who attacked you," said the Sergeant. "Yes, let's assume that for the moment."

"I think it was her," continued Conner. "She had very sharp features, her chin and nose." He paused trying to recollect any other detail about the girl. "She called herself Jessica, but who knows, maybe that wasn't her name at all."

The Sergeant raised an eyebrow, as if impressed by Conner's deductive powers.

"Okay," said the other officer, "anything else?"

"Yes," said Conner, "she wore a dress to start with, a turquoise dress, and then obviously this mask thing," he indicated the photo on the table in front of them, "and I thought she was crying at one point."

The Sergeant leant forward. "You thought she was crying? Why did you think that?"

"I saw a tear in her eye, through the eye slit of the mask she was wearing," said Conner. "It was there all the time, of course, but somehow it was more obvious when she had the mask on."

"Which eye?" asked the Sergeant.

Conner thought about it for a moment. "Left," he said, "her left eye."

He glanced at Caleb, who was still busy scribbling notes.

"Thank you, that's all for now, Mr Adams," said the Sergeant, stopping the tape. "We'll be in touch with you if we need anything else."

ALEX TOOK him back to her apartment afterwards and made him some tea.

"I should be angry," he said, sipping at the mug. "I should be angry at them but I don't feel anything."

"I know."

"Do you?"

"I know what it is like to feel nothing when you should be feeling everything."

He thought about the car crash that took both of Alex's parents; years later she had described feeling nothing but numbness for months afterwards.

"Yeah, of course you do," he said, "sorry."

"It's okay," she said, and smiled. "So, what are you going to do now?"

"What can I do? I need to keep going, for you and for SUMMER and for just everyone."

"And Poppy?"

"What about her? I don't want to think about Poppy, I can't talk to her about this. What is she going to think?"

"You need to tell her," said Alex gently, "before she finds out some other way."

"I know, but…"

"But what?"

"Alex, there's something else going on, it may be connected."

"What do you mean?" said Alex.

"There's something else I need to tell you, I've been getting text messages," said Conner. "It's really weird stuff; the number's withheld but whoever it is just sends me the message 'You are Cain'. You know, like as in Cain and Abel from the book of Genesis. I've been trying to work out what it means."

"Is it one of the lads in the band messing you around?"

"No, I asked them, but I knew it wasn't one of them, it just didn't feel like a joke one of them would have played on me."

"When did it start?"

"That day when Daisy did her presentation of all those designs, it was that evening."

They were silent for a moment and Conner buried his face in his hands.

"Talk to her," said Alex. "From what Daisy's told me, she has a good heart, tell her the truth, trust her with it."

Conner kept his face in his hands but Alex could see that he was crying.

"Okay," he said finally, "okay, I'll talk to her."

She came to him and hugged him, and he felt her love for him, her desire to protect him from further pain.

"I am so sorry, Conner," she whispered.

They stayed like that, motionless on Alex's couch for a minute longer, and then Conner stood up.

"Thanks sis," he said, "I'd better go." He moved towards the door of Alex's flat, but before he reached it he turned back to her.

"You know the thing that sticks most in my mind is that this girl looked like she was crying as she did what she did to me. I could see a tear in her eye, through the mask, like she was crying. I mean if she hated it so much why the hell did she do it?"

"I don't know, Conner. Go home and get some rest."

Conner left Alex's apartment in a daze. He'd been offered a lift, and his parents had wanted to pick him up and take him back to the family home, but he didn't want any of that, he wanted to be on his own.

He got on the train and sat by the window, and watched the countryside slip by. He felt dirty and guilty, and he didn't even know what he was guilty of. He could not remember the last time he had cried. He touched the scar on his chest, still raw and painful. He looked down at his hands and caught sight of the wristband he always wore.

"What would Jesus do?" he whispered, but he could feel no response, no emotion, no answer within himself to answer that question.

Eventually he fell asleep.

CALEB SPENT the next day forgetting tiny details. He had difficulty in concentrating on his day job, his mind drifting back to the crisis of the attack on Conner.

He had not mentioned it, but he was convinced that the attack on Conner was the work of the enemy. He knew the mark of his enemy well enough, and he could see it here. What he couldn't see was a clear motive for this attack. Of course this could stop Conner from performing, but it seemed like a crude and risky action if that was their motive.

There was something else, he was sure of it, especially in this reference to Cain, and he feared it was some hold, some leverage that the enemy had over Conner.

He prayed on and off all day, trying to sense the Lord's will in what had happened, asking for protection for this young man, but he was distracted and he felt no clear insight into what was happening.

Once his other duties were completed, he applied himself to the other challenge in his life – the identification of Bridget's killer, and more particularly, the man who controlled Bridget's killer. He was sure the assassin had not acted alone, but under orders. Dinner had come and gone almost as an inconvenience; he had had no appetite, not even for a helping of Mrs Wicks' apple and blackberry pie, and that was as good an indication as any of how distracted he was. They had talked together over dinner about everything that had happened to Conner and he was, as ever, reassured by her promise of prayers. That evening he felt restless and so he gathered his papers together and headed out into the bitter early evening chill, towards the SUMMER offices.

The sky outside the office windows had darkened enough to show up the stars, little points of light in the darkness, and he prayed for the Light to guide him now. When he got to the office he let himself in and sat at the same desk where he always sat – the idea of hot-desking made no sense to him at all – and he took the evidence he had out of his briefcase.

He spread out the material he already had on Bridget's killer, and next to it he placed the documents and six photos he had received from Orlando Shand. He was particularly drawn to the black and white images of the figure that Shand was convinced was the person who killed Bridget. Caleb Wicks studied the images carefully and after a minute or more he separated the four photos into two piles of three each. In three of the photos the man seemed to have a smooth face beneath what was no doubt a false beard, in the other three there was the faintest of lines, possibly a scar beneath the facial hair.

"Now what," he said to himself, "would Lewis, and Conner, and Alex make of you?"

He glanced back at the documents. There was a handwritten note on the cover of one of them with a question mark after it: "What have you done, MARTIN?"

He thought about the man who had visited Alex's café. If there was a conspiracy against SLaM, and even against Alex, could it be that the man who murdered Bridget was also the man who terrorized the customers in Alex's café? And if that were true, could it be that this was also the man who assisted in the attack on Conner.

"Oh, dear Lord," said Caleb sitting back and staring at the photos. He felt pleased that he might, at last, be getting somewhere, but everything he had discovered pointed to more danger for those he loved.

If all of his suppositions were true then "Joseph" was out there, acting against SUMMER now, and he was capable of murder.

Caleb knew it was urgent that they identify this man, and he hoped that through him, they would then be able to uncover the man holding the assassin's leash, the controlling mind behind all of this.

"My enemy," whispered Caleb, "I will find you, God willing, and I will stop you."

He thought back to what Orlando Shand had said about Bridget's comments; phone conversations between Martin Massey and someone else, someone who did not want to be disturbed too early in the day.

What was it Shand had said?

"Apparently, he told Massey only to call in future well after ten thirty in the morning."

But who would not want to be disturbed before ten thirty? Caleb turned it over in his mind, trying to find a way into this puzzle. His train of thought was interrupted by the arrival of Aiden.

"A late one tonight then, Caleb?" said Aiden.

"Trying to fit some pieces together you know," said Caleb. "What brings you in this evening?"

"Just needed to pick up some papers I left here," said Aiden. "So what are these pieces you're working with? Is this about what happened to Conner?"

"Indirectly yes," said Caleb thoughtfully. "I'm trying to find out more about Bridget Larson's killer, or more precisely, the person who gave the order for her to be killed by this man." He pointed to the photos. "I have some clues, but none of them make sense, yet; and my fear is that, yes, somehow Bridget's death is connected to what is happening to Conner."

Aiden stared at the photos on the desk.

"So you think this fellow is the monkey; but you want the organ grinder," said Aiden, "is that it?"

"That's one way to put it," said Caleb, smiling. "Actually you might be able to help me, can you think of a job that someone would have which would mean they don't want to be bothered before ten thirty in the morning?"

"Well, I'm not sure," said Aiden. "Perhaps he's a market maker of some kind; maybe based abroad in a different time zone?"

"Possibly, although I think he is based here in the city. By the way, how is the money going for SUMMER?"

"We'll be fine with the money, Caleb, leave that to me. What we really need is to make sure our main asset can function properly. It's all going to be pretty academic if everything that's happened to Conner damages him so much that he can't perform."

Aiden opened the safe they had installed in one of the cupboards and pulled out some papers.

"Nearly done with the company name change," he said. "SLaM is out and SUMMER is coming." He winked and then smiled at Caleb.

"I am looking forward to summer," said Caleb. "I sense that this current battle might be over by then. Well, goodnight, Aiden."

"Goodnight, and don't stay too late, Mrs Wicks will be wondering where you've got to."

"Mrs Wicks knows exactly where I am," said Caleb, sighing. "Although both of us wish I was at home, with my feet up, relaxing."

Caleb was tired, but he hadn't just come into the office to get some work done, and he was pleased to see Aiden leave, not for any personal reason but because he was expecting another visitor at the office with whom he wanted to have a private conversation.

Caleb wandered into the kitchen, made himself some tea and sat back in his chair.

It seemed to him that these new office chairs were designed

to be uncomfortable, as if, in keeping with the spirit of hot desking, no one should sit still for more than ten minutes at a time.

He breathed out a long sigh and was overcome with a feeling of weariness, confusion and even despair. It was really hitting him these days, and it wasn't just for lack of sleep. There was something else, something working against him, sapping the life from him. This wasn't the first time he'd experienced this feeling; it was, he knew, part of the battle. He shut his eyes for a moment and thought about Alex, and Conner, and Daisy, and this new friend of Conner's – Poppy. He didn't really know why, but he was very glad that Poppy had appeared on the scene, very glad indeed.

He woke with a start, the taste of disorientation in his mouth. He had lost thirty minutes, and the tea he wanted to drink was now cold. Now he had no time to prepare for the arrival of his guest. Whatever thinking and praying he had done would have to be enough.

He looked down again at the photos scattered on his desk, and then glanced up as the office door opened again, and, on cue, Lewis Ashbury appeared.

"Hello, Caleb," he said.

"Good evening, Lewis, thank you for coming."

Lewis laughed. "You're welcome. I was quite intrigued when you invited me to some clandestine late-night meeting at the office. Are you sure Alex or any of the others won't suddenly turn up unannounced?"

"Alex is at home group this evening," said Caleb. "We won't be interrupted."

"Okay," said Lewis sitting down, "so, any more developments on what happened to Conner?"

"I'm afraid not," said Caleb. "The police have drawn a blank so far, and young Conner has taken it quite badly."

"I can imagine," said Lewis. "Anything I can do?"

"I don't think so." Caleb shook his head. "But I do appreciate you coming in here for a chat."

"No problem." Lewis leant back in the chair next to Caleb's desk. "So what can I do for you?"

"I thought I might show you some pictures," said Caleb, smiling. "Let's start with something you'll have seen before." He spun round the photo-fit picture of the supposed window cleaner, and prime suspect for Bridget's murder so that Lewis could see it.

"Seen this a few times," said Lewis. "I presume this is just your warm-up act, is it?"

"Something like that," said Caleb. "We've all seen that photo-fit many times before, but what you won't have seen are these."

He spread out the images that Orlando Shand had sent him, and Lewis studied them closely.

"That's the same person," said Lewis.

"Yes," said Caleb, "I think it's very likely to be the same person, but there's more."

He took another piece of paper from his case, this was a drawing of a man in a long overcoat. There was a livid scar along his cheek.

"This," said Caleb, "is a rather sketchy drawing of a man who walked into Alex's café a year ago and upset some of the customers. This incident happened shortly after Bridget's murder."

Lewis laughed. "Oh yes, I remember her telling me about that. Didn't Alex tell him to get out? I wish I'd been there to witness it."

"That's right," said Caleb, "she did."

Lewis frowned. "You think it's the same person, don't you."

"Yes, I think it might be."

Lewis swore, and then apologized.

"Do you recognize him?" said Caleb.

Lewis peered at the pictures for a long time, and a recollection of his conversation with Martin passed through his mind.

Finally he said, "No, I don't recognize him."

"He never came to SLaM's office to see anyone?"

"No, I think I'd have remembered him," said Lewis quite truthfully.

"I'm sure you'll remember these though," said Caleb reaching into his briefcase again. He pulled out two slim documents, copies of the material Shand had sent him. One was a research paper that Martin Massey had commissioned, and the other his own report to the board of SLaM about how they could take advantage of, and make money from, the drugs and rave culture.

Lewis stared at them.

"Where did you get these?" he whispered.

"Bridget's solicitor sent them to me," said Caleb. "I think she took copies of these documents and sent them to him before she was murdered. Look at the note on the front of this document." He pointed at the report.

Lewis read it: "'What have you done, MARTIN?'" He looked up. "That's Bridget's handwriting, and the 'Martin' she's referring to is Martin Massey."

"One of your former employees?" said Caleb.

"Yes," said Lewis frowning, "yes I know Martin."

If Lewis had harboured any doubts about applying more pressure to Martin, those doubts were now gone. Now he was going to squeeze Martin Massey for every last drop of information.

Caleb watched carefully as Lewis took a deep breath and then picked up the drawing of the Assassin from outside Alex's café and stared hard at it.

"You were very fond of Bridget, weren't you," said Caleb.

Lewis was silent for a moment.

"I loved her," said Lewis finally. "I still do."

"I'm sorry," said Caleb.

"Don't be," said Lewis. "I'm glad of the chance to admit the truth."

"Tell me this then," said Caleb, "how much do you hate the man who killed Bridget?"

Lewis smiled, and shook his head.

"Oh, I try not to hate him at all. I don't dare hate him. If I did, I know it would consume me, and I'd spend the rest of my life trying to track him down, and either fail to find him, or probably get myself killed."

"Suppose you did find him," said Caleb. "What would you do then?"

Lewis grimaced. "Well that depends, doesn't it."

Caleb raised an eyebrow and waited for Lewis to go on.

"I am different from all of you, Caleb, I am not one to turn the other cheek. An eye for an eye, a tooth for a tooth, that's more my style." He took out a silver case, opened it and took out a cigar.

"Don't worry, I won't light it in here," he said. "Who knows what I would do if I found the guy. I don't think I'd know until the opportunity presented itself."

"So do you know what's going on here?" said Lewis, staring at Caleb. "And before you answer, I don't buy this bumbling old provincial solicitor act, you're much sharper than that even if the youngsters around you don't realize it."

"Okay," said Caleb, "I'll be honest with you. I don't really know much more than anyone else, but I believe we, I mean SUMMER and those associated with it, are under some kind of attack. I believe there is a spiritual dimension to this attack, I think the person who is organizing this attack is an associate of, possibly in command of the man who killed Bridget."

"And you think Martin has something to do with this?" said Lewis.

"I think SLaM, or at least some of your former employees, are connected with this, primarily this fellow Martin. I need your help to fill in some more of the gaps."

Lewis looked down at the photos again and then back at Caleb.

"Oh I can help you, Caleb," he said. "I'd be very happy to." He got up, put the cigar in his mouth and turned to go.

But Caleb Wicks wasn't finished with him yet. There was one more thing he was burdened with, one more thing that he now judged was worth the risk of saying.

"A moment more please, Lewis, I want to tell you something about Alex's parents, about their death and how it affected Alex. You must repeat this to no one."

"Okay," said Lewis, intrigued. He sat down again.

"The driver whose car killed Alex's parents had three times the legal limit of alcohol in his bloodstream. He was injured in the accident but made a full recovery. They locked him up for a period of time, but he's out now. Whilst he was inside, and for a short period after his release, Alex seriously considered visiting him, harming him in some way."

Lewis stared, and then laughed, nervously, shaking his head. "No, really? I find that very hard to believe. I mean, come on, she was only a kid. And besides, she would have forgiven – any of you would have forgiven. That's what you do, isn't it?"

"Well, I can tell you," said Caleb, "that at some point, before it all went too far she came to me and confessed that she had discovered the name of this man, his home address, the date of his release and his previous place of work."

"Really?" said Lewis. "How long after her parents' death was this?"

"Years later," said Caleb, "and by the time she came to talk to me about this, she tells me she had developed a rather comprehensive knowledge of poisons. I think she had decided that was going to be her approach."

"That's crazy," said Lewis. "Why are you telling me this now?"

"I want you to know that whatever you think of Alex, she does understand vengeance. It was a long time before she finally forgave this person; and she only did that to find release for herself from the anger and the guilt."

"Well that's good for her," said Lewis, stretching his face into a smile.

"It wasn't just good," said Caleb, "it was essential. Even the religious, as you call us, can feel anger, and the thirst for vengeance, the sweet thrill of pulling a trigger, plunging a knife, adding a few drops of poison maybe. Taking the life of the one who took a life we cared about."

"To forgive is to act in one's own interests," continued Caleb, "as well as those of the wrong-doer, to release a burden of anger that nobody should have to cope with. You carry such a burden."

"I WANT to carry my anger," shouted Lewis suddenly. "I want to feel that passion. I want to crush this man and destroy him if I can, because he murdered the woman I loved!"

"You think," said Caleb, unmoved by this outburst, "that the motivation to hate is a rich vein you can tap into, and you are right. But it will come at a cost, and you know that. In my experience, vengeful anger will feed on a person's character until they don't know who they are anymore, and none of it will bring back the dead. Tell me, what kind of life do you wish to live?"

"My own life, Caleb, my way."

"And what is your way, Lewis? What does it tell you about Bridget's murder?"

"I don't know," muttered Lewis, and then stood up. "You might be right, Caleb – all of you – but I do not choose to give up the energy and passion of revenge, even though it may harm me. I want that vengeance more than I want anything else."

Caleb rose slowly from the chair and picked up his coat and bag.

"I think you might discover something else that you want more than vengeance," said Caleb, deciding to play his final card. "I think you might fall in love again, and that love will force you into a choice about what you do."

Lewis was genuinely astonished. "Fall in love?" He laughed out loud.

Caleb smiled and nodded.

"Oh yes," he said, "don't tell me you have chosen to forfeit the potential for love in the future, surely you can still love?"

Lewis looked at him, speechless.

"What would anyone who might love you in the future think of your actions?" said Caleb. "What might you think of yourself? How, indeed, would you meet them if you were dead? If you really want revenge, that is what it might cost you."

"I'm not going to fall in love again," said Lewis.

"Are you sure about that, isn't the potential right there in you even now?"

"I'm not in love with anyone!" said Lewis, shaking his head.

"No, but there is someone you are fond of."

Lewis looked at him. "Are you messing me around?"

"No," said Caleb, "I am absolutely serious. I think you are fond of Alex and you will do all you can to help and support her."

Now it was Lewis' turn to laugh. "I'm not in love with Alex," he said. "I'm fond of her, I've wanted to sleep with her for five years, but now..."

"Now you just want to do what you can for her," said Caleb.

"It doesn't mean I love her, and anyway, you of all people

know she wouldn't even so much as look at me," said Lewis, with a rueful smile. "This is a ridiculous conversation."

"Well, maybe you're right," said Caleb, "but don't confuse morality with indifference. She is fond of you. Now I think I have said enough and I had better be heading off, I might see if there is any of Mrs Wicks' pie left. Goodnight, Lewis."

"Back to the wife, Caleb?" said Lewis.

"Precisely," said Caleb, winking, "back home to my wife."

He eased up slowly from his chair, picked up his case and coat, and wandered slowly towards the door. "Don't stay too long old chap!" he called as the door closed behind him, and Lewis Ashbury was left on his own.

12

———

ALEX KNEW that her company was running out of money.

She was no accountant, but then she didn't need to be to work out what the numbers were telling her. The cash was slipping away. It trickled like sand through fingers as the business incurred a hundred necessary expenses; each one was essential and each one was bleeding the business dry.

She was so immersed in it all that the ringtone of her mobile made her jump.

"Hello, this is Alex."

"Alex, how are you, darling?" Alex smiled at the familiar voice of Bernice, the old friend with whom she'd become reacquainted. "How's the dizzy world of global media entertainment?"

"Expensive," said Alex.

"Expensive?" repeated Bernice. "Well, everything that's worth having is expensive."

"Not everything; love isn't expensive!" retorted Alex, cringing as she heard herself.

"Alex," said Bernice, and she let out a long sigh at the end of the line, "every form of love is expensive, and I don't just mean in terms of hard currency. I thought you of all people knew that."

Alex didn't answer. She was too tired to engage with this now.

"Anyway," said Bernice eventually, "chin up, my dear. At least you are doing something you really want to do. Better to burn out than to fade away, yeah?"

Alex smiled, a call from Bats Templeton was actually a welcome relief after the stress of the past few days. She was glad to hear from her friend, and she told her about what had happened to Conner.

"Alex, my God, it's simply horrible," said Bernice when the story was over. "The poor guy, how is he coping with it all?"

"I think physically he's fine," replied Alex. "We'll know more in a few days when the medical results come through. Emotionally though it's hit him hard. I think it's going to take him a long time to recover."

"I'd be bloody furious if it happened to me," said Bernice, indignantly. "How dare they! So what are the police doing, has he been able to tell them anything? Have they made an arrest?"

"Wasn't much he could give them," said Alex. "I don't know what these people used on him, but it pretty much wiped his memory for most of the time he was there."

"I think you're right, it's going to take him a while to bounce back onto the horse again." She paused in mid-comment. "God, what kind of a mixed metaphor was that? Anyway, I think this rather impacts on what I was going to speak to you about."

"Oh, what did you want to talk about?" said Alex.

"Well, this party of course! But I'm wondering whether perhaps we shouldn't put the burden of playing at our event on your poor brother at the moment. Do you think it might be too much for him?"

"To be honest with you, I don't know what he will be able to manage in the next few weeks or even months. He's booked into a quiet place in the country, a sort of retreat, just to get away from it all for a few days. Maybe after that he will be able to face things again. He also had some strange phone calls and text messages as well, so that didn't help. It's really pushed him to the edge; I'm hoping that a few days away will do him good."

"Hmm, I'm not sure it would work for me," said Bernice. "I'd get bored pacing around some house out in the sticks somewhere, I'd want to be out there trying to find the people who did this."

"I'm sure you would!" said Alex, with all sincerity. "Or you'd be working off your feelings by climbing a mountain or immersing yourself in some fencing tournament."

"Oh gosh yes! Work it off with the foil. But then I'd still go after the people that did this." She paused for a moment, and then said, "I feel really sorry for him, Alex, I know you think I'm as tough as old boots, but I do have a soft sensitive side as well."

"Of course you do," said Alex, trying to sound convinced.

"No, it's true," said Bernice. "People don't realize this about me. They think I'm hard as nails just because I like to play a bit of sport."

"You can certainly do that," said Alex. "I think you learnt it all at school."

"Well, maybe," said Bernice. "But it's not all mountains and sword fights you know. Anyway, I need to get on; let's see how Conner is in a week or so, shall we? I'll talk to you soon."

"Look after yourself, Bernice."

"And you look after that brother of yours, darling, the poor thing!"

Alex put the phone down, and then, without thinking she picked it up again and looked for Lewis' number. She found it but paused for a moment with her finger over his contact name.

She did not really know why she was calling him, and so,

rather reluctantly, she put her phone down again and turned back to the subject of SUMMER's non-existent cash flow.

AFTER NEARLY FOUR hours of rehearsal, Conner rested his guitar on its stand, and looked at his fingertips; they were hard and red, and they tingled with the repeated plucking of strings. Normally the tingling gave him a sense of achievement, of work well done, but today he felt nothing. No achievement, no nerves, no excitement in the music – nothing.

"That's it," he said, looking over at bass player Al Weaver. The rehearsal had been scheduled for three hours, and so now they were an hour over.

Al responded by tossing an empty water bottle across the studio where it hit the carpet-tiled floor and skittered over towards Mark the drummer, who frowned at it.

"Had enough then, Al?" said Conner.

Al responded with a withering look. They had all tried to be careful with Conner, but tempers were frayed after such a long session.

Baz stretched over his keyboard and growled, "Why do we have to spend four hours on a three-hour practice?" He ran a hand over his shaved head.

The other two looked at Conner, silently asking the same question.

"It's because I'm such a rubbish guitarist," said Conner, smiling, "and I'd embarrass you lot if I didn't work this hard at it."

Baz laughed into his microphone, and the whole studio rang with the sound of feedback.

Mark glanced at the empty water bottle by his foot; then on an impulse, he guided his toe under it and, shouting at Conner, he flicked the bottle up into the air.

"On yer 'ead, son!"

The bottle spun in a high arc, and Conner leant forward so that it glanced off his forehead and onto the sofa by the studio door.

"GOOOOOOOAAAAAAAAAAL!" Mark and Conner shouted in unison.

Conner laughed. He had told them all not to pussyfoot around with him, just to treat him the same as ever, but it was hard for them, and him. He had started a lap of honour after his "goal" when his mobile rang, and he was still running when he answered it.

"Yeah?"

"Hello, Cain," the voice said with cool civility.

Conner stopped in his tracks. The others noticed his sudden change of mood.

"Who are you?" said Conner, suddenly full of indignation.

"I am the man who knows who you are. I know that you are a deceiver and a thief, and I know that your actions have compromised everything you would seek to do."

"What?"

"I know you!"

"I think you've got the wrong number, mate," said Conner, and switched his phone off.

When this had all started, he'd decided not to do the obvious thing and change his number, somehow the defiance of it appealed to him, but now he was beginning to doubt the wisdom of that thinking.

"What was that all about?" said Al.

Conner shook his head and forced out a smile. "Some crazy fan got my number."

"I wish some crazy fan would get my number," said Mark casually, "So who is she, this fan? I presume it's a she."

Conner didn't seem to notice him, he just stared out into the space in front of him.

"Hello, Conner," said Mark. "Earth to Conner, come in."

"What? Yeah, what did you say?"

The others smirked at him.

"Hey, you're not in love, are you?" said Al.

"No," said Conner.

"What about that girl you met in Paris?" said Baz. "Poppy, was that her name? What's going on with her?"

"We're just friends," said Conner.

Al looked at Baz, who looked at Mark.

"Really," said Conner. "I mean nothing is going on between us."

"What was her name again?" said Baz.

"Poppy," said Conner. "She's one of Daisy's friends."

"I thought you and Daisy were a thing," said Al. "What happened to that?"

"Daisy and I were never a thing!" said Conner.

"But Poppy?" said Baz. "Is that a thing?"

"Maybe," said Conner.

"Ah, there it is," said Al.

"Like I said," said Conner, "we're friends, we're not in love or anything."

"Just good friends," said Baz, and played some soft chords on the keyboard, the first bars of "I'm Not in Love" before coming in with a falsetto version of the lyrics.

Conner shook his head, but he thought of Poppy.

"Come on," he said, "let's get packed up and get out of here."

Al and Baz began putting their instruments away.

Mark wandered over to Conner who was unplugging a microphone.

"So go on then," he said quietly, "what is the deal with you and Poppy?"

"I don't know," said Conner, "it's all gone a bit sideways since I got attacked."

"Have you talked to her about that?" said Mark.

"Yes, I told her," said Conner. "She's been very understanding about it."

"But?" said Mark.

"But," said Conner, "it's not how she's reacted, it's me, I just don't want to go near her at the moment, I don't feel..."

Mark said nothing and waited.

"I don't feel right," said Conner. "I don't feel clean."

"I'm sorry," said Mark, "we all are. I know the others get a bit antsy with you, but we are all on your side."

"Thanks, mate," said Conner.

"I think you should try to hang on to this girl," said Mark. "She sounds like a good one."

"I don't know," said Conner loudly. "I don't know how I feel about her."

"Maybe I know how you feel better than you do," said Mark. "Don't let her go."

"Okay," said Conner, "advice noted."

In the car park, Conner declined the offer of a quick drink and thought about getting home. He wanted to have a quiet night, and a chance to think.

THREE MILES AWAY, Darius Lench sat in the driver's seat of a cheap little car with faded green paint that was just beginning to flake away at the wheel arches. The interior smelt of junk food and stale sweat, and he wrinkled his nose. His eyes moved over the crass design of the upholstery, the overly optimistic array of dials and icons across the dashboard, and he felt another wave of pure contempt for everything that he saw as cheap and igno-rant and stupid.

He hated this car. The garish interior spoke of thinly disguised poverty, but there could be no beautiful Mercedes tonight; he must not be noticed, he must simply blend in.

The neck pain he'd been suffering more frequently of late came upon him again and for the first time he resolved to talk to his doctor.

His mind turned to the job at hand. Conner Adams, the weak link, already compromised by Marie's attack, was espe-cially vulnerable right now, and he knew it was essential, urgent even, that he press home their advantage.

He drove to the corner of Conner's street. A previous dry run told him that there was an unlit space near this junction where he could park and prepare himself. His course of action would depend on whether he actually got to talk to the boy. He got out of the car and walked to the telephone kiosk a few metres away.

In his flat, Conner was sitting in front of the TV, nibbling a piece of pizza when his mobile went off again. He answered it without thinking.

"Hello?" he said, spitting pizza onto the floor in front of him.

Lench gripped the phone a little harder. The victim was there. The game was on.

"Do you think I have the wrong number now, Conner Adams?"

Conner did not answer, and so Lench continued.

"Be assured that I do not have the wrong number. You are Conner Adams, and you are lead singer in the band Joel's Garden."

"Yes, and you are?" said Conner. The familiar surroundings of his own home made him feel more confident.

Lench ignored the question and continued:

"And you have in your possession a 00L-17 acoustic guitar made by Martin & Co?"

This also was true.

Conner said nothing. He looked over at the guitar, sitting on its stand in his living room.

"Well?" said Lench with all the spite he could muster. "That is the case, isn't it? You do have in your possession a 00L-17 acoustic guitar?"

Eventually Conner answered. "Yes."

Then he waited. What else was this guy going to tell him?

"Are you there, Conner Adams?" said Lench in a clear, assertive tone.

"Who are you?" He was just whispering now. "What do you want?"

And Lench knew then that he had the boy, so he waited, counting slowly in his mind, *one...two...three...* before speaking in a slow, measured tone.

"What I really want is for you to die. I want your heart to stop beating and for you to die," he murmured, "but failing that, I want you to understand that your performances, your art, indeed all of the offerings to your God, are utterly without integrity. You are bankrupt, barren, worthless."

Conner could find no response to what was being said because his brain could not process any of it, other than to know that what the voice said was true. Something there in the back of his mind told him he was indeed guilty and that everything was compromised; but he didn't know why or how.

"Are you still there, Conner Adams?"

"What have I done?" said Conner.

"Why, don't you remember?" said Lench, feigning surprise. The boy was breaking, and Lench wanted to pile on the damage, as much as possible, right now.

"All those clever notes, all that beautiful music; all those songs played on your lovely guitar. Did it all sound wonderful in your ears? You hypocrite, Conner Adams, where did you get that instrument from? How did you get it?"

Lench hoped this was enough to provoke the boy into a more profound despair. He didn't know precisely what happened with this guitar, maybe it was used to sing deliciously profane songs, maybe it was stolen, or maybe it was in fact, the god that this boy truly worshipped, an idol in the place of the God he professed to bow before. He said nothing more, hoping that the silence, and the boy's own pain would do the work for him.

And in this assumption he was correct. Conner remembered, as if it was yesterday, entering the music shop, seeing the instrument, knowing that he was alone for a moment, and simply taking it and walking out.

It was an act of theft. He stole the guitar. It was a truth he had buried, covered over, left in his past, but it had come back now to haunt him, and what was worse, his enemies seemed to know all about it.

All the songs he'd sung, all the worship he had offered, all of it felt like dust now. His sacrifice, which he secretly felt so proud of, had been shown up for the hypocrisy that it was.

"Nobody knows, do they, Conner?" said Lench, pressing home his advantage. "We have already humiliated you, and now we will finish you."

And at that moment Conner remembered the little lecture he had given Poppy about how terrible stealing was, and how pleased he had been to show off his moral credentials to her, and his head fell.

He switched the phone off and looked across the room at the guitar, the instrument he loved, sitting on its stand, next to its case. The case he'd bought from the same shop a week later. He closed his eyes and thought of Poppy, and the tears rolled down his cheeks.

LENCH WASTED NO TIME. He was, on the whole, satisfied with his performance, and the boy's response, but now, he needed to drive the poison home with one last engagement. He remembered the words of his master:

"You must be bold, so that you can complete his humiliation..."

He turned up the collar on his coat, adjusted the sunglasses, wig and beard that Josef had applied for him and set off at a brisk pace down the road. This was the most critical phase of the procedure.

Conner was holding his guitar, just staring at it, when the doorbell rang.

"Oh, go away," he whispered. He wasn't expecting, and neither did he want, any visitors tonight. He tried to ignore the noise, but the bell rang again with an insistence that made him wince, so he pressed the intercom.

"Yes?"

"Delivery for Conner Adams," said a voice.

Conner pressed the entry button wondering what he'd ordered that he had forgotten about.

In the same place, but in another world, Conner's angel was provoked by the Spirit to move away from him, pass through the door to the apartment, and out into the corridor outside, where she saw a man in a long black coat entering the building.

He was attended by such a display of horrors that for a moment she paused and was quite still. She recognized in them instantly the remnants of her ancient brothers, morning stars now faded and perverted from their former glory.

One of them, presenting itself as a mirror image of the human it infested, stared to her as it passed with its host.

"Sister," it said, and in a realm outside time all was still and the thing stared at the angel with contempt in its heart.

The angel whispered a breath of prayer: *"Lord, Lord, deliver me from evil."*

The demon twitched, and some of the others with it shivered and clung to the one who had spoken.

"Our host," it whispered, *"our host has come for your boy."*

Then it looked away from her, and time restarted, and Lench walked up to the door of Conner's apartment.

The angel resisted the temptation to rejoin the one in her care. She had her instructions and she needed to fulfil them. She turned her back on the gibbering collection that accompanied Conner's visitor, and, just for a moment she interacted with the world, giving a light tap on a neighbour's door.

Conner, meanwhile, went to his own front door. He was still holding the guitar in his hand as he opened it, and there before him was a man with pale skin, long brown hair, a trimmed moustache and a rather bushy beard. He wore a trilby hat and reflective sunglasses that shielded his eyes, although the night was dark by now, and Conner could not see much of his face.

Conner stared at him.

"May I come in?" said Lench in an almost apologetic tone.

Conner recognized the man's voice immediately.

"Tell me who you are," said Conner in a quiet voice.

"I am the voice of reason," said Lench, raising his hat and bowing slightly. "I look for sin in the lives of people, and help them to atone." He smiled and stepped forward to the threshold. "I see you have the instrument there." On impulse, he reached out and gripped the headstock of the guitar.

"Let go of my guitar," said Conner, looking behind Lench down the corridor. He felt vulnerable and alone.

Darius Lench laughed.

"Your guitar, Mr Adams?" he said, still holding the end of the guitar. "Is that true, and if it is, what do you think is the worth of what you've done with it?"

Lench increased his grip on the instrument.

"It's beautiful though, isn't it?" he said. "Far too good for you though, don't you think?"

Conner felt his grip on the instrument weaken, and as he did so he heard the click of his neighbour's door open.

An old man, in black shorts and an old football shirt squinted at Conner and his visitor. He was holding a much-folded newspaper that showed a page with a half-finished crossword.

"Evening, Conner."

"Evening, Mr Brooks."

Mr Brooks frowned and then nodded at Lench.

"Evening," he said. "Only came out because I thought someone knocked at my door."

He stared hard at Lench, and then glanced at the guitar, which both Conner and Lench were still holding.

"Well, goodnight then," said Mr Brooks and with one final glance at Conner's visitor he shut his door.

Lench turned back to Conner and released his grip on the instrument.

"Listen, Conner," said Lench, grabbing Conner's attention again, "I don't think you should play that instrument again. Do you? In fact, I don't think you should be playing guitar at all anymore."

"I..." said Conner.

"Lay it down, Conner," said Lench quietly. "You are no longer worthy of it."

Before Conner could answer, Lench had walked away down the corridor and back down the stairs to the exit. He didn't even take note of the fact that there was no one in the lobby as he left.

Conner went back into his flat. He placed the guitar back on its stand and went into his bedroom. He knelt down on the floor and curled himself into a ball and wept, adopting the same position that Daisy had adopted when she crouched in the cubicle of a public lavatory, oppressed by the demons that harassed her.

The tears squeezed out of his eyes, and he shook under a sense of worthlessness, guilt and loneliness.

The visitor was right. He could not call this his guitar anymore, he could never call it his guitar again, and the visitor was also right that he could never play it again. Conner had stolen this instrument. He remembered all the details of that incident so clearly now, and he knew that all of his offerings, all of his music, was compromised, and worthless.

And all this just before the band was going to go on tour.

He went into the lounge, and as the tears formed in his eyes again he got a cloth from the instrument's case, picked up the guitar and gently wiped it, cleaning the dust and grease and fingermarks from it. He moved the cloth over the body of the instrument, and as he did so he thought, strangely, of the women who loved Jesus, who performed one final act of love when they went to anoint his body after the crucifixion.

With the body of the guitar cleaned he placed it carefully into its case. Then he went back into his room, opened the cupboard and dug behind the clothing to find and pull out his old rucksack. Then he began to pack.

DARIUS LENCH JOGGED BACK down the street to the little car. The last part of the mission was at hand, the part that he had been savouring the most, the part of the mission that would actually give him a great deal more pleasure than dealing with this feeble boy. He was going to visit an old acquaintance. He would afford himself this visit only because he believed that his master had allowed him to do this, to go and twist the knife one more time.

This would, he hoped, be the sweetest moment, a little innovation of his own. While some of his associates craved wealth or sexual gratification, his real lust was for the exercise of power, and the art of dominating another person. These were his pleasures, exercising a stronger will, his will, over those who were weaker than him, here was his treasure.

He felt the excitement well up within him. He could not touch her, he could not physically harm her, but then he didn't need to and in truth he didn't really want to now. He was permitted to present his dominance, to damage her mind and spirit. This would be like the swift insertion of a sharp instrument, a clean but very deep cut.

Eventually he drew up at the kerbside in another part of the town and looked at the lights in the windows of the building opposite. The evening breeze had turned bitterly cold now, and above him the stars were bald specs on a deep black canvas. He was reminded of his visit to Tarmo, and the bitter cold weather of the New Year.

Lench stayed in the car and reached for his mobile phone. This would be the last call on this number before he changed it. Before he could dial the number, the phone vibrated in his hand.

"Good evening, Marie," he said and paused, listening. "I see, well that's good." He listened for a couple more minutes.

"I am going to have to cut our conversation short, I have something that requires my attention. Yes, I will call you later, good evening."

He switched off the phone and breathed deeply; he needed to focus now. When he was ready, he hit the buttons with precision. He did not need to check the number; he had a good memory for the personal details of his enemies.

The phone was answered.

"Hello."

"Alex Masters?" he asked.

"Yes," she said, and she recognized the voice instantly, and he knew it.

"Miss Masters, I thought I would call to tell you that I have this evening, presented a member of your family with evidence of the gross sin that is manifest in their lives; can you guess who it is?"

In her flat, sitting on her sofa, Alex froze, knowing the caller and sensing the poisonous intent. But as Alex heard one voice, Angel heard many of them.

Angel shut his eyes and listened to the tortured chorus of the legion, speaking over and through this man, their host. He had heard them before, and knew them of old; this was the man who had accosted Alex and Daisy on that fateful day just over a year ago.

"What have you done?" she said, fascinated and horrified by his intrusion.

"It's not what I have done, Miss Masters," said Lench, sounding reasonable, "it is what your little brother has done that is the issue." He was thinking again about how best to administer the maximum amount of pain to this woman. Of all the individuals involved here, she was the one he hated most. She was the one he most wanted to debase and hurt. She was the one who had, in some sense, beaten him, humiliated him before his peers and brought him to his knees in ignominy before his master, and for that, she would pay.

"Are you there, Miss Masters?" he hissed.

"I don't believe you."

He laughed out loud. This was delicious, just the reaction he wanted.

"No, of course you don't, but then you cannot quite dismiss what I say either, can you?" His tone mocked her.

"What have you done to my brother?" Alex shouted down the phone, the anger kicking in.

Lench's mind filled with all of the degrading things he would love to do to her, but for now, he would have to settle with this little chat.

"Why, Miss Masters! Contain yourself. It is not I who has, how shall I say it, 'sinned and fallen short'."

In response to this, all Alex could do was shout questions. She had never felt so indignant, so angry, even when she had thought about her parents. She suddenly felt such a deep and overwhelming love for Conner, and a corresponding anger for this repulsive man who was again attacking her family and making her life a misery.

"Where is he?" she shouted, hot tears forming in her eyes. Her mind filled with images of her brother.

"Do you know," answered Lench in a mock-casual tone, staring again at the grotesque dashboard of his car, "I really have no idea. Perhaps he's in a blubbering mess on the floor, perhaps he's run away somewhere, I don't know where he is, or how he is–" He was cut off by Alex's outburst.

"What have you done to him?" she screamed at the phone, completely abandoned, completely desolate and desperate about her brother.

Angel watched, agonized, again restrained by the rules that governed his existence. He could not interfere, but he sensed the enemy. He could see what Alex could not: this man together with the whole menagerie of demons that plagued him, sitting in a car just across the road from where she lived. He knew she needed to finish this conversation, she needed to stop listening to this man, now.

Alex's grip on the phone tightened, making her hand ache

and her knuckles turn white. Lench spoke again again, but she wasn't listening. Instead with some force of will she placed the phone back on the receiver cutting him off in mid-sentence.

"Miss Masters, your brother is a–" She heard no more.

What had happened? What had Conner done? What had this man done to her brother? What claim did he have on Conner?

"Stop, think," she whispered to herself, shivering.

She called Conner, and there was no answer.

He wasn't with his parents.

She called the other people who might know where he was.

"No," said Daisy, "haven't got him here."

"I don't think he is here, my dear," said Caleb. "Bear with me a minute…" Caleb's voice trailed off. She could hear him mumbling to Mrs Wicks. "No, we don't know where he is."

She even found a number for Conner's new friend Poppy, but he wasn't with her.

She called each of the band members, who professed ignorance about Conner's whereabouts. Mark, who was close to him remembered the bizarre phone call that Conner had laughed off as a crazy fan.

She called Caleb again.

"He's not answering. I don't know where he is and I don't really know what's happened between him and this man. I think his mobile is switched off and I am worried about him."

She was trying to regain her composure. Caleb asked her a couple of questions about what this man had said, and how he sounded. Then the phone became silent and, in the silence, Alex saw in her mind's eye a picture of Conner again, as a young boy, the brother she had inherited. He had been part of the family she had gained, just as she had lost others. She found that she could not deal with Caleb's questions, and she whispered her apologies and put the phone down.

She called Conner's mobile again but got the answering service. She drove round to his flat, but no one was there. He had gone.

Alex spent a lonely night, with worry robbing her of her sleep. Worry for the brother she loved, worry for the business that needed his input, and worry that whoever it was who had terrorized her before had come back to haunt the people she loved.

13

———

If ever there was a fool's errand, this was it.

Poppy had never climbed this mountain before. She had never been to this part of the country before. She didn't know what equipment she would need; she didn't even know if her journey was a huge waste of time.

But still, she was here, and she was here because when she heard Conner was missing she remembered what he'd said to her and, for once, she had done the reckless thing, the impulsive thing, and set off to find him.

It was only once she'd arrived in the Lakes that she called Daisy to tell her what she was doing.

She stood at the base of the mountain and stared up. The summit was swathed in damp wisps of vapour, surrounded by what looked from a distance like damp green felt. Within the first half a dozen paces of her long walk to the summit, she was questioning her actions. Already the hard lumps of rock were pushing up through her soft shoes. The other people she saw all had proper footwear, and expensive looking waterproof jackets. These people were organized, they had done what she had not and planned for this visit. She wished she'd bought some boots first, but the urgency of this trip had compelled her to come here straight away.

At least she knew now why Conner called this land intimate. It was imposing certainly, but also somehow close, distant but also intimate and accessible.

She carried on up, understanding more fully why Conner said he loved this place, but that was small comfort as the rocks bruised the bones of her feet.

"What a stupid name for a mountain," she whispered to herself. "Harrison Stickle, what does that mean?"

About half an hour in, as the foolishness of the venture began to overwhelm her, a rainbow appeared. Just a short ribbon of colour set in the bracken ahead and she remembered the Kente cloth that she had admired with Daisy and Conner in Paris. Searching for any sort of encouragement, she accepted the rainbow as a sign of hope, a slender portent of success.

A stone path stretched before her, just lumps of rock wedged together to mark out the long, arduous climb. She began to ask herself why she was really doing this. Of course she wanted to find Conner, but why, why bother? What did it say about how she felt about him? And what if she did find him? What state would he be in, and what would she say to him? She couldn't make what had happened to him disappear; it was going take a long time for him to recover. She examined her motives for coming on this search, and when she really got through to the honest answers the word "love" seemed to come up again and again, and she tried to distract herself by looking at the colours of the landscape around her.

But for once, the colours did not capture her.

Conner was a nice guy, becoming a friend, and she thought that this was as far as it went, and yet, and yet, here she was, bruising her feet, breathing in the damp air, and staring at the sodden looking sheep that were scattered on the slopes around her.

Up ahead, water rumbled through ancient gulleys, cascading over the rocks and stones, setting up a subliminal roar that became a backdrop to all of the other sounds. It was not so very different from the more familiar rumble of the city. She looked at her map; this was Stickle Ghyll, apparently.

After ten more minutes all she could do was focus on the route ahead. Another ten minutes after that and she was breathless, her socks were soaking and she felt a pang of irritation at Conner, as if he was forcing her to do this, and, perhaps he was.

"Morning!"

Poppy looked up. The cheery voice came from a wrinkled man with gravity defying curls of white hair that poked out from the sides of his head. He was walking back down on the same path as her. He had a gnarled walking stick, mountain boots, and a plastic sleeve for his map.

Another organized walker, she thought, and felt embarrassed by her lack of preparation.

"Morning," she mumbled.

"Keep at it," said the old guy, cheerfully, "the summit is worth the walk."

"Really?" she said. "You think so?"

"Of course." He paused as he passed her, and smiled. "It's a bit of a slog to get up there, but for you it will be well worth it."

"Right," she said, "okay."

He carried on walking, humming to himself, and disappeared from view behind a rock below her.

"Right," she said again, and his words seemed to lift her, it would be worth it if Conner was up here.

She shook her head to rid herself of some clinging self-pity, and started walking again. Wet feet or not, she was going to get up this mountain, and if Conner was there she would find him.

On impulse she turned again to look at the old man she'd just spoken to, but she couldn't see him on the path, and without much energy to spare for curiosity, she faced forward again and kept climbing.

Poppy judged herself to be about halfway up, when the path opened out onto rough grassland, scattered with mounds, like a burial ground for ancient kings. Her map told her that the shining body of water she could see to the south was Blea Tarn. The wind moved across the grass, a susurrus that dislocated her from the reality of her mission, and the air was punctuated with the rattling call of a black crow. She stopped for a rest, and munched on a bar of Kendal mint cake. She had never come across this stuff before, but she'd bought it in a hurry at the station and it seemed to be required food for hill walkers. It was shaped more like a bar of chocolate than a cake, and each lump had an intense minty sweetness, almost too sickly for her taste.

The mist was beginning to clear now. There were two or three darker shapes above her, the different summits of the Pikes. Below, she could see along the Langdale Valley, a rolling patchwork of farmland, sectioned off by walls and hedges.

Her stomach did feel warmer for the sweetness of the mint cake; but the rest of her was cold. The muscles in her legs, shoulders and back were aching, and the wind teased her thin coat open, and blew against her jumper so that sweat on her tee shirt was icy against her skin.

"Please, be here, Conner," she whispered to herself as she set off again, labouring over the stubborn lumps of rock, the weariness in her bringing some honesty from within her. "I want you to be here, I want it to be me that finds you and rescues you, and holds you. I want you to talk to me, and I want to get warm again with you, and–"

"Morning!"

She looked up, startled from her soliloquy, as two smiling

figures, again well dressed in the right kit, came striding down past her. There was definitely a kind of unspoken etiquette amongst these hill walkers: one obviously said "hello" to fellow travellers. This wasn't like the enforced solitude of a cramped London tube journey. All of these people shared some common purpose, even if it was not her purpose.

At the end of a particularly steep climb she came up onto more rolling grassland. The ground was wet and boggy underfoot, and she thought she might have to throw her shoes away when she got back.

She blew her nose on an already damp and ragged hanky, and trudged off towards the peak on her left. The wind was quite strong now, whipping at her damp hair.

She wasn't thinking of anything as she made the final climb. It was just one foot in front of the other, an aching trudge up to the top. The speculations were gone, and the emotional responses were gone. She just needed to do this, as much for herself now as Conner. She didn't want to think about him at all, she didn't want to waste her energy on the emotional consequences of what she was doing.

At last she reached the summit. She was exhausted and nervous and triumphant, and she looked out to the other peaks across from her, shielding her eyes from the insistent, biting wind. She looked around the clumps of rock for any sign of him, but even as she had approached the top of the mountain she felt concern. This place just did not seem to have the kind of features she remembered Conner describing in Paris. Where was the little patch of green facing out to the northwest? The place where she stood was nothing but a mound of bare rock.

She collapsed onto the stone beneath her, feeling the chill of her damp clothes clinging to her. She bowed her head, and contemplated that this had been one of the most pointless miserable things she'd ever done in her life. Her shoes were muddy and scuffed and her feet tingled under wet socks.

A snatch of human voice caught her attention and she saw a couple of other walkers chatting across from her, one holding up a plastic folder.

Without thinking she tuned in to their conversation.

"Still time for the other one?" said one, breathlessly.

"I think," said the other, "we can get on to Harrison Stickle, then round Pavey Ark and down from there."

She turned back and stared, tear streaked into the breeze. Now that she had stopped walking she was really feeling the cold.

She shivered, and then frowned as one more confusion settled in her mind.

They were going to Harrison Stickle, and that meant this wasn't Harrison Stickle, this was some other stupid Stickle!

"This is the wrong peak," she said to herself. "It's the wrong damned–" But she stopped herself. She did not as a rule use bad language, and she wasn't going to start now.

She took out her map and her bar of mint cake and just sucked on the sweet end of it. Her tee shirt still clung to her, chill and wet, and the wind picked up again as she steeled herself for the next walk.

"I haven't come this far to stop now," she said to herself, staring at the peak just a few hundred yards away, "I am here for a reason."

A new sense of resolve formed inside her, and she scrambled down into an area dominated by boggy grassland. Lumps of rock stood like menhirs, half sunk into the earth. She headed off in what she thought must be the right direction, and was encouraged to see the two walkers who had been on Pike of Stickle clambering up the hill in front of her.

Slowly, painfully, she worked her way to the summit. Her

feelings for Conner now oscillated between passionate love and anger; she didn't trust either of these emotions, but she hoped that the anger wasn't in the ascendant when she did see him.

If she saw him at all.

By the time she had scrambled to the top and hunched down on the old slate and quartz rock, her emotions had calmed and she just wanted Conner to be there, only so the trip was not a waste.

The summit here was broader than the previous peak. She could see a few hardy walkers, hunched together, sharing their lunch. The sight of people eating made her feel hungry.

Now she was here, she didn't even want to search for Conner, didn't dare to discover that he wasn't here. So she just slumped down with her back to a piece of granite and looked around. The cloud hovered around the peaks nearby leaving banks of grey and green mountainside. She shivered again as the cold of the stone found its way through her trousers, making the bones of her pelvis ache.

If he's not here...

The statement came into her mind but she had no will to finish it.

If he's not here...

She did not have the mental energy to think it through, so instead she fumbled in her pocket and found the last fragment of the mint cake bar and just put it in her mouth. As the sweet taste burst over her tongue she whispered in a hoarse voice to herself.

"If he is not here, at least I've climbed two peaks in the Lake District today." And she took some comfort from the thought that, even if he wasn't here, he would find out that she'd come here to find him. The thought sparked a flicker of warmth in her heart.

She stretched her arms to make her tired muscles work

again and climbed to her feet, and then she looked out across rock and water, farmland and forest, the restless wind buffeting her; and she admitted to herself that the view, and the achievement of reaching the summit did make her feel proud of herself.

She looked over to the north and east, to Pavey Ark. This was the view he had mentioned, visible from the grassy ledge; it would have to be over the shallow rim of rock where she was standing. She told herself he would not be up here, a couple of thousand feet up in the mist and the rocks.

On a whim, she took out her mobile phone and rang him. There was no answer, but she imagined she heard a sound, in the air, in the moan of the wind and cry of the crows, an unnatural sound, like the voice of a cartoon character.

Poppy knew she couldn't put the search off any longer, and so she switched off the phone and walked further around the summit, searching for this little grassy nook he had spoken of.

Her mind was full of the foolishness of her mission, and the foolishness of Conner Adams, and the futility of it all. That was her defence, and a sudden blushing anger at him, the fool that he was. She told herself she hoped he wasn't here, that he didn't deserve all this effort, whatever he'd suffered. She conjured up the anger and hid behind it as she peered over a ragged lip of granite.

OF COURSE HE WAS THERE. Hunched up and staring out to the distance; and in the moment her heart softened, and she knew, of course, that she had been desperate to see him, desperate for him to be right there.

He was tucked into a corner of the rock face, sitting on some kind of groundsheet, facing out across the space to the next peak, and beyond that to the distant coastline. He looked like a little boy who had somehow lost his way. She could see that something had damaged him, see it inside him, and compassion for him welled up within her.

He hadn't noticed her yet, and now she hesitated. Would he want to see her? Could she help him overcome the thing that had driven him here, could she help him face it? She felt a sudden urge to go back, to avoid the risk, and but she knew she would never do that. She could not leave him here, not now, and so she climbed down over the edge of the rock, and he glanced up to see who was coming, and she saw his eyes widen as recognized her.

"Poppy," he said, "Poppy."

He watched her approach, the ginger curls hanging damp around her face, and the wet patches on the knees of the jeans, and the hopeless trainers, and despite himself he laughed.

It had crossed his mind that she might come for him but the idea had seemed foolish, an indulgence on his part. He watched as she came and sat down next to him.

"Are you laughing at me, Conner?"

"Yes," he said, "I mean, no, I'm just pleased, more than pleased, to see you."

"I have just climbed up two mountains to find you," she said, "and whilst this view is spectacular, I am cold and wet so I would really, really recommend that you don't laugh at me right now."

"I'm not," he said, serious now.

"Move over so that I can sit on the edge of that groundsheet." she said.

He moved over and she came and sat next to him, and they were silent for a moment.

"They're all looking for you," she said, eventually.

"I know," he said, "but you found me."

"Yes, eventually," said Poppy, "and I'm not doing this walk in these shoes again."

He looked at her wet, muddy shoes.

"We'll get you some decent footwear," he said, and put his arm around her.

She looked at him, and noticed the plastic tub on the groundsheet next to him. It contained a half-eaten sandwich and a few segments of orange, the remains of his lunch.

"I didn't know you have to *prepare* for a walk like this," she said. "It's like gearing up for an adventure in the Himalayas."

He smiled again. Sitting so close he caught again the hint of her scent; it reminded him of Paris and their last time together. He lifted up the box and she reached over, opened the lid and took one of the remaining orange segments. He was silent as she ate the fruit, just watching her eating, watching a bead of orange juice touching the corner of her lip.

"So," he said eventually, "how was the climb?"

"You really want to ask me that?" she said, licking her lips. "I've got the wrong clothes, the wrong shoes and I'm cold and everything aches. And I might have been here in time to share your lunch if I hadn't climbed up onto the wrong piece of rock to start with!"

Conner laughed out loud, and somewhere within him the dam broke. He laughed, and cried and laughed and shook his head, and she let him do all of this until he'd finished.

"So how are you doing?" she asked.

"You really want to ask me that?" he said, mimicking her comment. Then he said, "I wondered if you could answer some of the questions for me."

She frowned at him and then shivered again, and he felt her body shake as she sat next to him.

"Can we go somewhere warm first," she said, "then we can talk."

For Poppy, the return journey proved to be as difficult as the ascent. Her knees did not take kindly to the constant jolt of the descent and the boggy ground caught her a couple of times, submerging her feet up to the ankles.

The second time it happened Conner laughed, and then immediately regretted doing so.

"Funny, is it?" she shouted furiously. "Think you are so smug with your smart walking boots! You're the one with the problems, not me." Her voice echoed across the landscape.

"I know, I am sorry, Poppy, I..."

"Forget it," she said. "I'm sorry, I shouldn't have said that, that was really stupid."

"It's okay," he said.

"I'm sorry," she said again and he could see the tears forming in her eyes.

"Really," he said, "it's okay, you came for me, and it's okay. Come on, let's get back." He helped her out of the bog and she was about to say something else when she was interrupted by the rattled call of a sheep standing just a few metres from them.

"What do *you* want?" she shouted.

The animal stared at her, unmoved by her outburst, and bowed its head, bleating again; then it took two or three paces towards her.

"I think we'd better get on," ventured Conner.

"Well you've a better coat than I have," said Poppy, still staring at the animal.

They didn't say anything else to each other as they scrambled their way down past Stickle Tarn. The steep incline of the descent held their attention all the way back to the base of the mountain.

By the time they arrived back at Conner's car, Poppy was wet, tired, aching in too many places to count, and exhausted.

Conner got a spare jumper and trousers from the back of his car and offered them to her.

"Come on," he said, "let's get some food in the pub."

A few minutes later they found a corner in the lounge bar of the Sticklebarn Tavern, and Poppy changed as much of her wet clothing as she could. His jumper held his scent and it felt rough but warm against her skin. When she returned Conner looked at her, hair still a little damp, wearing his trousers and his jumper, which was rather too big on her. And all he could think was that she was beautiful in his eyes, and she looked even more beautiful today than she had been in Paris. Perhaps it was the fact that she was here, that she had made this much effort just to find him. For the first time, he wondered if there might be a way back from this. Her presence gave him hope.

The lounge was warm and humid, with logs alight in the fireplace. The wood hummed and cracked, and Conner got up and walked towards the bar.

"Hot chocolate," said Poppy, before he could ask her what she wanted, "and a ploughman's, please."

He returned with their food and drink and put it all on a low table in front of them.

"*Bon appétit*, as they say in France," said Conner.

"Thanks," she said, but she didn't move to pick up her food.

"Eat," he said, picking up the ham roll he'd bought himself. "God knows, you've earned it."

"Conner," she said, "I want to help you work this out. I don't know what I can do, but I want to help."

"Well you can eat the food I've bought you to start with," he said, a thin smile on his face. The truth was, the smell of pub food had made him very hungry too.

They ate for a minute in silence, listening to the spit of the logs and the pub chatter around them. Then Poppy looked up at him.

"So what were you going to ask me?" she said.

He looked at her and was quiet for a very long time, and then he spoke:

"A long time ago, I did a stupid thing. I'd forgotten I'd even done it. I did a stupid thing and now it's all come back to haunt me." His voice was so quiet she had to lean forward to catch his words even above the crackle of the embers in the nearby hearth.

"I took something that didn't belong to me."

She waited for further explanation, sipping at her chocolate. He smiled at her and she realized that she had frothy milk over her top lip. She picked up a napkin.

"Go on," she said.

"Remember I told you about when I was younger; all the stuff about drugs?"

She nodded.

"Something I did then is affecting me now."

"Go on," she said.

"You know I told you how some of my old mates used to steal things, and I thought it was such a stupid thing to do."

She nodded.

"Well it's true, I never stole anything while I was with them, but I did steal, once. I stole the guitar I use."

"You stole that guitar?" she said, frowning. "The one you use now?"

"Yes." His voice was quiet now and there were tears forming in his eyes. "I've been using it all this time, and it's not mine. It was never mine, I stole it from a shop and I had forgotten I had even taken it. It's the only thing I ever stole, one of the most expensive things I ever had, and it wasn't even mine. I mean it still belongs to the shop I suppose, the place I stole it from."

He stopped speaking and stared at the lip of the cup in his hands.

"Are you okay?" said Poppy.

"Yes," he said, "just thinking about what happened to me, it comes into my head a lot still, I think I'm just processing it."

"So, anyway," he continued, "a few days ago I started to get some text messages and calls from some guy I had never heard of before."

And he told her all of it; all about the sinister figure who had called on his mobile, and then visited him at his own home.

"He knows, Poppy," he continued, close to tears now. "I don't know how, but he does. And it's not really this guy, it's more that what he says is true. Everything I've done is compromised; I thought I was so clever, so talented, so *righteous,* but the whole thing was a sham. I can't play it now; I don't feel as if I can play anything now. I know we have a concert in ten days' time, and I can't do it. I don't know what to do."

They both sat in silence for a few moments, listening to the hiss and the crackle of the logs on the fire.

Finally, Poppy spoke:

"Is that all you've done wrong?"

He looked at her, with what Daisy would have described as his "stupid face".

"Eh?" he said.

"Is that all you've done?" she repeated.

"Isn't that enough?" he said.

"Conner, this is something you can put right," she said. "This man has acted to hurt you, but he has made you face the truth, and now because of that, you can do something to put it right."

He looked at her, and the truth of what she was saying seeped into his mind.

"These people," she said leaning forward, "whoever they are, they really don't have that much of a hold on you. They are just the accusers, they are not the people you have wronged."

She stared at him. "Conner, you owe them nothing, certainly not your fear."

"It's true," he said.

"But you may still need some other help," she added, "like Daisy did after Mr Wicks prayed over her. Prayer and reconciliation are wonderful but you'll also need some support for your mental and emotional health."

"I'll make sure I look after myself," he said. "I have heard all this from Alex, and I believe her, I believe you. Even the simple things like drinking enough water, and getting enough sleep."

"Sometimes it is the simple things that will help the most," she said, "but talking of help, I can help you as well, if you want me to."

"You've helped me so much already," said Conner.

"Maybe I have," she said, "but there is something else. I can take the guitar back to the shop, and give it back to them. Tell them what has happened. They can do whatever they want to about it, they can say 'thank you', they can call the police, but at least your conscience will be clear."

He stared at her, amazed, as if with a few words she had lifted a crushing burden from his back and he could stand up again.

"That's all very well," he said hesitantly, "but–"

"But what?" she cut in on him. "But what, Conner? There is no 'but', it can all be done."

"But what would I play?" he said.

"Another guitar," she answered. "We'll find you one."

"Do the right thing, Conner," she said, "and then you can properly discover the gift you have. And know that you are loved by so many people."

He seemed to brighten before her eyes.

"You can get through this," she said. "I am not belittling what you have been through. The abuse you received is something else, you may need time to get over that, and these things can't just be brushed off."

He thought about the mysterious figure that had visited his home. He realized now that he had been frightened and over-wrought. This man had talked him into believing that stealing this guitar was the worst thing that ever happened, the unforgivable sin. Now that he thought about it, this visitor hadn't even accused him of stealing the guitar. Somehow Conner had been taken in, overawed by all this puffed up condemnation, and now Poppy had come along with a sharp pin and, BANG...

But still there was something else not quite right. He stared at the table, the food and the drink, and he thought about the guitar.

"Yes, but there's one change I'd make to your plan," he said, "I need to take it back. Thank you for everything, Poppy, I mean it, but it shouldn't be you who takes it back for me, I need to face this, and they can do what they wish."

Poppy looked at him and nodded.

"Okay, Conner, that's good." She moved her chair back, stood up and came around next to him. "Now come here."

He stood up and she stepped towards him and she hugged him and he drank in all of it, everything she had to offer, and through her he felt all the love of family and friends surrounding him, and he felt himself, the deepest parts of himself, beginning to heal.

"Now I'm really hungry," he said, and they'd sat back down to finish their meal.

WHEN THEY'D FINISHED, he got up from his seat.

"I need to go for a walk on my own for a while if that's okay, just for a few minutes, and I think I'd better make some calls as well."

She nodded and he looked at her.

"What?" she said.

"Listen, Poppy, since we're being honest, whatever happens between us, I'm really grateful to you, I'll always be grateful for what you did for me." Before she could reply he turned and opened the door, and went out into the late afternoon sun, like a free man.

He called his mother and she asked him a lot of questions, first about the guitar and then about Poppy. Then he phoned Al from the band. All the guys happened to be together, and when, reluctantly, he admitted that Poppy had found him he could hear the cheers in the background.

Then he made one more call.

"Hi, Alex," he said.

"Conner? Are you okay? You're up in the Lakes, aren't you? Is Poppy with you?"

"Yes," he said, "she's here, and it's okay. We're coming home."

"Thank God," said Alex, "You know, Poppy said you'd be there, and I was pretty sure she was right."

"I'm doing the concert," he said. "I am sorry about all of this, but I'm okay, I'll be okay, I'll tell you all about it when I get back."

There was a pause before Alex spoke again.

"Okay, Conner. Take it easy okay and let me know when you are back home."

"Sure, I will."

"Have you spoken to your mum?" she asked.

"Yes, I've spoken to her, and to the band."

"You know Caleb will want to go over the details of this man's visit to you, every point."

"It's okay," he said, "I'm ready to do that, you know, this guy even tried to take the guitar from me, crazy."

"Well," said Alex, "save the details for a chat with Caleb, and look after yourself, okay?"

"Sure."

"And, Conner?"

"What?"

"It's good to hear your voice again."

"You too, sis, bye."

He switched off the phone and smiled. His sister loved him.

14

———

BARROW INSTRUMENTS LIMITED stood on a narrow street in Conner's hometown. The shop had been there for over fifty years; and Conner still went there occasionally to buy strings and put up posters advertising gigs for the various bands he had been involved with.

A couple of days after Conner and Poppy returned from the Lake District, Conner got up early and was waiting outside the door of Barrow Instruments when they opened for business at nine thirty in the morning. As soon as the bolts were drawn and the "closed" sign flipped over to "open" he walked in, carrying the guitar in its case.

His pounding heart contrasted sharply with the quiet, sleepy atmosphere of the shop in the first few minutes of opening and he was relieved to see that he was the only customer in the shop.

"Can I help you?" said the assistant, a fine-haired youth who looked younger than Conner. He was casually sipping on a mug of tea.

"Yes, I would like to return this to you." Conner indicated the guitar in its case.

The assistant put down his mug. "Do you have the receipt?" he asked.

"Well, no I've had it a while," said Conner.

"Is there some problem with the instrument, sir?" the assistant said.

"No, nothing is wrong with it," said Conner, tasting the adrenaline as his heart continued to beat. "It's just that I stole it from this shop about three and a half years ago, and I want to return it, it does not belong to me."

The assistant looked at him, unsure how to respond. Then he put down his mug and disappeared into the back office. Conner stood alone in the shop, listening to one of the keyboards piping out a prerecorded tune, and resisting the temptation to leave the guitar and run.

After a minute, he began to look around the shop. All of the available wall space was fitted with shelving, supporting woodwind, brass and stringed instruments, music stands, manuscripts stacked at crazy angles, and threatening to fall to the floor, and cardboard boxes of various sizes that might have held anything from drumsticks to flute cases to shiny new trombones.

Conner glanced at the sheet music books on display near the sales counter, some of them were new, but some of them had been on sale in their stands for as long as he had been coming here, the numbers on the price tickets almost faded to nothing. He wandered over to the stand and browsed through some of the Beatles material. He was about to look at some of the other acoustic guitar music when he realized that someone else was standing at the counter, staring at him. It so happened that the now rather elderly Mr Barrow was in the shop that morning, and he wanted to see for himself this customer who had stolen his stock, and now wanted to return it.

"Don't I know you, sir?" said Mr Barrow in a rather loud baritone voice. He fixed his sharp grey eyes on Conner.

"You might have seen me in the shop," said Conner, feeling distinctly awkward.

"Hmm." Mr Barrow looked skeptically at Conner. "No, I've seen you on the internet somewhere, you play in a band, don't you?"

"Yes I do."

"Well you must be famous if I've recognized you," said the old man. "Now, my assistant tells me that you are returning some property you stole from us, is that correct?"

"Yes," said Conner, indicating the guitar.

"Open the case for me, will you," said Mr Barrow, and Conner obliged. The owner peered intently at the instrument, saying nothing. The silence began to make Conner fidget.

At last he looked up again at Conner.

"Is it damaged?" he asked.

"No, it's in very good nick, really," said Conner honestly.

"You do realize that this is a Martin, a very valuable instrument," said Mr Barrow.

"Yes, I do," said Conner, feeling increasingly uncomfortable. "I'm sorry," he added.

"You are certain it's not damaged?" repeated Mr Barrow, ignoring Conner's apology.

"Certain," said Conner quite truthfully; he could feel his face going red.

Mr Barrow looked at the guitar again and looked at Conner again, peering at him intently, as if the boy were some kind of interesting zoological specimen.

"Well, thank you for returning it," said Mr Barrow.

"You're welcome," said Conner.

"But what," said Mr Barrow, "shall we do with you? Let me see."

Before Conner could offer any suggestions, the old man turned and paced across the floor, past the anonymous boxes and into the back office again. Conner thought he heard someone humming softly to himself, then the humming stopped, and the old man returned.

"Are you going to be famous one day?" said Mr Barrow.

Conner stared at him, nonplussed by the question.

"I don't know," said Conner. "Maybe."

"Hmm," said Mr Barrow, "well there is the raffle coming up I suppose."

Conner wasn't sure if he was supposed to say anything else, so he kept quiet and tried not to fidget. The old man rubbed his chin and scowled; then he jumped as if someone had nudged him in the side.

"I know what we can do." He opened a drawer at the counter and took out a thick permanent marker pen. "Now, would you please open the case and sign the headstock for me," he said, offering the pen to Conner.

"What? Why?" said Conner, completely taken by surprise.

"It is my business what I do with my property," said Mr Barrow sharply. "But for your information, the local Chambers of Commerce are asking me to provide something for their annual charity auction; and it's a confounded damn nuisance having to give up my stock for these things! But I would think a Martin signed by a local pop star should keep them happy. So if you would be so kind as to sign it, just above the sound hole, thank you."

Conner did as he was asked, signed the instrument and then handed the pen back.

"Right," said Mr Barrow, and he closed the lid of the case. "Now, was there anything you wanted?"

"Can I have..." Conner glanced around. "Can I have a set of new strings, please."

"Of course," said Mr Barrow and placed a packet on the

counter. "I presume you'll be paying for these rather than just taking them this time."

Conner paid, said thank you again, and went back home to tell everyone how it had gone.

THE CHARITY AUCTION was a citywide project, with a number of Chambers of Commerce joining forces, turning it into a major event. Despite his protests, Mr Barrow had been generous in the past in supporting what he privately felt to be a worthy cause and wasn't in the least bit sorry to be able to offer the guitar as his contribution, especially since he hadn't had to use any new stock. The auction was held in the Lancaster Ballroom at the Savoy Hotel in London. It was a risk to take the place, albeit for a much-reduced fee, but the event proved to be popular, and nearly all of the invited guests turned up.

Of some interest was a 00L-17 whisky sunset acoustic guitar made by Martin & Co and signed across the headstock by the talented young performer, Conner Adams of the band Joel's Garden. It was indeed a stroke of good fortune that by the time the auction was held; the band's recently released single was enjoying some success in the charts.

Interest in this particular lot was heightened by a rumour, alluded to in the programme, that Mr Adams had in fact stolen the instrument in his younger, more reckless days, and in the fit of conscience had since returned it to the shop. The donor of the guitar offered no comment on this speculation, and a good number of the guests, while disapproving of theft found that the story added some cachet to the item.

The guitar was purchased for £3,000 by an anonymous bidder, and everyone was satisfied with the result.

ALEX MASTERS SIPPED some tea and then yawned. She sat in Caleb office, nestled in the corner of the expansive sofa, draped as ever with an incongruous selection of Mrs Wicks' knitted covers. The sofa had always been a sharp contrast to the polished mahogany furniture and bookshelves of legal opinion that occupied the rest of the office.

"I'm not boring you, am I?" said Caleb.

Alex smiled.

"Just tired, and it's warm in here, and I suppose I feel relieved."

"Of course," said Caleb "Conner has been returned to us, in more ways than one."

Alex had sat on this sofa as a child and as a young woman. She had seen the knitted covers come and go, changing with the seasons and Mrs Wicks' evolving taste in styles and colours. This was indeed a safe place to be, but she hadn't come to Caleb's office to escape from the outside world, he had expressly invited her.

"Well, here I am," she said.

"Thank you for coming to see me, my dear," he said, fidgeting with his bow tie and sitting at his desk. "I wanted to have a chat with you away from the SUMMER offices. I do understand why you wanted a small 'hot desk' office, and I'm sure that's wonderfully efficient, but..." He paused.

"But?" she said.

"But sometimes a warm desk is better than a hot one; I think," he concluded and tapped the surface in front of him.

Alex raised her eyebrows and smiled.

"Anyway," he said, "I was wondering whether you could assist me."

"If I can," said Alex, "of course I will."

"You know it seems to me," said Caleb, "that as soon as one of our number resolves their difficulties, another becomes a subject for concern."

She looked at him and waited. Caleb always approached any topic from an oblique angle and she found it was best to let him get there in his own time.

"What I'm saying," he continued, "is that now young Conner seems to have got over his crisis I am feeling more concerned about one of our other friends."

She looked at him and raised an eyebrow, implying the question: *who?*

"Lewis," he said.

"Lewis?" said Alex, frowning.

"Yes Lewis," said Caleb. "I'm worrying about him because I have discovered how much he felt for your former colleague, Bridget Larson. Of course, they were lovers; but I did not realize that he also loved her, very much it seems. They had a history together, building up the business from the beginning."

Alex tensed slightly; she felt it in herself although she didn't show it.

"The thing is," he said, "I just wonder what his feelings would drive him to. Tell me, Alex, do you think he loved her?"

"Well, they were close," said Alex, she really hadn't expected this, "and when Bridget started seeing Martin Massey outside of work, Lewis found it hard to deal with."

"I am sure he did," said Caleb. "And that is part of the problem, you see. Based on what you've just said, I suspect Lewis never came to terms with the relationship between Bridget and Martin, and he certainly never really recovered from Bridget's death, or properly grieved for her passing, that's very clear. And I suspect he has not grieved for her properly, because he does not know how to grieve."

"I'm sure that's true," said Alex. "Yes, I think in his own way he did love her, they loved each other. But what do you want me to do?"

"Well, that rather depends," said Caleb, cryptically. "I'll try and get to the point, Alex. Lewis is angry about Bridget's death. I think he is so angry that he wants some sort of revenge on whoever killed her."

"Yes," said Alex, leaning forward, "I could have told you that."

"You are aware of this?"

"Yes," she replied.

"And you haven't done anything about it?"

"What can I do about it?" she said, sitting up straight now. "What do you think I can do about it, Caleb? Do you think I can just go up to Lewis and tell him to stop being so silly?"

"Well, maybe not with those exact words but, yes you could try that."

She was at a loss to know how to reply to this. Eventually she shook her head.

"I don't think I have that kind of influence over him, and I'm not sure I even want it. You know how things are between Lewis and I."

"Well actually, no," said Caleb, "I am not sure that I know how things are between Lewis and you, perhaps you'd like to tell me?"

"He's my employee. He has specialist knowledge and I want to use that for the benefit of the company."

"And that's all?"

"Yes, of course, what are you saying?" She was beginning to get irritated now. It seemed as if Caleb thought he could ask her any question he liked, including about her private life.

"I am not saying or assuming anything," said Caleb, "and of course your private life is your own business, but you should try to answer this question for yourself, Alex, even if you don't answer it for me."

"Well I'm not sleeping with him, if that's your thinking," she said.

For a moment he said nothing and then she interrupted him before he could speak.

"I'm sorry," she said. "I'm sure that's not what you meant."

"No it wasn't," he said, "and I am sorry if I was insensitive. I know most of what I say and do seems rather obtuse and even bizarre to you, but trust me, Alex, beneath all of that, I am serious, and I have my reasons. This is a war, and it is fought on multiple fronts in multiple battles. I think we're winning the battle for Conner, but the war is certainly not over, and whether he likes it or not, Lewis is now involved."

"In what way?" said Alex.

"I think," said Caleb, "that Lewis is being tempted at his weakest point, no surprise there of course, and that weakest point is his grief over Bridget's death, and his desire for vengeance."

"And you think I can help him through this, talk him back from the edge?" said Alex.

"I think you are the best and perhaps the only person who could," said Caleb, "because he is very fond of you, and you are, I think, very fond of him."

He continued before Alex could answer him.

"Now there is nothing wrong with that, why shouldn't you be fond of him, and he you? I think you two have formed a good friendship, and I am loathe to disturb this happy arrangement but I believe that the temptation to go off on this vendetta is growing in Lewis' heart and you are the person who can stop him from doing something really stupid."

"Which he might." Alex shook her head.

"Indeed he might," said Caleb. "I think he believes that Martin Massey knows something about Bridget's murder and I think he will go to any lengths to find out what that something is."

"And if he finds this murderer," said Alex, "you think he'll go after him?"

"I think that's very likely," said Caleb. "The temptation will be too much for him."

Alex put her hand to her mouth. "No, I don't want him to end up hurt, or worse."

Alex's mind filled with images of Lewis arguing with someone, maybe the man who had visited her first café. It was easy for her imagination to finish the scenario with the worst possible outcome.

"So you see," said Caleb gently, "I really want to persuade Lewis to think again. It is not going to go well if he threatens Martin Massey; and it's going to be a lot worse if he goes after Bridget's murderer. But I think only you can reach him, if you want to."

"So, I need to talk to him about it," said Alex.

Caleb smiled and sat back in his chair. "As soon as you can, yes."

"Okay," said Alex, "I'll talk to him, but it's up to him in the end. If he wants to go off on some damn fool crusade to avenge Bridget's death, that's his choice."

"At least you will have done what you can," said Caleb.

"Now," Alex paused to remember some part of the conversation she wanted to return to, "what was it you were saying about Daisy? Are you worried about her as well?"

"Before we talk about Daisy," said Caleb, "there's something I want to show you. Could you come and have a look at this, please?"

She pulled herself up from the sofa and came over to his desk, where he had laid out the photo-fit of Bridget's murderer, which Alex had seen before, and the CCTV images that Orlando Shand had sent him, which she had not.

"Where did you get these?" she said.

"I bumped into Bridget's lawyer," said Caleb. "He has taken her murder very personally, and has tracked down these images from some local CCTV, taken on the day she was killed."

"Is this the man who killed her?"

"He thinks so," said Caleb. "What do you think?"

"It could be the same person as the photo-fit," said Alex. "But I can tell you one thing – I've seen this person before."

"Really, where?"

"This is the guy who came into the café," said Alex. "I think I recognize his face, and I can see the scar he had in some of these images. It is him."

Caleb was silent for a long time.

"I am going to show these images to Conner as well," he said, "and if he thinks this is the man who played a part in the attack on him, then we can connect him to all of these incidents, and we have a name: Joseph."

"Will you go to the police with this?" said Alex.

"Yes," said Caleb, "but I also want whoever is directing him, whoever ordered him to do these things. Leave it with me, Alex, I'll let you know how I get on, and as ever, thank you." He smiled.

"You're welcome," said Alex. "Now I had better be going, thanks for the tea." She picked up her coat and bag and they both stood and walked across the room, and Caleb reached out to open the door for her, but before he turned the handle, he placed his hand on her shoulder; when she looked at him, she thought he was actually going to cry.

"This thing with Lewis," he said, "I'm not playing games with you, Alex, God help me, I never want to do that. I have watched you and cared about you for nearly twenty years, and I, well," he was lost for words for just a moment, "well, look after yourself, dear, and if I can help you, you only have to ask."

He leant forward and kissed her lightly on the cheek. "Take care, my dear, and bless you."

"It's okay," she said to him, "I know you love me, and I trust you."

As she stepped out into a cold spring morning her phone rang, and five minutes later she had accepted a dinner invitation from Lewis.

15

———

THE FOUR MEMBERS of Joel's Garden waited out of sight and listened to the crowd. They clustered at the side of the stage, feeling the energy of the fans and hearing an occasional comment from one of the crew.

The support band had got a good reception from the crowd but they'd only served to whet people's appetite for the main event, and now the stage was empty and the audience was getting restless. The whistles blew and huge balloons bobbed sideways across the heads of the crowd; the canned music vied with the increasing volume of human noise.

"Hands in," shouted Conner above the din. "Okay?" he said, looking at each one of them. This was it, the biggest concert they had ever played; two thousand people were standing just metres away, expecting the best that these guys could give.

"Your kingdom come, and your will be done," Conner whispered to himself; then he stepped out onto the stage, clutching a brand new guitar. As they all moved across the stage the lights dimmed, and thunder rolled through the house as the sense of expectation in the crowd welled up to the surface. Conner could hear and feel the roar of the people as he picked his way in the darkness up to the centre of the stage.

He stood, transfixed by the heat and the vibration of sound, all of it coming at him, the people baying for the set to start. A single bass note began to blend in with the crowd and Conner clutched at the microphone, waiting. And then for a moment, just for a moment, he forgot everything – the lyrics, the set, the chords, everything. He remembered that he had spent these last few years playing songs with a stolen guitar, and he remembered how incredibly angry he still was with whoever it was who had done *that thing* to him. He thought about photos that might, even now, be on a website somewhere, spreading from computer to computer, phone to phone. He thought about his sense of worth, his body, his blood, abused by these people and he was angry, and that hadn't gone away, at least not yet. And then he thought about Alex and Daisy and Caleb and Poppy, especially Poppy who was beautiful in his eyes, and who knew about all of it and still loved him. He closed his eyes and recommitted himself, whispering what should have been a private prayer in darkness:

"All for you, Jesus, all for you."

But this was not a private prayer. His words were snatched up by the PA, amplified out, and that prayer carried out over the crowd who roared their approval; and then two drumsticks cracked together:

Snap snap snap snap

Conner's hands jumped into the first chord, instinctively, responding to hours and hours of practice, and then the lights came on and the whole stage was bathed in revolving circles of white light, and acting on instinct, the band leapt into the first song of the set.

At the back of the auditorium, Daisy, Alex, Poppy and Aiden were standing by one of the bars watching the show. Caleb, though invited, had politely declined, citing the fact that he did not wish to be the oldest person in the building. Even from this distance, Alex could sense the liberation in Conner's performance, and it blessed her to witness it. ,

"So where is this party we are going to afterwards?" shouted Poppy above the noise.

"Hotel near here with a big function room," replied Alex in an equally loud voice. "Conner tells me that a lot of bands use it for after-show parties; it's always good to have some big event just before a new album comes out, we've invited a lot of press people."

"You coming to the party?" said Poppy in Daisy's ear.

"No If I did I'd end up staying there until about three, and I have to be up early in the morning for a meeting with an online vendor for our merchandise."

"So you getting the bus home?" said Poppy.

"Got a lift, haven't I," said Daisy smiling. She grabbed Aiden's arm and he turned to her, a look of mild shock on his face.

"Aiden has to get an early night so he's all bright and ready in the morning for another battle with the numbers," said Daisy. "He's taking me home."

On stage the songs came with smooth energy, and Conner, full of the sense of his own freedom, played and sang the set of his life. He even indulged in a little bit of crowd surfing. This wasn't part of the script and left the other band members bemused and cycling through the chorus of one of their songs as they watched him tripping and staggering over the hands and heads of the crowd.

Halfway through the set he remembered his mobile, and, digging it out he screamed at the crowd:

"SAY *CHEEEEEESE!*"

A thousand voices rose in a cacophony of noise, and arms

waved. The people at the front tried to climb on top of each other to be at the forefront of Conner's picture gallery.

Later, when he sent the pictures through to Poppy, she saw a sea of faces full of intense joy, celebration, and passion. She looked at the images and knew that Conner was on the journey back to wholeness, and the climb up two mountains, and the cold and the sore feet had all been so worth it.

AFTER AN ENCORE that had the whole house shouting themselves hoarse, Daisy and Aiden said their goodbyes and headed for the exit while Alex and Poppy dug out their stage passes.

The evening was cool, noticeably so after the muggy heat of the concert hall.

"So, did you enjoy that?" said Daisy, still buzzing from the atmosphere.

"Yeah, it was great," replied Aiden.

"You don't sound very sure."

She took his arm; it was something she did when she walked anywhere alone with a man she knew. She felt him tense slightly at her touch.

"Sorry, do you want me to let you go?"

"No, please don't." She felt him tighten his grip on her arm. "It's just that nobody has held my arm for a long time."

"Well you enjoy it, mate!" she said. She had decided that Aiden was okay really, once you got past his spreadsheet façade.

They walked across the road to the multi-storey car park and found the graffiti-covered entrance. In the rank darkness of the stairwell Daisy tightened her grip, and she had to almost run to keep up with him as he mounted the flights of steps to the level where he had parked earlier.

They were a few feet away from Aiden's Audi when Daisy heard the "pop" of the remote locking. It was a reassuring sound, Daisy liked being driven anywhere by a man she trusted; and Aiden was just that, a little boring maybe, but safe, and that was all she needed at the moment.

She sat in the front passenger seat and settled down. The car had the scent of calmness and order about it, and the engine breathed into life when Aiden pressed the ignition. A collection of numbers, in cool blue light, appeared across the dashboard.

"This is a posh car," she said. "I thought we were all short of money."

"I had an investment that matured last year," he said, "and I've always wanted an Audi."

"It's nice," she said, feeling herself relax in the seat.

They were both silent as the car eased away and some silky jazz emerged from the sound system.

"You okay with jazz?" he said.

"Yeah, it's fine," she replied.

"If you want to put something else on, you can you know."

"It's cool," said Daisy, "leave it."

Daisy wasn't feeling very lively, and some calm jazz and the smooth interior of Aiden's car suited her mood.

Aiden was definitely the quiet type, so she didn't expect there to be much talk on the journey home. She looked out of the window and watched the streetlights sail past. Light flicks of rain began falling, smearing on the glass and distorting the images around her. Strangely, it was when she felt this secure, this relaxed, that she became aware of the growing unease deep within her.

In recent months she had gained the self-awareness to be honest, and so she had begun to examine the web of motives, desires and resentments that had governed her life. There was a lot there that she did not like. Not least the occasional flare of jealousy, aimed at Poppy and her flourishing relationship with Conner. It was stupid really, because Daisy didn't want him like that, but jealously wasn't a rational emotion, and if she thought about it for more than five seconds, she knew Poppy was good for Conner, and she, Daisy, wanted to work with Poppy, they created wonderful garments, and she knew it.

But there was something deeper inside her as well. She thought back to the presentation she'd given, to the cigarette she'd smoked beforehand, the nerves, and the sense that she was different from them, this Christian club, these nice people she really loved. Sometimes the one she felt the most affinity with was Alex's friend Lewis.

And now here she was with the safe accountant, a man she trusted but felt distanced from, excluded.

This guy isn't going to be any more than a convenient ride home, she thought, *Mr 'Dull and Dependable'.*

She wasn't very proud of her feelings; she owed Aiden, especially after he had been the one to argue the case for her trip to Paris.

"You're quiet tonight, Daisy," he said, breaking in on her thoughts.

"Yeah," she replied, dreamily, "what else you got in your juke box?"

She tapped the sound system.

"Take your pick," he said.

She flicked through the titles and found some Norah Jones.

"Can I put this on please?" she asked.

"Sure."

Soft evening songs filled the car, and Daisy felt her eyes closing. Maybe this wasn't a bad place to be. She looked across at Aiden, to see if there was anything at all about him that she could find attractive.

"Where do you come from then, Aiden?" she asked.

"Where do I come from?" he said, laughing. "North London."

"No," she said, "I mean you sound Irish."

"The answer is still North London," he said. "But it's okay, I know what you mean. My parents are from Shannon originally," he said. "Moved here, had my sister and I, moved back when we left home. I did my degree in Accountancy and then ended up working for one of the banks in London."

"So, is that when you moved into the area where Alex lives?"

Aiden was silent, and she looked over at him again. He was thinking, wrestling with something. She knew he was deciding whether to tell her something, to let her in, and immediately she craved his secret. She wanted him to tell her what it was that pained him so, she wanted someone to let her in.

"Tell me," she said, turning to him, "if you want to."

Eventually he spoke:

"I didn't move there straight away."

And he said no more, and she was quiet, her arms folded, waiting for him to say something more.

Aiden stared out at the road ahead, and let out a sigh.

"The thing is, Daisy," he said, "I didn't move to Alex's area straight from college. I lived, we lived, somewhere else first."

"We lived?" Daisy perked up,. "You were living with someone?"

"I was married. I married a girl I met while I was at university."

"Wow," said Daisy," I thought you were just an accountant."

She scolded herself for saying something *that* stupid, but he actually laughed, out loud, like it was some kind of release.

"Sorry," she said, "I mean, I didn't mean that." She shook her head. "I meant I thought you had always been single."

He smiled at her apology.

"You thought I had always been single? Well I haven't done anything to dispel that idea, have I? It suits me, you know, for people to think that I am too much of a number cruncher to be going out and meeting people and having a life."

"I didn't know," said Daisy. She was itching to find out what had happened to this woman that Aiden had married. Her mind buzzed with the possibilities, maybe one of them had a steamy affair and the whole thing had fallen apart.

"There's a lot of things that people don't know about me, Daisy," said Aiden. "Perhaps it's time I told somebody about them."

"You don't have to talk about it if you don't want to," said Daisy, hoping that he would.

"Well," he said, preparing himself, "why shouldn't I tell you? I mean, I've spent most of the firm's cash on you, I might as well give you some of my treasure as well."

"When I started my second year at college," he said, "I met a girl called Catherine. Everyone knew her as Cath. Anyway, to cut a long story short, Cath and I fell in love and at the end of that year we got engaged."

Aiden stopped his story; they had arrived at Daisy's flat.

"Maybe I can tell you some more another time, if you still want to hear about it."

"Are you serious?" exclaimed Daisy. "You can't stop now! Okay, look. If you need to go then go and cuddle a spreadsheet then fine, but if you don't have to then come in and have a coffee and talk to me." She got out of his car and stood with the door open, staring at him.

"Okay, Daisy."

Daisy had found a smart one-bedroom studio to rent near to the SUMMER offices. It was small but she could do what she liked here, and at least she now had a sofa and couple of chairs for visitors to sit on. She ushered him in.

She had turned the main living space into a work area. Her old circular table had survived the move from student digs and sat at one end of the lounge. It was, as usual, covered with drawings, pencils, pastels, design books, a beer bottle and some coffee cups, and a few samples she had brought back from Première Vision. A few of the designs were now stuck to one of the walls, creating a collage of half coloured pictures.

Most of the sofa was covered with paper of some sort: books, magazines, drawings and sketches. It was about as far away from Aiden's idea of a working environment as possible; and he was horrified and fascinated in equal measure.

She had made some coffee, and in her enthusiasm to hear more of his story she had rushed it, thrown too much coffee in, and the resulting brew was so strong it made his eyes blink. He had to ask for some sugar. She returned and sat next to him on the sofa.

"Tell me about it, Aiden, I want to hear all of it from the beginning," she said.

He looked at her, and she felt as if he were weighing her up, deciding how much to say.

"Tell me what happened," she said.

He put the spoon down, and stared into the black liquid.

"Cath died a year after we were married," he said. "We found out she had pancreatic cancer."

"My God, that's terrible," said Daisy, who knew nothing about cancer except that some people died from it. Without thinking she placed her hand on his. He did not try to remove it.

"I don't really tell people this story," he continued. "I mean Alex knows, but it's not something I talk about."

"It must have been devastating," she said.

"Well, there was a lot of pain and hospital appointments," he said. "I don't talk about it now, partly because it's too painful and partly because people sometimes don't know what to say. And I just want to be ordinary; I don't want people to feel sorry for me. I just want to get on with life."

"But you're still very sad, aren't you?" she said.

He looked at her, and nodded and sipped his coffee, and Daisy could see that she had brought him to the edge of tears.

She looked away, around her room, finding interest in anything else, giving him a moment.

"Cath was the most wonderful person," he said. "She had a vision, just like Alex does. She had a dream to go and serve the poorest and most desperate people. I don't know what drove her like that; it was simply what she wanted to do. When she left school, she had a year out and spent some of that time in Uganda, working with orphans in a place called Jinja. She wanted to go back there after she graduated." He grimaced as he sipped the thick coffee.

"She studied medical microbiology and wanted to use some of her skills. In our third year we began making plans for our wedding. Anyway, it was about then that Cath started to develop some problems; and when she went to the doctor, they referred her to an Oncology specialist, who told her she had the cancer."

Daisy had a sudden feeling of being out of her depth. She had wanted someone to let her in, and yet now that they had, she realized what a responsibility it was. She was more used to everyone holding in their rubbish, keeping it sealed tight, and just talking about the fluff. Usually if anyone ever did let it go, it was her, she'd been the one who poured out her heart, but now she was the listener.

"Anyway," he continued, "that wasn't all. Cath also tested HIV positive."

They both sat still for a moment, and a car murmured past outside, and the boiler in Daisy's apartment powered down to stand-by. They had not noticed the noise until it stopped, enveloping them in an intense silence where the usually unnoticed sounds could be heard. Pipes gurgled, water and air in metal, radiators ticked lightly as pressures eased and temperatures cooled. Somewhere outside, far away, a motorbike whined distant and angry, its potency fading as the sound drifted away from them.

"They checked her for that when she discovered the cancer," said Aiden. "She hadn't had unprotected sex; in fact she had never had sex at the time." He paused. "The only conclusion we could come to was that she had become infected during her year out, working with some of the AIDS orphans in Uganda. I thought she would be bitter about it, I certainly was. I was angry with God and angry with whoever had given her this thing. It broke something in me, but we loved each other and we got on with it. And then she died and I was angry with God again, and I still am, but I get on with it. Sometimes when I wake at night all I want to do is scream, but I never do. I never scream and I never cry. Ever."

"What do you do?" asked Daisy.

"I look at figures, spreadsheets. I do my job."

Daisy watched him closely. "So you don't really love all the numbers and budgets for themselves? I mean I thought you lived for all that."

He laughed. "I like what I do, but I don't live for it, Daisy. And have you tried sleeping with numbers? Have you tried having dinner with numbers, and telling them your dreams, your feelings?"

She stared at him as his voice rose.

"Can you argue and then make up with numbers? Can you make love with numbers? Do they bleed when you cut them and cry when you hurt them?"

"No," she said.

"It's my job," he said, "to look at numbers, and they are important, but they're not everything."

"Well that's a relief to hear you say it," said Daisy.

"Let me ask you a question," he said, "have you ever

wondered why I argued for you to be given a chance with this project of yours? I mean now, not at some point in the future." He waved at all of the drawings around the wall.

"I don't know, maybe you thought it was a good idea?" she said, sensing the indignation rise within her; she didn't want him to see her as some kind of charity case.

"Oh, don't get me wrong, Daisy," he said apologetically, "I think what you have done is fantastic, and that's the point really. Everyone needs the opportunity to take their chance, before it's too late."

She nodded.

"When Cath found out that she was going to die," he said, "it took away the other dream, perhaps the most important dream she ever had. She had always wanted to have children; she wanted to be a mother. But with the cancer, that dream slipped out of reach for her, and for both of us. She even thought she would lose me as well. Not that she ever would have."

"You wouldn't have left her," said Daisy.

"No, I wouldn't, and I didn't."

"You're a brave man," said Daisy.

He shook his head. "I'm not sure I am. Some people thought I was brave, after she died, but I wasn't. I nearly did leave her. God knows, I was that close. And then when she died I gave in to the despair, time and time again. I didn't feel brave. I felt angry and broken. I withdrew into myself and just worked, and worked, and that's all I did, all I've done since then. It's the people around me who are brave, the ones who want to fulfil their dreams, and take a risk, and make a difference: Alex, Conner and you. Cath had some dreams, but she wasn't able to fulfil all of them. I want other people to have that chance. I want that for Alex, and I want that for you."

Daisy sipped her coffee, then sipped it again.

"Is it too strong?" he said.

"I'm going to put some hot water in this," said Daisy.

"Make some more," said Aiden, "make it the way the rest of he world makes coffee, I don't think I know what I'm doing."

She returned with a fresh cafetière and two mugs.

"I thought," she said, "at one time you and Alex would get together."

"Alex and I, yes," he stopped and paused, "I love Alex; and it took me a long time to work out that the love I felt for her wasn't like the love I'd felt for Cath. In the end she's like a sister, a friend; some people are dear to us, but just not in that way." He put his hand on his heart.

"Yeah, that's true," said Daisy. She thought about Conner, and then she thought about Bill, and the differences in her feelings for the two of them.

I'm going to be honest now, Daisy," he said. "With this Paris thing, it really was quite speculative, you know. A real wacky idea and there was quite a big part of my head telling me that it was stupid to spend the company's money on it." He watched her for a reaction, but she kept still and watched him.

"But then again, it's not that stupid an idea, it might work; and more to the point, you wouldn't get another chance. Because if they'd said no, or 'come back next year' or whatever, you might not have stuck around with us, and the moment would have passed. I didn't want your moment to pass, Daisy."

"You must have loved her so much!" Daisy blurted out. "You must have!"

He laughed. "Oh, I did, and I don't regret one moment of my time with her. She was the girl I loved, and I got to be with her. I got what I wanted and there's many people who can't say that."

"You really loved her," said Daisy again, and Aiden nodded and put down his mug, and closed his eyes, and Daisy could see the moisture collect and fall, down his cheeks and she came and she put an arm around his shoulder and drew him to herself, and they sat in silence for a few moments. She thought he was going to speak again when he moved slightly; but instead his whole body shook, and he began to cry.

He stayed like this for long minutes and she felt the tears on her shoulder, the moisture on her tee shirt, and compassion welled up within her like something waking from a long deep sleep, and she felt a kind of love for this man. It was a love she had never felt before. She supposed this was what people called compassion, and she was amazed that such a feeling could exist in a world that, until recently, had seemed so hollow and uncaring to her.

16

ON THE EVENING that Alex was supposed to have dinner with Lewis, a storm of such ferocity blew in across the city that she was tempted to stay at home, close the curtains and camp on the sofa for the evening.

But she found within herself that she did not want to stay at home.

If her visit had been *purely* business, a discussion of strategy or a review of figures, then she would have done just that. She would have called him, full of apologies, talked matters over on the phone, and stayed in the warm. But somehow she knew that this was more than business; what else it was, she did not know, but she did want to visit him.

She was getting dressed for the evening when the rain had started. The wind picked up, the clouds gathered, and then the water drops fell, and soon those drops turned to hail and fell with a thunderous power that drowned out everything else.

As she looked at the different outfits spread across her bed, the phone rang. After years as a PA, Alex had developed the habit of reacting quickly to a ringing phone and she ran into her lounge, unclothed, but aware that the curtains were drawn against the storm outside.

"Hi, this is Alex."

"Alex, it's Lewis, I was wondering whether you still wanted to come over; I don't know what the weather is like where you are but it's blowing a gale here."

Before she could answer, the whole room was suddenly lit by two flickers of lightning, illuminating everything – the furniture, walls, mantelpiece – all revealed for a moment in silhouette. She paused before speaking.

"Of course I still want to come over," she was interrupted by a deep rolling rumble of thunder, "I'm just getting changed; I'll be with you soon."

"Are you sure about that? We can re-schedule," said Lewis.

"No I want to come," she said, "and I'll see you later."

Alex was on the main road heading out of the city when the rain really started to come down hard, smashing against her windscreen. Through frantic wipers she could just make out the smudged images of red taillights in front of her. The storm made such a racket in the car that she switched off the radio and concentrated on driving.

For some reason, which she could not fathom, she was feeling sad. It wasn't the prospect of an evening with Lewis; that was something she was looking forward to, it was something else.

She searched her mind, and her heart and she remembered her parents, and her sadness crystalized around the memory of them. She thought about Daisy, and the damage that had been done to her, and Conner, abused by some anonymous assailant, and Bridget, who, like her parents, had paid the ultimate price.

Why did life have to be so hard? Why was it all so unfair?

But there was no good answer to these questions and at some level she knew she had to accept that this was how things were. But God had placed a defiance in her, it manifested itself in the desire to resist the despair and the weariness, and in the face of it all, to lament, to be kind, to have courage and to love.

In the safety of the noise of her car, she opened her mouth and spoke out.

"I will not give in, and give up; no." She repeated the word again and again, gradually louder: "No. No. NO."

She felt like a child trying out a new toy. Then she screamed, with all of the sound that she could muster against the cacophony around her.

"NO!"

And the rain crashed again into her line of sight and the traffic continued at a steady crawl.

By her side but outside the car, Angel observed her, sensing her pain and her passion. He wasn't unduly concerned. She was suffering and learning, and somehow this was as it should be. She had travelled through a furnace of experience, and it had not consumed her; rather it had purified her, and made her strong.

Neither was he as worried about this visit to Lewis Ashbury as he might have been. Angel was no fool, of course; he could perceive the emotional, and even sexual tension that ran between these two. He could see these things clearly in Alex that she could only just perceive herself, feelings and desires she did not want to admit to, let alone face and process. He could see these deep things within her as easily as he could penetrate the rain and glass and metal and watch her physically, sitting in this car as it moved along the road. He listened to her utter that single word, "no", and he heard her scream, and he felt just a tiny fraction of the compassion that God felt for her now.

Finally, her car rumbled over the wet gravel in front of Lewis' house. The wind of the storm had eased away, but the rain still fell. Alex stopped the car, switched the engine off, and bowed her head. She whispered a prayer of thankfulness for a safe journey, the rain still sounded as if a thousand birds were pecking and scampering just above her head.

She picked up her bag and her coat and stepped out of the car, avoiding a puddle of water. She could smell the scent of the rain on the plants and in the earth around her and feel the water drops pattering onto her head, so she hurried up to the front door and pressed the bell. A heavy drop of water fell from some creeping ivy arranged around the lintel and slipped in between the collar of her blouse and the back of her neck; the shock of the cold moisture made her shiver.

"Come on, Lewis," she whispered.

After a few moments she located an impressive knocker and rapped it twice, hard. It made a very satisfying *thunk, thunk* sound that reverberated from the door and into the structure of the house.

Almost immediately she saw a figure through a glass panel in the door hurrying towards her. The lock clicked and the door opened.

"Alex, come in, come in!" He stepped aside and she walked into the warmth of Lewis Ashbury's home.

"Can I take your jacket?" he said.

She realized she had not even put the jacket on, just carried it with her to the house. She passed the jacket to him and he led her through to the lounge. The air was full of the aroma of cooking food, and her stomach rumbled with hunger.

The lounge was warm and the rain a distant roar now. She looked around the room. Robin's egg blue walls gave the space a light airy feel, and she was surprised to see those walls hung with a number of Norman Rockwell prints. She would have guessed Lewis to be a little too cynical for the kind of vision that Rockwell's prints required.

A large cream carpet lay over the dark wood of the floor,

framed by a couple of comfy armchairs and a sofa. The room had a working fireplace and flames fluttered around some newly arranged logs.

"Want something to drink?" he said.

"Yes, please."

"Water, or fruit juice, or I can get you something a bit stronger after that journey."

"Just water, thanks." She smiled at him.

"Make yourself at home; I'll be back in a minute."

He disappeared, humming to himself, and Alex moved over to the wall to look more closely at the prints. She studied two of them before lingering at a larger one, hanging above one of the chairs. The picture showed a little boy who may have run away from home, sitting with a police officer on the chrome seats of a classic American diner. There was something delightful and innocent about the picture; the suggestion of safety and reconciliation, even for the prodigals. It was an appealing thought, and Alex was moved by the vision of it.

She tried to imagine herself as the little boy who had run away, but she couldn't connect with the image in front of her. In Rockwell's world the little boy would be going back to his parents, and she was never able to do that.

She remembered Alice, a kid she knew from church who'd run away from home and lived on the streets for a few days before being taken in by the Salvation Army. The Rockwell print was an idealistic image of what might happen to a runaway. And yet, this is what happened to Alice, so people could dare to hope, even in the face of the brutality and tragedy of the world.

"Thank God for the Salvation Army," she whispered under her breath.

"Do you like Rockwell, then?" Lewis had returned with the drinks.

"When I'm feeling hopeful," she replied. "I like art that suggests hope, and love."

He nodded, thoughtfully.

"These are all quite new," he said. "I've always had a sneaking admiration for his work, but it's only recently that I have found the courage to put them up. Come and sit down."

He put another log on the fire, blew gently on the embers and sat in the other armchair across from Alex. Flames licked around the wood even as he settled into his seat.

"I saw an old colleague of ours recently," he said.

"Oh, who was that?"

"Martin Massey."

She stared at him. "Really? Where did you see him?"

"Oh," said Lewis, "I dropped by to return something I had of his, a briefcase from the SLaM days, he'd asked me to look after. I thought it was time he had it back."

She looked at him as he stared at the fire with a frown on his face.

"Did you tell him what you're up to now?" she said.

"Oh, we talked about a few things," said Lewis. "Me working for you now, he found that very amusing as you'd expect, but mostly we talked about Bridget and what happened to her."

Alex sensed he wanted to tell her something more so she deliberately said nothing and waited.

"I did love her, very much," he said. "They say absence makes the heart grow fonder. I used to think that was sentimental rubbish, but now..."

"Now you're a wiser man," she said.

"Maybe, but not wise enough to get over a dead colleague."

"Perhaps you have to admit to yourself how much she meant to you first," she said.

"Your friend Caleb said more or less the same thing to me,"

said Lewis, smiling. "Her murderer is still out there," he continued. "The police are never going to catch him."

"No," she said, "maybe they won't."

"Caleb thinks it's the same guy who came to your café," he said.

"So do I," she said. "He also thinks it might have been the same person who was involved in the attack on Conner. He's spoken to Conner and me about it. All three incidents, it's the same person."

"It's interesting," said Lewis, "if it is the same person, he could easily have killed Conner, in fact he could probably have killed any of you, but he hasn't."

"God," said Alex, "I hate this, these people who seem to want to destroy us, who are they?"

"I think old Caleb is intent on finding out," said Lewis. "He's focused on that now, but he thinks this murderer has a boss, and that's the prize he's going after."

"But we've no idea who that is," said Alex.

"Probably the creep who confronted Daisy and you in the car park all those months ago," he said. "But that's Caleb's target, mine is Bridget's murderer."

She looked at him. "For God's sake, Lewis, please be careful."

"Why? Why should I be careful?"

"Caleb told me you were still very angry, he's concerned for you."

Lewis burst out laughing.

"Bless him," he said. "So did he send you along here to try to talk me out of doing anything stupid?"

"You were the one who invited me over, remember?" she replied.

"Indeed I did," he said, conceding the point, "and I'm very pleased that you are here."

"But yes," she said, "Caleb did want me to speak to you. He is concerned about what you might do, and frankly so am I."

"You are?"

"Oh, come on," she replied, "you know I'm concerned for you; I always have been. I don't want you to get hurt. Besides, the company needs you at the moment, and I like having you around."

"Well, I like working for SUMMER; and I like working for you, Alex."

He sniffed the air. "I also like to eat, and I think dinner is ready."

Lewis served a very passable satay sweet potato curry, remembering that Alex was a vegetarian. The portion he gave her was more than she would normally eat, but she cleared her plate and as she did so, they talked about the old times at SLaM, and Lewis talked about Bridget and the relationship they'd had, both professional and personal, over the years.

He'd prepared a fresh fruit salad for dessert and Alex took some. They went back to the lounge with some coffee, and Alex decided to return to the subject of Lewis' quest for justice for Bridget.

"So let's talk about what you are going to do then, shall we?" she said, as they settled into their chairs.

She looked straight at him, and he stared back at her and he remembered again the desire he'd felt for her when she joined SLaM. He'd always known she would be unattainable, and yet what was it that Caleb had said?

"...don't confuse morality with indifference. She is fond of you..."

"Lewis?" she said.

"Sorry," he said, "yes, what I am going to do? To be honest with you, I don't know. I could go back and lean on Martin again, try and force him to tell me what he knows, if he knows anything else, or I could do the sensible thing and back off, leave it alone, let the police do their work."

"Tell me about Martin's connection to this," she said.

"At first I thought Martin had arranged for someone to kill Bridget," said Lewis, "because she was rapidly going off the SEEKA project, and I think she might have threatened him."

Alex's eyes widened at the suggestion.

"Martin? Arrange to have someone killed?"

"Yes, well, I dismissed the idea pretty quickly," he added. "Martin was ambitious and greedy, but a killer? No, for all his faults he wouldn't do that."

"You know it's us they're after, don't you?" said Alex. "Not you. You could get away from all this if you wanted to."

"Are you serious?" said Lewis, leaning forward. "I'm not going anywhere. You and your holy huddle are the people I'm closest to now. There isn't anyone else, you're my tribe, and I'm on contract with you, so no, I'm not going anywhere."

"And apart from all of that," he continued, "these are probably the people who killed my lover and ruined my business. That's why I want to go after them, I really want more than justice, Alex, I want vengeance, I want them to suffer and to die, the people who did this. That's what I want."

In the fireplace the blackening logs popped and crackled.

"Please," she said, suddenly, "don't do it."

"Do what?"

"Don't go after them: Massey, this Joseph, any of them, whoever they are. I don't want you to go after them." She was sitting forward now, looking straight at him.

"Why not?" asked Lewis, staring back at her.

"Because, I don't want you to get hurt."

"Why shouldn't I avenge Bridget if I want to?" he said. "Or even die trying? Why shouldn't I do that?"

She knew he was forcing her into admitting what she really felt. But she did not answer him because she didn't know herself. Eventually he stood up and walked over to the window; the wind had settled and the rain had softened to a steady patter on the glass.

"Because it's better to love the living than avenge the dead," she said finally.

"That sounds like the kind of thing your old friend Caleb would say."

"Don't go after this murderer," said Alex. "The police have Conner's testimony as well as all the other evidence, let them do their job. And whoever these people are, they haven't destroyed Conner, all they've done is make him stronger than he was before."

Lewis smiled. "Well, I think Conner's new friend Poppy might have had a hand in that as well."

"Yes," said Alex, "that's true."

He continued to stare out of the window.

"Please, Lewis, I don't want you to get hurt!" she said loudly, and before he could respond she continued. "Okay, okay, I am fond of you, I care what happens to you, that's all the truth I know."

They were both silent for a long, long time, and then he let out a long sigh.

"Okay, okay," he said, "here's the deal. I'll leave it alone, for now. But if anything happens to you or your brother, or Daisy, or even old Saint Caleb, or any of you, so help me, I am going to go after every last one of them; and I won't stop till one of them gets me or I've got all of them. I've lost one person I love to these people, and..." his voice caught and he coughed, "...and she was the most precious thing I had." He swallowed.

Alex stood up and moved slowly towards him and then without any more reflection on what she was doing she put an arm around him and kissed his cheek. He moved away slightly from her as she did it.

"Don't forget," he said, "I'm not like you; I'm not like any of you."

"I know who you are," she said. "I was your PA for five years."

They stood for a moment watching the rain fall onto the windowpane.

"Thank you for a lovely evening," she said. "I think I should be heading off now.

He nodded and turned to the door. She followed him out and they walked back to the front of the house where Alex collected her coat. Before she left she hugged him, somehow managing to combine both passion and reserve in the act, and then she let him go and he opened the front door.

"Drive safely," he said.

She nodded, and hurried out into the pattering rain.

She waved as she left and then her car she disappeared down the road into the distance.

After she had gone Lewis went back into his house and lit a cigar, and sat watching the flames in the hearth while he tried to work out what he really thought of Alex Masters.

17

———

DURING THE FOLLOWING WEEK, for the first time in a long time, Aiden began to talk about Cath. The facts broke out like water from a crumbling dam. A detail here and there, as much as he felt able to share, and then a little more, and then some more until it was a rush of as many things as people wanted to hear.

For a few people, not least Caleb Wicks, the truth made some sense of that which had seemed incomprehensible – the silent pain of Aiden Kennedy, the quiet, hidden sorrow with no root or reason.

With his past revealed, Aiden walked with a lighter step and a straighter back. Even now he could not quite say why he had kept quiet so long, although most of those close to him did not press him too hard for reasons.

In all this liberation, two facts went almost unnoticed. First, although much of the burden was lifted, he still felt the pain, he had still lost the one he loved and in his most private moments, he still grieved. Indeed he grieved all the more as he felt another dam of sorrow burst within himself, unfreezing a process that had remained unfinished.

The second thing was the fact that it had been Daisy who

had unlocked Aiden's secret. It was a mystery of circumstance and personality, and no one, not even Caleb, tried to fathom it.

Nobody at SUMMER had time to reflect too much on what Aiden had said though, because in the middle of all this, Conner's band released their album. It attracted muted praise from the critics who baulked at some of the more overt religious content, but the people loved it, and it charted in its first week. Even Darius Lench had to suffer the indignity of seeing a fleeting mention of Joel's Garden in his morning paper. The success of the album was a team effort. The band had worked hard, and Lewis had worked his contacts, and helped them find their way around the maze of retailers, distributors, production companies and radio stations.

The atmosphere in the office reminded Lewis Ashbury of the heady days of two years ago when his company had introduced the SEEKA project. He made phone calls to old friends and colleagues in the music business, opinion formers and journalists were invited to listen and provided with interviews. Conner switched from guitar practice to interview to TV appearance and back to guitar practice in a bewildering cycle, and the media enjoyed the narrative of the boy who made good after a checkered past. Most of the interviewers wanted a version of the stolen guitar story and in the end he had the script off by heart.

Meanwhile Daisy and Poppy had their own work to do. The production schedules for their clothing lines were in place in time for the launch of SUMMER's ethically traded clothing, to be known as "SUMMER Fare".

Aiden and Alex had been working hard to secure the acknowledgement of the World Fair Trade Organization, with Caleb drafted in to decode any legalese that crossed their desks. The whole operation buzzed with energy and expectation.

Daisy and Poppy arranged to have the weekend off together, and Daisy even agreed to come to Poppy's "dialled down" service, as she called it, the Quaker meeting on Sunday morning.

On Friday evening, with everyone at last heading out to play, or home, Aiden sat at his desk and opened up some files, to review the weekly income figures. The money was, at least, beginning to come in and he realized, much to his delight, that for the first time in months, a week had gone by and no one had asked him about the financial situation of the company.

It was a very healthy sign.

* * *

DAISY WAS in a relaxed mood when she joined Poppy for the service at the Friends Meeting House on Sunday morning. She felt no need to have all her defences raised. She imagined this would be a good chance to sit and reflect, to switch onto autopilot while this gentle contingent of the religious types did their thing.

She brought her own presuppositions to the meeting, and so she had expected them all to be sitting in rows, facing in the same direction, staring at an altar. But they weren't like that at all, and the idea of having everyone *facing each other* unnerved her at first. At Daisy's insistence they chose seats near one of the walls and in a corner.

"You'll be okay," said Poppy, who could see Daisy staring around her. "Believe me, you are not going to be the centre of attention."

"I'm not dressed for this," she whispered to Poppy. Daisy was wearing one of her favourite Day-Glo tee shirts, complete with sunflower, a rather loose black cardigan and a short tartan skirt.

Poppy turned to her and looked straight into the wide blue eyes. "Just relax, you will be fine."

Daisy took a deep breath and looked at the little knots of

modestly dressed people coming in. Some of them nodded and smiled at Poppy and her, but none of them made a fuss about what she was wearing.

Daisy tried to take Poppy's advice and relax. She was here now so she had better make the best of it, whatever that might be.

There were long periods of silence. This in itself was a strange experience for her. She assumed that a church service was like a variety act, with some singing, and listening to someone read the Bible, a bit of preaching and maybe some prayers. As the silences continued, her mind flitted from the designs to Aiden and then to Alex.

Gradually she did begin to relax and look around the room they were sitting in. A couple of years ago the silence in this place would have driven her mad, but now she was beginning to learn to be at peace with herself, and so she did not feel so threatened.

She was just studying the wooden ceiling panels of the room they were in when one of the old guys in the congregation rose very slowly to his feet and looked around at the others.

"What's he doing?" whispered Daisy to Poppy.

"He's going to share something with us," said Poppy.

Daisy stared at the man, wondering what it was that he going to share with them all. She imagined the old guy producing a big jar of sweets and passing them round. Maybe, she thought, it was his birthday and he had some cake with him.

The man held a small shiny book in his hand and he fumbled through the pages. The steady precision of his movements fascinated Daisy, the measured way in which he found the place he was looking for, the slow rhythm of his actions; these things seemed to lend weight to whatever he was about to say. She was unused to watching anyone do anything without hurrying and the sight of it mesmerized her. His face suggested answers to questions that were important to her, but she didn't know what they were.

"I would like to read a few verses from the Gospel of John." He had a surprisingly strong voice that echoed lightly against the walls. The rest of the room was silent.

The old man recited the tale of Jesus and the Samaritan woman at the well, and Daisy listened to the story and a little smile came to her face. She had never realized that there were women with attitude in the Bible. She found herself liking this busy, no-nonsense Samaritan woman who had bantered with the Messiah, and had had five husbands before this encounter.

Respect to you, thought Daisy. In her mind she began to imagine this lady, busy about her daily chores, sparring with the Son of God before getting back to the house with her water.

The old man continued to read, but seemed to be coming to the end of the story.

"Then," he read, "the woman left her water jar and went back to her city and said to the people there, 'Come and see a man who has told me about everything I ever did.' Could this man be the Christ?"

He shut his Bible and with deliberate care and looked around at all of them.

"I think this story may have a particular significance for someone here," he said, then he eased down carefully on his chair, his descent managed by the shaky hand of his wife.

Nice story, thought Daisy, pondering on the Samaritan woman again. No doubt this lady was a well-known fixture in the town, and would be going round to all her mates, telling them she had met the Messiah, a man who knew about the events of her life – everything she had done.

The rest of the town probably imagined she was introducing husband number six, she thought.

As the service continued, some of the old man's words echoed in her mind:

Come and see a man who has told me about everything I ever did. Everything I Ever Did.

And then like a jolt in her heart, Daisy remembered her dream, the events of her life, all the things she had done; she remembered the hand that had appeared at the end of the dream, with the ragged flesh. She'd recognized even then that her restless brain had conjured up an image of the hand of the Messiah, still sporting the hole from the Roman nail, and she thought about the series of dreams that had preceded the image of that hand, images showing her everything she ever did, everything that had been done to her. She remembered the last words of the story.

Could this man be the Christ?

Daisy frowned and fidgeted. Then she looked at the people around her, thankful that still none of them paid her any attention. She felt observed, as if someone just out of sight was taking a keen interest in her.

Well, she wondered *could he be the Christ?*

She thought about the derision with which she had treated Christians and their beliefs. She thought about the way in which she had laughed at Alex and teased Conner. Even in her wounded state she'd still had her pride, and she had treated all of them as weak, feeble individuals unable to hold their heads up and fend for themselves, unable to live without of their Jesus prop.

And yet she had been the one on the floor of the lavatory, sobbing her heart out as those things, these "demons" as Conner called them, interfered with her.

Even then, maybe even now, the chains she thought this Messiah would bind her with were heavier, and scarier, than the damage she had endured in her life. At least that damage came with some freedom; at least the demons left her free to despair.

But then again she had been loved! She'd been loved! By these people, family and friends, and that love had been like water in a thirsty land. Almost too sweet for her, that she should be so valued when she knew she had no value, that she should be so loved, when she knew she was not lovable.

And here was this man who told her everything she'd done and still loved her, she had learnt it through Alex and her crew, these people who cared about her and these people, like Alex, Conner, and Caleb and the rest of them, people who showed her what it was to love.

She was aware of Poppy glancing at her and then looking away, but Daisy did not move. She did not want to answer any questions at the moment. The sense of being watched continued, but she did not feel judged or condemned or lusted after, she simply felt loved.

What a fool he must be! she thought suddenly. *What a fool to love me so much!*

And yet he did.

I am acceptable. I am loved, as I am, not as someone I might strive to be. I am loved as I am.

The revelation smote her heart, its point sinking deep, deep into the very core of her being. She had not even realized that any of herself existed at that level, where this truth now resided.

She sat and absorbed this transformation for several minutes before she leant over towards Poppy.

"That was me," she whispered, still covering her face with her hands. "That was me, all that stuff about the Samaritan woman, and Jesus telling her everything she ever did. I had a dream like that."

Poppy stared at her.

"Okay," she said, "how do you feel now about it?"

Daisy looked out over the sea of faces. The meeting was coming to an end, people were talking to each other, getting up and moving around. She got up herself and looked over to where the old man sat.

"That was me!" she said in a clear voice that carried across the room. Everyone stared in her direction; most of them looking for the first time at this wide-eyed, stranger that Poppy had brought with her.

She moved out from her chair and walked down to the centre of the room, and everyone watched her as she crossed the aisle and walked up to the chair where the man sat next to his wife. He was holding tightly to his stick, staring at Daisy as if she were an apparition that had appeared before him.

She leant down. "That was for me, those words."

The old man looked up at her, startled by this visitor from another generation and culture. "Well then," he said, "God bless you."

"Yeah, and you, mate." She bent over and kissed him on the cheek.

The old man looked like he'd received a mild electric shock and remained seated for some time after that.

18

———

THE ASSASSIN FLICKED off the lamp and listened to his own breath as he moved slowly, back and forth, rocking on the edge of the bed. The mattress squeaked and the rumpled blankets rustled together. He went through this procedure whenever he felt lonely or depressed.

Just recently this had been happening more frequently. Other people might shed tears, but he could not remember the last time he had cried; it must have been years, decades ago. He could no longer remember how to cry, the concept was alien to him.

There was a streetlight just outside his room and the dull glow shone past the half-opened blinds at his window. The light moved across his vision as he rocked backwards and forwards; orange stripes raking the wall of his room. Looking down, he could almost pick out the shape of his exercise equipment in the shadows on the floor.

He picked up one of the dumb-bells in his left hand and went to work with it; back and forth, back and forth, grunting through the motion. In the course of this exercise he looked around the room, and then back to the grey blanket, and the faded colour photo placed on the bedside cabinet.

He had spent quite a bit of time recently looking at the face of his mother, trying to scratch together some comfort from it amongst all of the violence. It had been a gross indulgence, and he despised himself for it, not least because it left the legion within him restless and angry at his flirtation with the comfort of human love.

Many times the legion had told him to throw the photo away, rip it into pieces and flush it down the toilet, toss it in the trash. But every time he had resisted. This photo was the only connection he had with his history, his heritage, the only thing that allowed him to still think of himself as human. Some of the people in his trade forgot how many people they murdered; he did not. He had killed forty-six people individually in his career, the first being the man who murdered his mother and the last, the woman from SLaM.

Killing Bridget Larson was the first time he had made a mistake. The first time he had killed the wrong person, and the first time one of them had laid a finger on him during the act. He would bear the evidence of it for the rest of his life, on his face, and in his heart.

Back and forth went the dumb-bell. Then he changed to his right hand and started again, back and forth through the routine. He looked up at the slats of light on the wall, like a series of scars, like the scar on his own face.

He had built his life around the control and application of violence. This was his craft, and he was good at it, but after nearly twenty years he was getting tired, tired of being a killer and tired of having to face the condescension of people like Lench – people born with rank and privilege.

He could feel that tiredness in his bones as well. He could not now wait motionless on a cold night without feeling pain, without feeling the ache of the tension in his muscles. It wasn't a lack of fitness; it wasn't even just physical deterioration. He was beginning to feel as if his time was running out; a feeling accentuated by Lench's decision to sideline him in favour of Marie. He was starting to brood, the pressure in his head building as the walls closed in.

Around him and within him, unseen, the spirits lingered, uncertain where this current line of thinking would take their host, hungry for the opportunity to bring him to a frenzy again, to torment his frayed personality and satisfy their own lust for violence. They repeated their essence in whispers to him:

"We are violence, and the love of violence. Violence will bring resolution. Rage is the condition. Violence is the solution."

He closed his eyes and listened to their ancient call, the frustration, and he feared and loved what he heard.

He threw the dumb-bell down onto the carpet with a dull thud, and the slight incline of the floor caused it to roll towards his feet.

He turned to his other comfort, his other routine, hoping to find solace in it. He opened the drawer of the bedside cabinet and removed the soft grey cloth that contained the instrument of his trade. A customized .45 calibre 13-round handgun with a silencer that he had designed himself. *"Surely,"* the voices told him, *"this is your friend, your only friend."* Friend, confidante, intimate. This gun was his companion, the one he broke bread with, in the form of the bodies and blood of his victims.

He thought again about Darius Lench as he unfurled the cloth and looked at the instrument of his trade. Lench had been trying to silence the Christian group by breaking the boy, using his new tart, Marie. She was from Lench's world of course, clever, smart, another City type; no wonder Lench had *preferred* her.

But she had failed, as he secretly hoped she would. They had been too subtle, again. Trying to dirty the boy with photographs, upsetting him with lame accusations of theft. It was pathetic. Well, the boy was still on his hind legs singing his little songs with his friends, and stealing the hearts of teenage girls, and Lench's new whore was in disgrace, consoled only by the fact that the police had not worked out who she was. Indeed, the fact that her firm wanted her to take up an assignment in America for a few months had come as a blessing. She needed to get out, and Lench was more than happy to let her go.

Josef despised them both, and then he found himself despising their cause, the cause he thought he wanted to live by, and the revelation came to him, at last. He realized, dimly, that he was having a crisis of faith. Having been a willing and faithful servant to Lench, and to the master for all these years, he was beginning to wonder what it was all for. He could feel the horde within him fidgeting at the heretical thoughts flitting through his mind.

He looked down at the gun in his hand. He was able to say, without any hesitation, that he loved this weapon more than anything or anyone else in the world. It was beautiful in his eyes, a symbol, a maker of the sudden and devastating violence that he craved. He began to clean the weapon with the soft cloth, touching and caressing the metal, reminding himself of its solidity, the sureness of its grip.

Gradually, the tension in his mind began to subside and he felt his pulse rate settle. He replaced the gun with loving care and flicked on the TV.

For the sheer perverse amusement of it, he settled on an episode of *Crimescene*, a programme where the police asked the public to help solve crimes. There was the usual parade of petty criminals and thugs, turning over post offices and raiding factories on payday. He despised them all with their ugly faces and their impoverished ambition.

The presenters reached the final item, and Josef Durand reached for the remote control in advance of some idle channel hopping. He was about to press the button when a photo-fit image appeared that made him pause, and then stare in mute shock.

He was looking at a very blurred image of himself.

The presenter began to speak:

"Some of you may remember a disturbing case that we featured on the programme a couple of years ago. The murder of Bridget Larson was a particularly brutal act, and one that left police wondering at the motive of the perpetrator."

Josef leant forward and concentrated, listening to every word. So far there was nothing here that was new.

"Bridget was murdered in her apartment when she disturbed an intruder." The presenter continued speaking and a picture of the apartment appeared on the screen. "The police are keeping an open mind on the motive for the killing; it may be that Bridget simply disturbed a burglar, although nothing was taken. So far no one has been arrested for Bridget's murder, although a number of people were interviewed at the time."

"Ha," Josef barked out a laugh despite the tension he felt within himself. "Including that idiot Martin Massey," he whispered.

That had been another of Lench's mistakes, letting that soft arrogant fool Martin Massey get so involved with the group. Josef had singled him out as the weak link, the one most likely to blink, most likely to talk if the pressure got too much for him.

The presenter continued talking:

"But now, new evidence has come to light, we think the man in this photo-fit is called 'Joseph', and he may well now have a scar on his right cheek from a wound he picked up at this attack."

The blurred image of Josef from the CCTV appeared again

on the screen. There was no doubt it was him, but now they had a name as well.

The screen flicked back to the studio, and the presenter muttered something reassuring about violent crime being a rare thing, and for no one to get too worried. The closing comments were lost on Josef who was now engulfed by a rushing, boiling, sensation that closed out all sound. The veins on the side of his neck bulged and his hands clenched at the bedclothes.

They had his name now.

They had his name.

Around and within him the spirits hammered his skull, sensing a rare opportunity to bring their host to the absolute pitch of rage.

In his fractured brain Josef tried to make the connections. Who spoke that name? Who knew it?

It would have been someone who knew Bridget, and also him. Someone questioned by the police. So who might have buckled under renewed pressure? Who could have blabbed to the police, given them a name, his name?

Of course there was only one person who it could have been.

"MASSEY!" he spat in his fury, then he scooped up the dumb-bell and flung it with all his might at the TV screen. It shot across the room, not even dipping before it exploded into the screen sending shards of glass over the carpet.

He knew he should stop and think. He knew he should consult with Lench. He knew that there were so many good reasons to pause, to think, and to do the wise thing, the considered thing. Lench's voice was even now, in his head, urging caution.

He ignored the voice. Not because he wanted to but because he knew there was nothing he could do to calm the rage inside him now.

He stood up and crunched his way across the broken glass to

his wardrobe. He pulled out his work clothes, the anonymous uniform of his trade, and then he picked up his car keys and the weapon.

Some years ago he'd tried to resist the anger, to bring some discipline to his life by practising meditation, but the horde would not allow him even a moment of silent self-reflection, it was impossible. All he could do at times like this was submit.

Then, for a reason he could not fathom, he walked back to his bedside cabinet, opened a drawer and carefully, carefully picked out the photo of his mother. He slid this into his pocket and then he walked out of the cramped room into the bitter, clear night.

IT IS ten thirty at night. The Assassin sits in his car, staring at the total darkness that is Martin Massey's flat. The man is either out or asleep. His car is still in the communal garage, so maybe he has just had an early night. The Assassin's handgun sits snug inside the specially sewn pocket of his jacket. He does not touch the weapon once it is in place, until he needs to use it.

He checks his watch, and listens to his breathing, uneven, urgent despite his attempts to calm himself, and he waits. He thinks he will move when he is ready, but that decision lies with the host within him.

At just before a quarter to eleven he is walking swiftly and quietly towards the building. The main door of the block isn't even shut properly, and affords him the easiest of access. He has opened the door of Martin Massey's apartment before, and can do it now without even using a torch. Now he is working he feels relaxed and alert, playing to his strengths again.

He thinks of all the questions he will have to answer when what he is about to do is discovered. Lench will know it was him, and Josef won't simply acknowledge it, he will own this act in front of Lench, he will revel in what he has done. He will defy his former leader to his face, because Lench has now lost his respect.

He remembers the layout of the place from his last visit, and he smiles at the realization that unless Martin had reorganized the place, he would be able to move around, even in the darkness, with perfect ease.

He is in the lounge, listening for any sound, a creak, a breath, the rustle of clothing. There is no sound, the apartment does not feel occupied; the Assassin has a hunch for these things.

He pulls a small, narrow-beam torch from his pocket and flicks its beam around the room. Immediately in front and to the left of him, he sees a sofa and two armchairs, exactly as they had been on his previous visit. There is the hi-fi system on a glass shelf in an alcove, and there a widescreen TV and set-top box, flickering with numbers in different shades of green and blue.

To the right is the bedroom. The door is slightly ajar. He turns the torch off and removes the weapon, silently sliding back the safety catch. He recalls that the hinges of the bedroom door whine when it is opened slowly and so he pushes it, with a smooth swift action and then stops it immediately when it stands just over half open. He now has a view of the room; the small dressing table over by the window seems rather effeminate for Massey, but there is no accounting for taste. The wardrobe is still there to the right, the bed directly in front of him. He moves to get a better view of the bed and raises the gun.

But he can already see that it is empty.

He can hear his own breathing beginning to labour at the frustration within. For a moment he is tempted to smash the place, but he rejects the idea. Destruction is a slow and noisy process, and would not satisfy him. It is murder, done well, quick and silent that is the meat and drink he craves.

He tries to calm himself down; there is no point in losing composure now, he can leave without a trace.

He takes one pace back towards the living room area again when he notices a piece of paper left in the middle of one of the sofa cushions. It has been ripped from a TV listings magazine, the page for this evening's viewing. He can see that the listing includes details of the *Crimescene* programme. His curiosity is aroused and he shines the torch onto it. On the paper, around the edge of the print are three hastily scribbled words in small capital letters:

IT WASN'T ME.

The Assassin switches the torch off. "Liar." He mouths the word, and then mouths it again, although in his heart he knows that the scribbled words are true. Massey is too much of a coward to betray him, and what would be the point of doing so now? For all his weaknesses, Martin Massey is not a vindictive person, neither was he a fool.

That means someone else has mentioned his name to the police, or someone has let it slip in a careless moment. He stops and, in the silence, thinks. He listens to his own breathing and thinks back. Not many of the others in the group even know his name, Lench had at least granted him that concession when the Assassin had become useful to him. There are a couple of the long-term members who he knows will also be loyal to his need for discretion, and apart from that, the woman Marie is the only other person who knows that name. But she won't give him away, even if she hates him, her professional pride, and her reputation with Lench would stop her.

Unless she has done it by mistake.

He walks to the bedroom window and looks out through the crack in the curtains to the stale yellow streetlight and the pavement below. He thinks back to their assignment, when they worked on the boy, Conner. He thinks about the conversations they had when the boy was drugged, when he was starting to regain consciousness.

And now he feels the host stirring in him, jibbering, fidgeting. He hears his breathing again.

"Marie," he whispers the name. "Anne-Marie."

He takes the scrap of paper that Martin has left and walks into the study. He finds a pen and scribbles two words on the other side of the scrap of paper, leaving it face up on the desk.

STAY SILENT.

He wants Massey to know that he believes him. But he also wants him to know that he, the Assassin, was here.

He replaces the pen and moves silently to the exit. He eases his way outside, and closes the door. There is no sound, and there are no witnesses.

Four minutes later he is sitting in his car again, listening to his breathing. He grips the steering wheel tight with his leather gloves. He can feel the urge coming upon him again, welling up within him, the desire that cannot be resisted.

"Oh Marie," he whispers again. The reckoning that perhaps was always going to come will fall due tonight.

But then another thought comes to him, another desire. Now he really is off the leash, he is going to pay a visit to one other person first.

ALEX MASTERS HAD COME to the conclusion that running a media company was easy compared to knowing how to handle personal relationships. Family, friends and colleagues all slipped into and out of her mind. The hot mug of tea in front of her was not going to solve these problems, but still it was a comfort to her.

She tried to reconcile the success of SUMMER with her own

inner longing, still nagging her – some ambitions fulfilled, others still waiting.

Her mind moved on to other concerns. She thought about the men she knew. There was Aiden, and the undeniable truth was that while she liked him and she respected him, she simply did not love him, at least not in the romantic sense.

She had talked to Daisy about him recently.

"There is so much to admire in him," she had told Daisy.

"That's pretty lame," Daisy had replied. "Admiration isn't going to make you want to go to bed with him, or choose him as a partner."

"I do like him," Alex had replied. "And he knows what's going on with the business, what's going to be good for SUMMER."

Daisy had rolled her eyes. "Alex, you don't fall for a guy because he is good with a spreadsheet."

No indeed, thought Alex, staring in the darkness at her bedroom ceiling, *you do not.*

She whispered the words to herself:

"You don't fall for a guy because he is good with a spreadsheet."

She could never imagine herself with Aiden, not in that way. It wasn't so much that it was an indecent thought, quite the opposite in a way, the idea just didn't interest her.

And the irony was, it had been Daisy of all people who had sat and listened to Aiden, confessing his secret past life. He had said nothing of it to Alex, not even in their most intimate moments two years ago. She could not help feeling a twinge of jealousy at the thought of it.

Then there was Lewis. She did love Lewis, she knew it deep down, but the idea of being with him seemed shocking, much more indecent than being with Aiden. It didn't help that she'd spent five years of her life keeping him at a distance while they engaged in a very professional relationship. He had asked her about her feelings for him once, and, taken aback by the question, she had said she wished their relationship to remain entirely professional, and he had always respected her wishes.

She admitted only to herself that she hadn't actually answered his question; she had not talked about her feelings in her reply to him because she had no wish to do so. She had been his Personal Assistant, and undertook the duties that the position required. But she knew what she felt, and that tension would always be there.

She thought about Lewis being here with her now. She thought about him speaking to her, imagining him smiling at her. Somehow the darkness of the room made such things possible to contemplate. How she needed the wisdom of God! How she longed for the love that had eluded her so far.

"No," she spoke out into the darkness suddenly, scolding herself. She would not go there.

Who was Lewis anyway? An older man who had doubtless bedded plenty of women, including the infamous Bridget Larson. Alex found herself wondering how she could possibly compete as a lover with someone like Bridget, what could she offer Lewis that Bridget had not already given him? It was a horrible thought and she didn't want to linger on it for any length of time, even though the answer, obvious and powerful, lingered at the edge of her consciousness.

Love.

That was the irresistible answer to all the questions. But if those questions made her nervous, it was the answers that made her really feel scared.

Angel stood in the corner of her room, sensing these thoughts in the distance, seeking constantly to be open to the will of his master. Vehicles came and went along the main road outside Alex's flat. The night was inevitably a quieter time for him. Alex was safe in this place; he did not need to sleep but the quietness wasn't unpleasant to him.

The phone rang. It was rather late for a call, but Alex knew that some of her friends didn't get ready for bed at ten thirty, like her.

It was Bernice.

"Alex!"

"Hey, Bats, how are you?"

"Oh, you know how it is for me, dear, always looking forward to the next adventure. Anyway, look I'm afraid I've got some bad news, we're going to have to postpone our little surprise party."

"Oh, that's a shame," said Alex, but her thoughts weren't on the party. Bernice's call would provoke a conversation she had been contemplating for a couple of days now.

"I'm glad you phoned though," she said. "I've been meaning to ask you something."

"Oh? Well you've got me," said Bernice cheerfully.

"I was just wondering how you were getting on with God and with the whole spiritual side of things."

"Oh, why do you ask?" said Bernice.

Alex hesitated; she wanted to be honest with her friend.

"Well you know my aunt and uncle have kept in touch with your folks, you know how these old guys chat to each other."

"Yes, I know," said Bernice. Alex thought she could detect a hesitation in Bernice's voice.

"Well, your guys were saying that you had got out of the loop a bit. I think they were worried about you."

"Oh, they do worry, bless them," Bernice laughed, "and I guess it's true. It's difficult, Alex. Maybe I'll talk to you about it sometime. Mum and Dad think I've moved right away from spiritual things, but that's not true, it's just with God and me it's complicated."

Alex could believe that, things always got complicated.

"We'll talk about it sometime," said Bernice. "Anyway, look I'm sorry about the event, I've got a work assignment coming up. It's going to take me away for a while, you know, around the world a bit."

"Oh," said Alex, "so you are going on a bit of an adventure then after all? So how long are you going to be away?"

In the spiritual realm, Angel is hardly aware of the call. His senses are reaching out, even now, towards a car that has stopped outside Alex's flat; a man gets out of the car and is even now making his way into the building. The spiritual presence around him screams like the grinding of metal, it is a sound both terrible and familiar.

Angel has witnessed the presence of the host before, and would never forget the experience.

"I'll be back in a few months," said Bernice.

"We should stay in touch," said Alex, "and organize something when you are back."

"Definitely!" said Bernice. "Cheerio, stay safe!" And with that she rang off.

Alex thought about going off to bed. It was a shame that Bernice was going to go out of her life as quickly as she came in. She thought about her mate, and her mind drifted to Conner, and the horrible conversation she had had with this man who had tried to destroy him. And as she sat there, the thought that had been bothering her began to crystalize in her mind.

And in all of this, she did not hear her front door opening.

When had those horrible texts and calls to Conner started? Why had he said the person who was abusing him looked like she was crying? She shook her head, surely that wasn't possible, surely this idea conjured up in her mind right now was nonsense.

She thought about her friend, Bernice, Bats Templeton, and she tried to remember her name, her full name.

If it were possible for God's messengers to panic, Angel would have done so now.

It wasn't the thoughts going through Alex's mind that terrified him, it wasn't even the boiling horde that were even now just a few metres away. It was their host, who had somehow broken free of the shackles that held him. Who knows what he might do next? And so Angel did the only thing he could do. He flung himself down, prostrate before his master and desperately interceded for the woman in his care, praying for her even as the Assassin moved with quiet grace across the hallway of her apartment.

Alex picked up the phone again, and dialled Caleb's office number rather than his home number; she didn't want to disturb him now, but she did want to leave him a message.

"Caleb," she said, "I need to talk to you about this woman who abused Conner. I have a horrible suspicion that I might know who it is. Can you call me sometime tomorrow please? Thanks."

She replaced the phone and put her face in her hands, overwhelmed by the sense of anger and hate that would have driven her friend to do these things. Alex shook her head, grieving for what had happened to Conner and for what her friend had become.

And all the while the Assassin watched and listened. Hearing the sobs, watching the shake of Alex's body as she wrestled with this betrayal.

The legion formed and re-formed itself, spirits gathering and parting to make way for one single entity, which rose to the surface – a ravening monster.

"We are violence and the love of violence," it hissed. *"He comes here to do what must be done."* It indicated the man.

"You cannot harm her," said Angel. *"You are under authority before the living God, and you must not touch her."*

The whole legion recoiled, shivering at the mention of the Lord's name; the man who hosted them seemed to twitch slightly.

"*He comes,*" said the voice from the host.

"*Why?*" said Angel. "*Why did you bring him here?*"

"*The host does as he sees fit,*" said the voice, and then it laughed and laughed as it sank back amongst its fellows – a manic, desperate sound, submerged in echoes of rage.

In her lounge Alex blew her nose and reached for her tea. She was so tired, so exhausted by all of this. She wished life didn't have to be so hard, so full of loss and anger and disappointment. She sipped her tea and called out in her uncertainty.

"Oh God, is this really true?" she said aloud. "Is it Bernice, is this who she is now?"

"Yes, Miss Masters," said a voice, "it is true, that's what she is now."

The voice of the Assassin made her jump and tea slopped over onto her pyjamas.

She felt the adrenaline launch in her; she could taste it even as she looked up to the door of her lounge to see a figure standing there.

The figure remained motionless for a few seconds, before he took a single step into her lounge and closed the door behind himself.

"Miss Masters," said the Assassin, "I admire you. Our leader has consistently underestimated you."

Unable to stop shaking, she slowly put the mug back on the table in front of her.

"Jesus, into your hands do I commit myself." She tried to whisper it just to herself, but it came out too loud.

"Now there's a dangerous prayer, Miss Masters," said the Assassin taking another step forward. He looked at her, and then around the room, taking in the furniture, the ornaments, and the woman who was sitting in front of him, shivering with fear.

Alex stared back at him, this was the man who had come into her café; she recognized the voice, the scar, even the smell of him. And she believed she was going to die here, tonight, by his hand. She forgot about Lewis Ashbury and Conner and everyone else she loved. She felt breathless and nauseous, and lightheaded.

The Assassin closed his eyes and listened.

"Are we alone, Miss Masters?" he said.

"Yes," she whispered.

While his gaze was away from her, Alex remembered the Lord's Prayer and she started to whisper the words to herself, this time in silence.

"Our father, who art in heaven…"

He stepped forward so she could see his face more clearly in the light, the pale angry scar across the right cheek. She moved through the words of the prayer and he remained silent, waiting for her to finish.

His face remained expressionless but Alex could see some deep, deep sadness locked up inside him, suppressed. For a moment he looked to Alex as if he wasn't sure why he was here. She looked at his face and his hands and she wondered at the sense of loss in his eyes. And at that moment she was amazed to find that she felt compassion for him.

"You poor man," she said, when she had finished her prayer, and her voice sounded loud in the silence of the room.

He opened his eyes and stared at her.

"What did you say, Miss Masters?" His voice was calm, measured, and she tried to place the accent, Germanic, maybe.

This was the man who had killed Bridget, who taken part in the abuse of her brother.

"What did you say?" he said again.

She tried to answer but her voice would not work. Then she let out a murmur as he moved, in one stride, so that he stood almost directly over her.

"I am sorry," she said and shut her own eyes, expecting the single blow that would snuff her out.

But the blow did not come and when she opened her eyes again he had moved away from her and was looking at the items on the mantelpiece. He had removed a gun from his pocket and seemed to be fixing something to the end of it, she had no experience of these things and she thought it might be a silencer.

Angel also watched, and if he could have cried he would have done so now. How could this man come here? How could he be permitted to simply finish this life, her precious life, which had delivered much and promised so much more? Where was the Lord in this?

Angel's mind filled with a vast expanse of indignation and a deep sense of the offensiveness of it all. In his soul he cried out to his God, out of the anguish and the love that he felt for Alex Masters. And in his torment, the timeless, intimate voice of his God spoke to him:

"Why don't you just worship me Angel? As she has done."

And she was, he could see it, sense it.

In the perverse quietness Alex moved on from the Lord's Prayer and now she found herself remembering words from her very earliest days in church; words that had become a comfort to her then, and maybe could comfort her now. She whispered them in her mind:

"Therefore with angels and archangels, and with all the company of heaven, we proclaim your great and glorious name, forever praising you."

The Assassin flicked on the torch and sent its beam around the room. He radiated such a deep sense of agitation that she could not look at him for more than a couple of seconds.

"...forever praising you, and saying..."

"You are praying to your God," he said. He did not look up. The low, calm voice carried a menace with it. He looked down at his gun, and pulled up the safety catch.

She didn't answer him, she didn't stop, and she felt herself move beyond fear. If this was it, then so be it.

"Holy, holy, holy, Lord, God of power and might..."

She wanted to keep saying the words, but now she faltered. Angel watched her as her lips went still, and silence filled the room. Then he looked away because he did not want to see a person that he loved die. As one final act for her, he took up the prayer, speaking out words of praise, acting in obedience to his Lord.

"...*God of power and might...*"

The Assassin raised the gun with a perfectly steady hand and looked her over once more, his victim. She really was quite terrified of him and he was pleased to see it. He watched her breast rise and fall beneath the gown, a steady rhythm. He considered the possibility of a little entertainment with her but he knew he would not violate her. She had shown compassion for him, and he could not remember the last time he had known such a thing, although he knew exactly where that compassion would have come from. Only his mother had shown him compassion, only she had offered him anything akin to love.

"...*heaven and earth are full of your glory...*"

He was intrigued by the fact that, even in this moment of crisis, the woman in front of him had found something in her heart for him.

He placed the torch on the mantelpiece behind him and as he did so something caught his eye. He studied the items there again, the carved elephants and the photograph of her parents, a painting of sunflowers on the wall.

"...*Hosanna in the highest.*"

. . .

ALEX WATCHED him as he studied the photograph of her parents. While he stared at it she was almost overcome with the urge to run, to get help, to do anything to get out of this situation, but the desire ebbed away as quickly as it had risen, and she recognized it for the foolishness that it was. The waves of nausea settled, she took a deep breath, and Angel watched as the spirit hovered over her, and with an inspiration not of her own making she spoke.

"Who are these people?" said the Assassin.

"Those were my parents," she said, "my father and my mother."

"They are dead now," said the Assassin as if such a thing were self-evident. She wasn't sure whether this was a question or a statement, but his attention came back to her. His gaze was steady, motionless. The spirit hovered over her and she looked directly at him and said, "My parents died when I was ten."

The Assassin frowned, as if he was trying to solve a riddle she had told him. The gun remained steady. She could taste the adrenaline in her mouth and her breath came in short bursts.

He turned back to the photograph and moved over to it, studying it intently.

"Your mother's skin colour is darker than your father's," he said. "Please explain this."

Alex found that she had lost her voice, and had to swallow a couple of times before she could speak.

"My mother was Indian, but my father was white British."

"Your parents were of different nationalities."

"Yes."

"And your mother died when you were ten," he said.

"Yes."

She followed him as he picked up the photo and held it in

the beam of torchlight. The gun glinted in the half-light beside him.

"Your mother died when you were ten," he said again.

"Yes," she said, "both of my parents died when I was ten."

He placed the gun on the mantelpiece and reached into the inside pocket of his jacket. He pulled out a slip of card, a photograph, and held it next to the photo of her parents.

She could just see that the photograph he'd pulled from his pocket was the image of a woman. The photo was in colour but faded, as if it had been exposed to the sun for too long.

"Your mother died when you were ten," he repeated again, almost now in a whisper, still with his back to her.

"Yes," she said. She said the word very quietly and he only just heard her over the sound of a car driving past on the road outside.

Angel looked on fascinated, horrified. The legion within this man were now restrained, withheld by some spiritual authority. It was a mysterious sight as they pushed and writhed, like excited dogs, straining at the leash.

JOSEF TURNED BACK TO HER. She was a beautiful woman, and he wished he had not seen her beauty. He wished he had not seen the photograph of her parents, and he wished he had not discovered that her mother had died when she was ten.

"How did your mother die?" he asked.

"She was killed in a car crash, a drunk driver hit the car my parents were travelling in."

The Assassin nodded.

"Did the driver of the other vehicle survive?"

"Yes," she said.

He was silent for a whole minute, maybe longer, and then he said, "Did you consider killing that person, out of revenge?"

She paused for just a moment.

"Yes," she said finally, and he nodded.

"You are not so very different from me, Miss Masters," he said, and sighed. "I think you may even understand me rather better than Darius Lench does."

He looked down at her again. "I presume, you did not kill this person," he continued, maintaining his calm tone, "because you would consider such an act to be immoral."

She nodded and shivered. She wanted this to be over. She felt very tired and she needed to go to the bathroom.

At last he spoke again. "My mother also died when I was ten." He placed the photo of her parents back on the mantelpiece and walked over to her and she shivered.

"Stop shaking, Miss Masters," he said and placed a hand on her shoulder. "I have decided that I am not going to hurt you. Look at this please," he said, handing her the photograph of his mother.

She stood up and took the faded Polaroid from his hand. In the picture she saw a woman with long blonde hair, standing on what might have been a quayside; she was wearing a short skirt and a skimpy top. The woman was smiling, and held a cigarette in her right hand.

"This is a photograph of my mother," he said. "She was murdered. Like you, I considered revenge. Unlike you, I took that consideration through to action and killed the man who murdered her."

Alex said nothing. Her eyes moved between the faded Polaroid and the eyes of the Assassin.

"Did you ever grieve for her loss?" she said. "Did you ever shed tears?"

"I do not cry, Miss Masters," he said. "I do not mourn the dead."

He reached out his hand and she gave the photograph back to him.

"And yet," he said, as if still trying to solve a puzzle, "in this place I feel..."

He paused and his closed his eyes for a few moments and frowned, as if considering some complex puzzle.

"Please bear with me for a moment," he said finally, and he sat down cross-legged on the carpet. He breathed deeply a couple of times, while she stood staring at him.

"Sit down and relax, Miss Masters," he said. "I am nearly done with you."

He looked again at his photograph and then placed it carefully on the table between them and stared at it, as if it was an icon he might pray to. He was silent for a few moments, completely ignoring her as she sat down on the sofa. Then, as she watched him, he let out a strained howling noise, like an animal in pain. This sound continued in regular bursts for perhaps three or four minutes; it wasn't a loud noise, but Alex found it both pitiful and disturbing. As he released this noise, he rocked gently back and forth, shaking slightly.

He gradually became silent, and the rocking died away until he was perfectly still. Then with one graceful movement he rose to his feet, picking up the photograph as he did so, and placing it back in his pocket.

He turned around to the mantelpiece and took the gun and as he did so he placed a small item like a plastic counter where the gun had been.

He turned back to her.

"You are crying, Miss Masters," he said, and she realized there were tears on her cheeks.

"For whom are you crying?" he said.

"For you, of course," she replied without thinking.

"Do not waste your tears on me," he said.

"But there is still hope, even for you there..." She faltered as he raised a finger to his lips.

"Hush," he whispered, "hush, lest I change my mind."

She stared at him in silence and he looked at her with an impassive gaze before he spoke again.

"That's better," he said, and he placed the gun in his pocket.

"Good evening, Miss Masters," he said, "and goodbye." He walked out of the door, closing it quietly behind him, and when he had gone, all was silent.

Alex looked around her room, wide-eyed and shivering. She shivered again, violently, extravagantly and then ran to her front door to make sure it was shut and locked, and then she went into her bathroom.

WHEN THE IMMEDIATE crisis was over, she called Bernice. The phone rang, and rang, and then went to messages.

"I know who you are," she said. "Leave me alone, leave us alone."

She paused for a second, undecided, and then she said, "And listen, for your sake, this is important. A man has been here, the man of violence. He knows you, and he is angry at the moment, so be careful."

She shut off the phone and let out a long, long sigh. She felt exhausted, and cold, and still frightened. She checked every lock in her apartment and then she went to her room and climbed into bed thinking she might rest for a few minutes, but within moments she was asleep.

19

A DAY LATER, Caleb Wicks had planned to have a bit of a lie-in and a relaxing day off work. But instead he lay in his bed, wide-awake, again, at a time when most civilized people were still asleep. He had hoped for an easy day, getting up at a leisurely pace and then spending a little time in the garden with Mrs Wicks. Instead he was unnaturally alert, his heart beating. He had been summoned again by the Lord.

"What kind of gift is this?" he muttered to himself, grumpy and full of self-pity, as he looked around the room in the pre-dawn darkness. But this thing drove him now. He went into the study, and closed the door behind himself.

"Deliver the warning."

It was five thirty-eight in the morning.

He wrestled and struggled with this thing in his prayers for about twenty minutes, all that time spent on his knees. It took him several minutes to get up and walk off the fierce tingling in his legs as he limped into, and around, the kitchen. By six he was back in his study.

Taking a fresh sheet of paper he drew out a series of circles, and in each one he wrote a name: Alex, Conner, Daisy, Poppy,

Lewis, Aiden, finally his own name. Spinning out from the circles were other names; "the Assassin", the man who had murdered Bridget; "Martin", Alex's hapless colleague, and "the adversary" as Caleb chose to call him. Here was a man who had wreaked havoc two years ago and seemed to be doing the same thing again.

Alex had decided not to call the police after Josef had visited her, but she had called Caleb and told him her suspicions about Bernice, and the visit from Joseph who, by accident or more probably design, had spoken the name that she thought sounded like "Darius Lynch" during their conversation.

"Who are you, Mr Lynch?" he whispered. "And why don't you want to be disturbed in the morning?"

He remembered Aiden's comment: *"Perhaps he's a market maker of some kind..."*

In Caleb's imagination market makers were young men in their mid-20s with loud voices and even louder jackets. Could this man be like that? He also had a vague idea that the image was now dated, that computers managed all of these markets now, twenty-four hours a day.

So did the market still rely on people to fix prices at certain times of the day?

The alarm went off in the bedroom and he heard Mrs Wicks stir. It was seven o'clock in the morning. He was still no further forward in his thinking, and Dora's appearance at his study door was a welcome distraction.

"Do you want a cup of tea, dear?" she said with a sweet smile and a knowing look in her eye, really she was much better than he was at mornings.

"Yes please, that would be lovely," he said. "I need any kind of inspiration I can get to try to track this fellow down."

"Have you tried doing a search on the internet for him?"

Caleb Wicks looked at his wife and smiled.

"Well?" she said.

"You know," he said, "that was the very next thing I was going to try."

She looked at him for a long moment. "I'll get you a cup of tea."

He fired up the computer and tapped "Darius Lynch" into the search engine, but nothing came back from that.

He tried all kinds of combinations of words like "banker", "market maker", "City", "Lynch", "Lynche".

"Traders," he mumbled. "Surely it's all done with computers now, twenty-four hours a day."

He tried putting in "daily price setting" and stared at the results.

"Gold," he whispered, "of course."

He tapped in another couple of searches and then he sat slowly back in his chair.

"Oh my Lord!" he shouted and leant back in his chair. "Oh my Lord!"

His outburst was enough to bring Mrs Wicks running to his study again, dressing gown flapping at her sides.

"Are you okay?"

"I'm fine." He waved at her without looking up, scribbling on another sheet of paper. Then he turned to her and smiled.

"I think I've finally tracked down our friend Mr Lench."

"Really? Well, I'm very pleased to hear it," she said. "Do you want another cup of tea?"

"Thank you, my dear. Oh, one more thing," he said, "I am afraid I am going to have to drive into London today. I hope that when I come back we shall be able to do a bit of gardening."

"Drive into London?" she said, staring at him. "Whatever for?"

"I don't think I'll really know until I get there," he said.

"Oh I see," she said, "it's one of those trips, is it?"

"I'm afraid so," he said. "I'll get back as soon as I can."

"I should think so too, Caleb, you did say you were going to help me in the garden today."

"Nothing but this would stop me," he said. "I have a little bit of business to attend to and then when I get back we can really get down to it." He scribbled some addresses down on a sheet of paper in front of him.

"I really would rather stay here," he said, "if I could."

"I know you would," she said. "But go and do what you have to."

"Thank you," he said.

"Do you think it's nearly finished now?" she said with a sigh. "All this present trouble?"

"I think so," he said. "I think we're coming to the end game now, but please do pray for me, I have one more challenge to face."

She came to him and kissed him on the forehead. "Of course I will," she said. "I always do."

<hr>

CALEB CRAWLED through the traffic into London. It was an unpleasant trip ahead of what was likely to be an unpleasant encounter. He fell foul of the rush hour and the congestion charge, and halfway in, he witnessed a minor accident on the other side of the road. One vehicle bumped into the back of another, and the ensuing argument made the situation worse than it would otherwise have been.

As he approached the centre of the city the traffic slowed even more. It took him half an hour to drive the final mile to his destination, the London offices of Stern, Shearman and Partners, one of the constituent members of the group of organizations that fix the price of gold twice a day.

When he did find their office, he paid for and parked in a space some distance from the entrance before walking back to the small forecourt in front of the building. Two vehicles were parked in a small space at the front of the building.

One was a stationery supplier's van, but the other was a Mercedes Benz SLK 350, and when he looked at it, he felt the hairs at the back of his neck prickling. This was it; this vehicle belonged to his adversary, and all he had to do now was get to this man, meet him alone and confront him with everything.

He had to face this man, to get his attention. He didn't want to just walk into the building and broadcast his presence, and the best alternative he could think of was quite reckless and, for a man like Caleb Wicks, almost offensive. But perhaps, he thought, this was a moment for recklessness.

He walked back to his own car, and got into the driver's seat.

There was no barrier to the car park but the reception door was clearly visible with an intercom system for visitors. Caleb crawled back up a narrow street towards the front of the office, then he swung the car gently into the parking area so that his bumper was pointing at the Mercedes, and then he pulled on the handbrake. His insurance documents were in the glove compartment where he always kept them. He said one final simple prayer and watched as the light of the morning sun shone on all of the expensive cars parked in front of him.

"God forgive me, and protect me," he whispered. "Father in heaven, may your Name be glorified, may your kingdom come here on earth..."

He slowly released the handbrake.

"...may your will be done here on earth as it is in heaven. Give me today every resource that we may need..."

He put his car into reverse.

"...and forgive us our sins, as we forgive those who might sin against us. And lead us not in to temptation..."

He eased the car back, inch by inch, until his bumper nudged the bumper of the Mercedes. He thought he noticed the other car move very slightly, but it may have been his imagination. Immediately the world was filled with the urgent warble of a car alarm. The indicators on the Mercedes flashed, and Caleb knew that he was now committed.

"But deliver us from every kind of evil, for yours is the kingdom, the power and the glory now and forever; amen."

Caleb moved his car forward so that, when this was over, he would be able to get away quickly, and he made a point of not looking at the building, he didn't want to see if anyone was watching him. He got out of the car and went to the intercom at the front door. The Mercedes' alarm had stopped. He found a small button on the grille at the front and pressed it.

"Hello?"

"Hello, can I help you?" said a distant crackling voice from the loudspeaker.

"Hello there. I am afraid I seem to have had a bit of an accident with the Mercedes in the car park. Is the owner there?"

"Who did you say you were?" asked the distant voice.

Caleb repeated his story, and waited. There was evidently some conversation going on within the office.

"I think that's Mr Lench's car. I will tell him what has happened. Were you here to see someone?"

If he still had any doubts they were now dispelled.

"In fact it was Mr Lench that I was here to see."

"He usually has no appointments before eleven" came back the voice.

"Can you tell him that I represent a company called SLaM. I think he will be happy to see me; and he does need to see if there is any damage to his car."

The intercom went silent. Caleb Wicks waited, fidgeting with his car keys as the minutes passed by.

Just as the whole exercise was becoming embarrassing, he saw a figure striding towards the door.

This was him, he knew it. Lench was lean, with the look of a man who was aging well. Caleb studied the steel blue-grey eyes, revealing nothing, the immaculate hair, just beginning to silver at the temples, and a kind of aggressive formality that would have intimidated lesser men.

Darius Lench walked up and looked at his car and then he looked down at Caleb.

"Who the hell are you?" said Lench. "And what did you do to my car?"

"I am the legal representative of SUMMER," said Caleb.

Lench paused, and then looked at his car again, and then back at Caleb. His arm twitched as he tried to suppress a twinge in one of the muscles.

"Perhaps the name SLaM might mean more to you," said Caleb. "We were called that once."

Lench looked at his car again, weighing up the situation in his mind. "You have not damaged my car, so I think we can consider this matter closed."

He turned and walked back to the office building. He'd gone four paces when Caleb spoke again.

"I am also here as a representative of Bridget Larson's estate."

With some considerable exercise of will, Lench continued to walk back to the office. Bridget Larson was history, officially he had never heard of her, and there was nothing to connect him to her murder. Again he heard the old man's voice.

"And I am also here to represent Conner Masters."

Still Lench walked on. Let this man throw as many names at him as he wanted, he did not believe there was anything to connect him to any of them. The mobile phone he had used to call Conner Masters was gone, and there was no CCTV at Conner Masters' flat, so his visit remained unrecorded.

He was at the door when the voice came again from behind, one last time:

"I also represent Miss Alex Masters, the lady you assaulted in the car park of her apartment block eighteen month ago. I have to tell you that she is now thinking of pressing charges for assault. I understand you got a parking ticket for your troubles that day as well."

Lench actually had his hand on the door, but now he stopped. This man knew about the parking ticket and his meeting with the two women. That was more complex, that would need some management. The time was twenty minutes to ten. He had maybe five minutes to conclude this matter before he needed to prepare for the price-fixing meeting.

"What did you say your name was?" said Lench, as he turned back towards this man who had hit his car.

They faced each other again; and in that moment Lench remembered the dream, he remembered the surgeon's table and that the growth on his stomach had contained the faces of his enemies. He recognized one of those faces, looking at him right now.

"Caleb Wicks, director and legal adviser to SUMMER." There was no offer of a handshake.

"Why don't we sit in my car, Mr Wicks," he said. "We can talk privately there."

Lench fished out his keys and with a gentle "pop" the automatic locking jumped. Lench opened the driver side door and got in. After a moment of hesitation Caleb got in on the passenger side, and shut the door.

"Are you recording this?" said Lench before Caleb could say anything.

Caleb found this almost amusing. He wasn't that much of a secret agent. It also occurred to him that his adversary, sitting just inches from him now, had an interesting smell about him, a blend of cigar, expensive cologne and something else, something just about to go rotten.

"No, no, Mr Lench," he said, "this meeting is very much off the record. I shall not be relying on recordings for what I have to say to you. I will be brief because I know you are a busy man, and today's gold prices will require your attention. What I want is for you to leave us all alone, and by 'us' I mean those associated with SUMMER, particularly my clients: Alex Masters, Daisy Masters, Conner Adams, Aiden Kennedy and Lewis Ashbury. Whatever you are doing please stop it, immediately."

Lench burst out laughing and shook his head.

"I really have no idea what you're on about," he said.

"Let me tell see if I can convince you otherwise," said Caleb. "Firstly, we know that about a year and a half ago you were involved in an incident in which you assaulted Alex Masters outside her home. We have two witnesses who will testify that you did this, including the traffic warden who gave you the parking ticket."

Lench listened in silence, thinking about the time, thinking about the cost of the barrister he would use to minimize the fallout if these people chose to take him to court. Caleb went on.

"Secondly, we have this very unpleasant business with my client Conner Masters. Now I shan't insult your intelligence by pretending that I can link you to the young lady who so meticulously abused Conner, and perhaps," he continued, "in return you will spare me your denials."

Lench regarded him impassively. The old man hadn't really said anything to worry him yet.

"And then there was your own visit to see Conner," continued Caleb. "Did you really think you could go and see Conner and remain completely undetected? In a way you were, there is no visual evidence that you were there, no one got a clear sight of you, the CCTV is going to see how an anonymous bearded figure in a coat and sunglasses, and even if we could prove your presence there, and make a case against you, I wouldn't want to throw poor Conner to the wolves of your defence team."

Lench could not resist a smile. It was true that the barrister he would use, if that became necessary, would tie young Conner in knots. The old man carried on chattering away:

"No, there's no evidence that you were there at all," said Caleb, "except for one crucial detail. All your planning, Mr Lench, was perfect, of course, but you took one action while you were there that you had not planned, allowed yourself one simple indulgence."

"Your little games are boring me, Mr Wicks," interrupted Lench. "Say what you have to say and be done with it."

"It was the guitar, Mr Lench," said Caleb immediately. "The very thing that you hoped would bring Conner down was, in fact, your undoing. Oh what a history that instrument has had! I understand you play a little yourself."

"I am really not sure what you are talking about," said Lench.

"Oh, I think you do," said Caleb. The smell of the cologne was really beginning to irritate his sinuses.

"Somehow you knew that the guitar had compromised the boy," said Caleb. "I have no idea how you found out, and it doesn't really matter now, but I have to hand it to you, you really did try to make the best of that information. For a while it looked like you really had broken the boy; and you quite rightly guessed that that would have been the end of SUMMER."

"Really? I'm sorry to hear that," said Lench, smiling slightly again. "So is that all you have to say, Mr Wicks?"

Caleb sat back away from the smell. At least the seats were really comfortable, much more so than the ones in his car.

"Not quite," he said. "I think I need to tell you just a couple more things about that guitar; as I said, it's had quite a history. You may not be aware that Conner took the instrument back to the shop he stole it from. Funnily enough he had just finished cleaning it before you arrived. The owners decided to get young Conner to sign the instrument and then they added it to a charity auction. With Conner's signature on it, they were able to raise a good price for it, since Conner's band are doing rather well, in fact their album is in the charts at the moment, and apparently it's all over social media. It's not my taste in music of course, but good luck to them."

Caleb paused, he wanted this to sink in, and he wanted Lench to realize what he was saying here.

"Now you have seen this instrument. In fact, I understand from Conner that you even tried to take it from him. Do you remember? I was so intrigued by the story that I ended up buying it at the auction myself. An expensive purchase, but as I said, the money went to a good cause, and of course I wasn't just buying a good guitar, I also bought a little bit of you, Mr Lench." He leant forward, lowering his voice.

"The boy, Conner, had just cleaned it, and there were only two sets of fingerprints anywhere on it. An acquaintance of mine has taken a copies of them for me. I am sure one set will be Conner's but I think the other set, taken from the bridge stock will be yours."

Lench looked like he might deny the suggestion but remained silent.

"Under the circumstances," said Caleb, "I consider that purchase to have been a bit of a bargain. I am sure you can see why."

Lench stopped smiling and glanced at the dashboard clock.

"Do you have any more to say, Mr Wicks? Because your time is up."

"I'm nearly there," said Caleb, "and I know you are busy, so

I'll be brief with the rest of it. What I know is that Martin Massey had an association with you that is now severed. Massey made phone calls to you, at least one of which was from his office phone rather than his mobile. We can trace that call and investigate the owner of the number he dialled. If that is traced to you, we will use it as evidence for another more serious charge that might be levelled against you."

Now this was a long shot, and Caleb knew it, but he thought he'd throw it in for good measure, and he also felt obliged to speak in Martin's defence.

"Oh, and before you go after poor old Martin Massey, I will tell you now that he is not at home. Of course, you may know this already. Additionally none of this information has come from him; he has stayed annoyingly tight-lipped through this whole business."

Caleb Wicks sighed. He had the strangest sensation, as if he had to tell some sad news to a small child and he wanted to do it gently.

For a moment they were both silent.

"Is that it?" said Lench, finally. "Well I would like to say it's an impressive range of charges, but it doesn't really amount to much does it, Mr Wicks? You work in the law. Would you take this on as an assignment if you didn't have to?"

"Now," he continued before Caleb could reply, "let me tell you something else, Mister *Wicks*", he spat Caleb's name, "I shall return the compliment and not sport with your intelligence. You know who I serve. When I act for my God, I do so in the arena of contemporary culture. And do you know what? We shall always win in that arena. We shall appear to be more daring, more fun, more radical, more cool; we have more rebels and showmen and freaks than your God will ever have."

"Heaven for the climate and hell for the company, Mr Lench?" said Caleb.

"Something like that, yes," said Lench with a smile. "We are stronger, and more focused, and more powerful than you will ever be, hamstrung as you are with your notions of love and forgiveness. When some of your friends make wild and unfounded accusations about us, we shall be conciliatory and look innocent. We shall look like victims and the church will look like fools. And still we will have our magicians and our daredevils, our intrigue and our liberty. And what will you have? What will you be? Bickering amongst yourselves. Your church is safe, irrelevant, neutered. Pathetic! You shall never beat us. Now, good day to you, sir. As you rightly guessed, I have business to attend to."

Caleb pondered these last words. They contained some seeds of truth and he felt their sting, but while Lench was ready to finish, Caleb had one more card to play; everything depended on what he would say next. He was about to respond when Lench spoke again.

"Get out of my car." The locks clicked up again.

Caleb obliged, but his thoughts were on delivering this one final comment, to make sure this man understood what he was saying. He lifted himself out of the passenger seat knowing that if this next revelation didn't crack Darius Lench there would be nothing more he could do. He turned back to Lench who was looking at his watch.

"Oh, there's one more thing, I almost forgot. Your friend Joseph, you know who I mean? Were you aware that he visited Alex Masters two nights ago?"

Still Lench looked at him, impassively, but Caleb could detect just a slight twitch in his right eye.

That's more like it, thought Caleb.

"Apparently Joseph, or whatever his name is, went to see Alex Masters," said Caleb, leaning in through the open car door, speaking quietly now but with as much force as he could muster. "It seems they had a nice chat and he decided not to kill her, but I have no idea what he did after that, do you?"

Lench stared at Caleb blankly and interior of the car became a bubble of silence.

"The expression on your face tells me you have no idea about this visit," continued Caleb. "Well, I am sure you will appreciate that I am not a liar. One of your magicians, one of your daredevils, visited Alex Masters, probably against your explicit instructions. He went there to murder her but in the end chose not to, perhaps he was saving his passion for someone else?"

Lench looked into the abyss of unresolved issues and difficulties. What had Josef done? How much, if anything, had he said about Bridget's murder? Or the group? And where had he gone afterwards. He realized that he had not heard from Marie for the past thirty-six hours. There was nothing unusual in this, but he resolved to give her a call.

"Are you now finished, Mr Wicks?" he said, sounding tired.

Caleb leant in just a little further.

"Listen carefully, Darius Lench," he said, "you might think you have this all covered but you do not. Alex Masters knows who abused her brother. She has guessed that her friend Bernice and your associate, Marie, are the same person. Your man Joseph has gone rogue. Now, I will ask you again – what do you think Joseph did after he visited Alex Masters? Did he pay Martin Massey another visit? Perhaps he visited your acolyte, Marie Templeton, to discuss the fact that she let his name slip. You might want to contact her when we've finished this conversation."

Lench suppressed an intense desire to reach for his mobile phone. He forced himself to stop thinking about the implications of this conversation, and to get rid of this man once and for all.

"I'll tell you what, Mr Wicks," said Lench, spreading his smooth palms in a gesture of magnanimity, "I know you've come a long way from your little provincial town to make your request and I am inclined to grant it; let's call a truce shall we? I will leave you and your associates in peace if you will do the same for me and mine."

Caleb was about to answer when a few words poured out of heaven and shouted in his mind:

"If you think I came chiefly to bargain for my friends," said Caleb, "then you are wrong. The main reason I came to see you is because God has required me to give you a warning. You must stop your evil practices and repent, and turn away from the devil. You must do it today, right now, because if you don't, your life will be forfeit."

Lench stared at him.

"Get out," he said, and turned away again.

"Take this seriously," said Caleb. "I doubt you'll get another warning."

"Good day to you," said Lench. "Now please close the door of my car, and go away."

"I am sorry," called out Caleb. "Don't be sorry, Mr Wicks," said Lench. "I congratulate you, you've won, for now. And winning is everything, *everything*."

Caleb didn't turn back. He kept walking, briskly, towards his own car. He felt bruised, and raw. He did not feel like the winner. Nobody had won, at least not in terms of this encounter.

The wind had strengthened and blew down the narrow street, and a disposable cup rolled and bumped down the road towards him. He leant into the breeze, and breathed in the smells and warmth of the mighty, restless city.

When he got back to his car he was amazed at how uncomfortable the seats were after the luxurious feel of the Mercedes. He pushed the fate of Darius Lench to the back of his mind, and drove back to the parking space he had used earlier; the ticket that he had bought was valid for a few more minutes and he was praying that the space was still free.

LENCH WAS ALREADY THINKING about the calls he needed to make, strategies to deal with Josef, and the need to speak to Marie. He was thinking through the actions required for damage limitation. "Life goes on," he told himself, "and so does business. Nothing changes."

"Nothing changes," he muttered to himself. "I do not repent and I do not change."

After the stress of the morning he was not surprised to feel the familiar pain return, in his chest and down his right arm, more intense even than before, and he began to feel a little light-headed as he fumbled with the security lock at the front door of the office.

20

—————

Lewis Ashbury stood on the rough ground encircling a rusted bin at the end of his garden. The clouds had gathered and there was a breeze blowing in from the north, giving the cold air a sting that made him grimace.

Over the years this old bin had seen him finish off weeds, brambles, twigs, and compromising documents of all kinds. Lewis did not trust his secrets to the refuse collectors; after all, he reasoned, rubbish can be stolen, dug up, examined.

He was holding some photos in his hand, and he was thinking about Bridget.

He recalled that, in death as well as life she broke all the rules. She had been outrageous and determined and successful and he had admired all that she had achieved. He had loved her and he missed her, and finally he had allowed himself to feel real sorrow over losing her.

It was the exploration of that sorrow, a final facing of the truth that had drawn him to this act of remembrance.

He tossed the two photos onto the dried kindling, each representing a facet of her life: Bridget the model, and Bridget the businesswoman. But he would best remember her as Bridget the survivor. She had often called herself that.

"I'm a survivor, Lewis, don't you forget it."

The irony of the remark brought the sting to his eyes again. He had cried more times in the last few days than he had in twenty years.

Unbidden, a memory came to him of them both together just after SLaM had started. They had worked stupid hours, willing this business into existence, living and breathing their company. Then one day they had just shut the office and left, driving to the airport and not even knowing where they were going, passports in hand. They booked flights for a long weekend in Budapest and there they had seen the sights, eaten the food, drunk the wine, and had delighted themselves with what the city had to offer, and each other.

Lewis poured some petrol over the two photos and threw a lighted match onto the wood. The first one took immediately, the hungry flames soon licking at the image of her.

He wanted to say the words but just as he was summoning his courage there was a noise behind him, and he turned to see Alex Masters standing at the end of the garden, waving at him.

"I'm glad you could make it," he said, and smiled. He beckoned to her, and just the sight of her conjured up more tears, but he could hide these behind the smoke now pouring up from the bin in front of him.

She came and stood next to him and looked down at the blackened curls of the photo, and he accepted the tissue she offered him.

"Aiden tells me the latest numbers are looking pretty good," he said, poking around at the flames.

"I think we're going to be okay," said Alex. "Thank God."

"And Poppy and Conner," he said, laughing, "I hear they're doing pretty well also."

She nodded and smiled.

"I'm glad you're here," he said without glancing at her, "I really am. God, you were one hell of an excellent PA, Alex Masters." He sighed.

"These pictures were precious to you," she said, "why are you burning them?" One of the photos was now not much more than blackened flakes, fluttering in the wind.

"Oh they were precious to me," he said, "but now I think it's time to give them up."

He wiped his eyes again and looked up at her.

"I think the timing for this is good," he continued. "It feels like we are in a season for new beginnings, fresh starts."

"Yes," she said, "I think it does."

Lewis turned back to the flames, and Alex took his arm as she stood next to him, feeling the breath of heat on her face.

"I suppose you know all about this," said Lewis, "mourning for those you've loved."

"Yes," she said, "I do." She held on more tightly to his arm and together they watched as the flames reached the second and last photo. The centre darkened and lifted, blistering as the fire found its way through. They watched Bridget's image fade, and then what was left of the paper curled and lifted in the breeze before it finally broke up and floated away.

EPILOGUE

NEWS ROUNDUP

LONDON BULLION MARKET members Stern Shearman and Partners have announced the appointment of Mr Daniel Fallon to the position of Lead Market Maker for their Precious Metals Group. The appointment was prompted by the recent untimely death SSP executive, Darius Lench. At the time of his death, Mr Lench had been facing allegations of market fixing, and the appointment has been seen as an opportunity for Stern Shearman to draw a line under a particularly turbulent period for the firm. Industry observers are expecting a clear-out of the existing team once Mr Fallon is in place.

WestComm Financial: Commodities Briefing

JOHN AND AVELINE TEMPLETON who are currently serving with us in Burkina Faso have been granted compassionate leave to return to the UK following the tragic death of their daughter Bernice. We would ask you to pray for John, Aveline and the family at this time.

Four Points Gospel Mission Newsletter

FLEDGLING MEDIA FIRM SUMMER has posted impressive trading results in the last quarter. CEO Alex Masters has hired industry veteran Lewis Ashbury to help with their music division; and a strong showing from this area of the business together with a successful launch into the Fair-Trade clothing sector has meant that the sun is definitely shining for this new start-up.

WestComm Financial: Media sector briefing

STAY IN TOUCH

You can stay in touch with Andrew Chamberlain by visiting my
website at:
www.andrewjchamberlain.com

And on social media at:
Twitter@storycraftpress
Instagram@thestorycraftpress

And on Goodreads at:
https://www.goodreads.com/andychamberlain